Nonlocality
A novel of entanglements
By Jason Dias

"We may say that there is at present no occasion and no reason to speak of causality in nature – because no experiment indicates its presence, since the macroscopic are unsuitable in principle, and the only known theory which is compatible with our experience relative to elementary processes, quantum mechanics, contradicts it."
John von Neumann, 1955

Wheeler: "Feynman, I know why all electrons have the same charge and the same mass!"

Feynman: "Why?"

Wheeler: "Because, they are all the same electron!"

From Feynman's Nobel Prize in Physics acceptance speech, 1965

One

"I think it's strange," Yvonne said. She closed the paperback book and put it in her lap. Little did she know it would be the solution to everything, and everything that needed solving was happening right now.

"Not so strange, really," said Val, her husband. "It's just different."

"I never did like science fiction. Asimov isn't so bad usually, but this..."

They drove through the snow. It was December seventeenth, nineteen seventy-three, Valery's birthday, and they were going out to meet some friends for dinner. Valery wore his smoking jacket and a repugnant yellow bow-tie, Yvonne a black gown. The snow was starting to pile up and so was the traffic.

"We'll be late for the meeting," Yvonne complained.

"Don't worry, darling. They won't wait for us."

"That's what I'm afraid of. The science fiction was always your thing. Mystery is mine."

"Agatha Christie isn't going to be there personally, you know," Valery chided.

Yvonne sighed, lifted the book back out of her lap with a sigh. "Three genders?" she wondered aloud. "What sort of pervert must this Asimov be?"

"Not so perverted," Valery said. "It's a mystery. You will have to finish the book to understand it all. It all makes sense in the end."

Traffic had slowed to a crawl now, the main street jammed. Valery mistimed a light, got stuck in the middle of an intersection. He leaned on the horn, hoping to get the drivers in front of him to tighten up a little bit.

He said, "I don't think we-" and that was when the snowplow coming from the cross-street hit them, sliding through the fresh snow. It hit the passenger side, lifted their gold-colored LTD off the ground and slammed it into the empty school bus next to them.

The book flew from Yvonne's hands on impact, out the exploding window and into the street. It would be decades before she remembered it. Glass pattered down around the settling wreck and Yvonne thought two things at once: how much the falling glass was like the delay between turning off the hose and its last spray landing around you, and how impossible it was that she was thinking anything.

Thank God I had my seatbelt, she thought, disconnected. Her breath turned into white haze in front of her as she turned to look at Valery.

He had not survived the crash, that was clear. His neck was broken and there was too much thoracic trauma. "Val?" she said anyway. "Val, why aren't you all right? Why didn't it work?" She didn't know why those particular words fell from her lips. Soon she would forget having said them.

Dazed, Yvonne scrambled out of the ruined front windshield, embedding glass in her palms and her knees. *This isn't right*, she thought. *This isn't how it's supposed to be.*

"Miss, you all right?" The snowplow driver had climbed down from his cab, unhurt except for a bruise across his face, diagonal, from what sort of impact Yvonne could not have said.

"I'm fine," she said, sitting down on the curb. Snow confused the air all around her, making her uncertain. "But you killed my husband."

The driver was on the other side of the wreck from her, could not come around to the front without going all the way around his truck. He peeked into the car from the back. By now they could hear approaching sirens but in this traffic it was going to be a while before there was any help.

"It was his birthday," Yvonne said, mostly to herself, mostly unaware of the crowd of onlookers who melting into being out of the snow at all such events. Someone threw a blanket over her shoulders, someone else sat with her and put an arm around her. "We were going to a mystery dinner. He was thirty-seven."

Snow whipped around. Fluids dripped out of the bottom of the damaged car. A wrecker was on the scene before emergency services and the driver just stood there doing nothing, orange lights spinning. Then there was a medical technician crawling over the wreck, another ambulance arriving from the opposite side street, a swarm of police starting to direct traffic away from the area. The noise of car horns was like the snow: swirling, impenetrable.

"Miss, can you walk?"

Yvonne did not hear the tech talking to her. "I think she's going to faint," said the woman with her arms around Yvonne.

Things moved fast after that. The techs carried Yvonne into an ambulance and whisked her away, the sound of the siren so loud it was like silence. She lay in the little cot, cold and still, and the techs put an IV into her arm.

"What's wrong with her?" one of the men said.

"Nothing, not a scratch on her," said the other.

"She came out of that car?"

"Yeah, see the cuts on her hands and knees from crawling through the windshield glass? Otherwise no bruising, no cuts, no welt from the seat restraint, nothing. At the least she ought to have a bruise right here, right temple, from where the plow hit the car. Ought to have lurched right - well, stayed in place while the whole car leapt left, smacked her head. Nothing, though."

Yvonne did not listen. This was all impossible, and that was important somehow. The IV flowed into her arm, feeling like cold.

***

The sense of wrongness had faded sometime between being admitted to the hospital and being wheeled down in a steel-sided wheelchair to identify her husband's body. Yvonne had been into lots of morgues, seen plenty of bodies and blood. The life of an ER doctor was one of abnormal experiences. But looking at Val was different somehow.

The wounds she could take. She had seen enough. They just made her hands itch for gauze pads and bandages and a good needle. But her husband was gone. Twelve years together, twelve good years.

She whispered, "That's him, that's Valery."

"Valery Leskov?" asked the pathologist.

"Yes, that's him."

"Thank you, Mrs. Leskov," the doctor said. "I'm sorry for your loss." He said it like a thoughtless courtesy, the same way you said *thank you* when someone passed the salt.

"It's doctor," she told him, feeling instantly inane.

"I'm sorry. Doctor Leskov," The doctor said, more sincerity in that apology than in his condolence. He looked at the nurse who had hold of her chair handles, and she whisked Yvonne away.

"That's funny," the pathologist said when she was near the door. Yvonne heard, though, without understanding.

"Yes, Doctor?" his nurse prompted when he did not elaborate.

"Well, on this form I could have sworn it said the wife had died and the husband was coming to identify her."

"Well, he does have a woman's name," the nurse suggested.

"Hm. I suppose that could be it. Must've been my imagination. This all looks correct, after all, and papers do not change between one glance and the next, do they?"

"No, Doctor." Yvonne might have imagined that part, because now she was out in the hallway, too far away to hear.

The air was heavy inside the hospital. While the chair did not move fast, Yvone still felt the density of the air against her skin, the wind of it moving through her hair. The hallways stank of antiseptic, a comforting smell, home. Her legs were cold. Her whole body was cold, really: the thin hospital gown kept out little of the cold, and her bare shins broke her trail through the thick, chill air.

The nurse did not try to make any contact with her, just pushed the chair like she was a cart of groceries at the Safeway. Stood behind her on the elevator. Made banal chatter with a pair of orderlies from the psychiatric ward. This was not her hospital and nobody knew her here.

Finally, Yvonne was in a room. Two beds divided by curtains. The nurse helped her into bed but she needn't have: Yvonne felt tired, sedated a little, but in perfect health. Still, she accepted the help, let herself be covered, requested an extra blanket. Even that could not keep out all the chill but it helped.

Finally, when she was alone except for an unseen roommate praying the rosary over and over again in a muted whisper, at last Yvonne let herself cry. The tears were furious, a wave of them like off the wake of a big, fast boat, spilling over and clutching her chest. She cried as silently as she could for as long as she could and reflected absently that at least the tears were hot.

***

"You should be able to go home sometime this afternoon, Mrs. Leskov."

"Doctor," she corrected.

"Hm?"

"It's Doctor Leskov."

"I see. In any case, there's no reason to keep you here. Physically, aside from a few cuts, not a thing wrong with you. Of course follow up with your regular physician in a few days if you have muscle aches, especially about the neck. If you like I can prescribe a mild sedative to help you through the next few days." The doctor looked at her strangely, looking at the paperwork as though something were missing.

"No," she said. "No, that won't be necessary. I think it's best if I just try to get through it the old-fashioned way."

"Whatever you think is best," her doctor said. He was a youngish man, younger than her. Tall, round glasses like John Lennon, earnest face like Ringo. He tucked some papers into a brown cardboard file, clipped it to a board at the end of her bed. "It happens sometimes, you know," he said, "but I wish to Hell we could understand why."

"What does?" Yvonne asked.

"People walk away from accidents that should have killed them. Walk away clean, not a scratch on them, even though everyone around them is... well, sorry to be insensitive. I should just let you rest. But damned if I didn't wish I knew what leads it to happen this way."

"It doesn't, though," Yvonne said when he was gone. "It doesn't happen this way. Never. It's impossible." She had worked emergency rooms for a dozen years. Since she was twenty-four her days had been sudden illnesses, cuts and scrapes, blood, contusions, broken bones and worse. And it never happened this way. There was no reason for her to have been completely spared and her husband, her love, to be dead. They had been in the same car at the same time for the same incident. It was impossible.

She lay in the bed waiting for the nurse to come tell her she could leave. She might have gone whenever she felt like it only the nurse had all her clothes, her purse a bystander had rescued from the wreck. Her watch, shoes. Rather than make a scene Yvonne just waited for the paperwork. She could practically envision each step being taken one by one, each form, each signature. Each interruption. Yvonne would be low priority.

So lunch came and went. Yvonne ate chicken soup and lime Jello and waited. Slept a while and waited. Woke up and waited. Eventually the nurse brought in her clothes and a packet of forms to sign, helped her dress even though she didn't need it, wheeled her out to the hospital doors through the heavy air even though she might as well have walked, put her into a taxi.

Yvonne opened her file, read through the incredulous accounts of her absence of injuries. The doctor had gone ahead and written her a prescription for a sedative, not a mild one, and she balled that up in one hand, tossed it out the taxi window. Even if she had wanted it, the dose was appropriate for a man twice her size. It would not so much have helped her sleep as kept her in a coma.

The snow had stopped. New York was not a pretty town the day after a snowfall. The stuff on the ground got trudged through, driven over, spattered with sludge from the roads. The stuff on roofs got the grime of soot and engine dirt. It was a smelly, dripping, dirty mess, and it matched Yvonne's feelings perfectly.

"Quantum mechanics is certainly imposing. But an inner voice tells me that it is not yet the real thing. The theory says a lot, but does not really bring us any closer to the secret of the "old one." I, at any rate, am convinced that He does not throw dice."

Einstein

Two

Walter wasn't doing well.

"Look, there's Asimov," Hugo said boisterously.

"Heard him from a mile off," said Peter, and it was easy to believe. The great man was there ahead of them, holding forth amidst a hoard of fans. At the moment they shouted random words at him and he wrapped them into bawdy limericks.

"He'll probably do Gilbert and Sullivan next," Walter said wanly. They were all three growing mutton-chop sideburns in Asimov's honor but none were quite old enough to pull it off, just nineteen. For Peter and Hugo the most interesting thing about their favorite writer right now was he had a girl on each arm, not bad-looking ones. Friends were catching the moment on film, cameras snapping all around.

They stood in line nearly an hour to get books signed. Asimov was obviously pretty tired by the time their turn came around and there was a cutish redhead making eyes at him but he stayed, signed their books. "Real fans," he told them, "buy hardbacks. I'm proud of you." Then he was off.

Walter had a copy of The Foundation Trilogy, a big book with white and black squares at the bottom, like a chessboard. He held it to his chest as if protectively, but it was not the book he was protecting.

Hugo had a copy of The Stars, Like Dust, another monochrome book except for the titles, which were in red. He looked at the signature inside and smiled. "Not worth much," said a fellow conventioneer in passing, and it was true. Asimov had probably signed a thousand autographs today and probably would sign a thousand more every day he was in a convention hotel lobby. But it was worth more than money to Hugo.

The End of Eternity made up the third of the black and white covers, this one with the titles in purple. "He wrote my name in it," said Peter, proudly. "It's like we're friends."

Walter turned his head suddenly. Nobody was there but he had been sure someone was watching.

"Let's go to the hotel bar and have some beers," Hugo suggested. "I'll bet it's full of writers."

"Nah, they all drive out to better places to drink and dine," Peter argued, but they went anyway. The night was getting old by now and they were able to squeeze in. Had there been anyone famous, a conversation would have been impossible.

Peter and Hugo drank beers, foamy and cold and good. Walter just stood, eyes and ears wide. Now when he looked there was always someone in the edges of his vision but they were real people and they only looked at him because he looked at them. Walter tried to smile but it was a sickly thing, made of sinew and worry.

He looked again. There was definitely someone there, the red-haired girl. She was watching him. She had green eyes, big green eyes, and sharp teeth. Only she wasn't real. She could not possibly be there amidst all the real people and certainly could not be standing there watching him through the crowd. But wherever he turned his head, she slowly settled into his peripheral vision.

His friends were laughing and joking and telling stories, but Walter sat with his eyes shut, trying not to think about the green-eyed girl.

"You were waiting for Isaac, weren't you?" he said to her.

"What's that, Wally?" Peter asked him. "We all waited for Isaac. You got your book signed. Say, are you well?"

"No, I don't think so."

"Let's go up to bed," Hugo suggested. He was sort of their leader. He was tall, good-looking in an austere way.

He had a crew-cut and horn-rimmed glasses, wore short-sleeved shirts with the top button left undone. When they had to deal with ordinary people, Hugo spoke for them, being by far the best at getting along with run-of-the-mill humans.

The convention had been his idea. They had all finished their undergraduate degrees in math this year and would be starting their graduate programs in a few days. A little time to indulge their science fiction hobby had seemed in order and the convention was close.

Their room was on the fourth floor, the cheapest available but the lap of luxury compared to the dorms they were used to. Three young men could fit in a small enough space, at least for a short time. There was one bed. Hugo and Peter shared it and Walter crashed on the floor between the bed and the wall. They knew other rooms had as many as ten people crammed in.

Walter supposed he should be comforted but he could not sleep, not well. He kept dreaming of the girl, the redhead, and when he woke up the dreams did not stop.

***

Morning came. Hugo woke first, steamed up the shower. Then Peter took his turn. Walter just lay on the floor, wrapped in a spare blanket.

"You really are sucking wind," Hugo said looking down at him. "Think a nice breakfast would perk you up?"

"I don't think so. You guys go on down without me."

"You sure?"

"Yeah, if I get hungry I'll just suck on the Brylcreem you buttholes probably left all over the bathroom sink."

"Gross, man. Seriously gross."

They hooted like that was the best joke ever, or one of Asimov's dirty limericks. It was one of the last times they would all laugh together.

"Well, if you're sure..." Peter wasn't so keen to leave him.

"Go on, Petie. I thought I saw a cute chick eyeballing you last night. She would have totally gone for you except

Asimov smiled at her and she forgot all about you. You should go try to remind her."

"Yeah, right."

He seemed to be better, more his self for a minute, so Hugo and Peter left him there in the hotel room. Walter got up onto the bed for while but then decided the floor was more comfortable. From the bed he kept wondering who might be watching through the window, wondering if there were any gaps in the curtains. Actually from down here he kept wondering the same thing, it was just easier to tell himself "no."

Half a day later Walter left the hotel, took the bus back to school and went to his dorm room. It was quiet there, just one other student ready for the Fall term. And for a while he felt better. The red-haired girl could not possibly have followed him home from the convention. Why would she even want to? For a couple of days nobody bothered him.

And nobody checked on him.

***

"You look like crud," Hugo told Walter, Monday morning. It had taken ten minutes to get him to answer the door.

"I'm sorry I split on you, man, only... I guess I don't feel too good."

"What's that on your shirt?" Peter asked him.

"It's toothpaste," Walter said, shy. "I thought maybe the polyprotein substrate might reflect the nonambient wavelengths, make her stop watching me."

"Come again?" said Hugo. "Hey, have you even been eating? You look like a sack of sticks."

"Guess I don't remember."

"What do you think?" Peter asked Hugo. Peter was not the leader. He was short, a little over five feet, and he had a baby face and braces. His hair was always a mess no matter what he did. He favored Western shirts with faux mother of pearl snaps for buttons and jeans that were a size too small. He looked like exactly what he was, no matter what he did: a kid who was good at math and bad at people.

"I think," said Hugo, "we ought to talk about going to the hospital."

"I'm not that sick," Walter protested. "Come on, I'll eat something, I promise."

"Three times a day?"

"Yeah, I guess so."

He was as good as his word the first day. The second, he huddled at the back of his dorm room under a blanket and started scratching in a notebook. At first it was drawings. He had no special talent for drawing and, even if he had, he'd not have been anxious to show them off. By the end of the day, though, he was pretty sure he could describe the watching girl better with numbers.

"Walter, dinner. Come on, chow hall's open for business. They got steak fries tonight." Hugo liked steak fries better than anything. Walter had once, too.

"Busy," was all Walter said.

"Too busy to eat, Wally? Come on, you promised."

Walter said nothing, kept scratching.

Hugo skirted through the room - there was junk everywhere, all over the floor - and lifted one of the blankets and then another until he could see Walter underneath, notebook in hand. The pencil danced between the lines leaving a trail of numbers in its wake.

"What's this, chum?" Hugo asked.

For the first and the only time in his life, Walter hit somebody. He smacked his best friend in the mouth, cutting open his own knuckles on the man's teeth.

"Oh, no-" he said right away, his voice full of shame and panic, but his body did not match his mind. His fists balled up, one of them bleeding. His shoulders rolled forwards. He hunched over his dropped notebook. "No, I'm sorry, I don't know why I did that..."

Hugo said nothing, just stood there dumbstruck, too shocked even to be angry. He stood silent for a full minute, then two. Finally Walter caved under his own internal pressures, snatched up the book and went back to scrawling, Hugo forgotten so long as he did not interfere.

"Don't eat, then," Hugo said. "See if I care."

He left calmly, went back to the room he shared with Peter.

"Is he coming?" Peter asked. His eyes swept over Hugo's mouth, lingered on the blood.

"No. We can't wait any longer. I guess we have to call him an ambulance."

"You mean, have him sent to the nuthatch?"

"Yeah, I guess."

"Will he hate us?" asked Peter.

"I'd rather he lived to hate us than starved to death in his room loving us."

"Guess you got a point."

"Yeah, guess I do. Lend me a dime."

"Stop telling God what to do with his dice."

Apocryphal, attributed variously to Niels Bohr and Enrico Fermi

Three

"Ah, Mrs. Leskov. Please, sit down," the psychiatrist said, double-checking his paperwork.

"It's doctor."

"Oh, I see. What are you a doctor of, if I may ask?" The psychiatrist was very doctorish, as though a child had drawn a cartoon of what a psychiatrist should look like. Everyone else on the ward wore scrubs unless they had labcoats over suits. He wore a tweed jacket unselfconsciously, sported mutton chop sideburns and round glasses, and smoked a pipe.

"Medicine," Yvonne replied quietly, keeping her eyes on his as she sat down in the aluminum and plastic chair across from him.

"I see," he repeated. "Well. I'm Doctor Weatherly, as by now you must have surmised. Your brother listed you as next of kin?"

"Yes, our parents have been dead for years. Heart attacks in both cases. We were raised by an aunt and uncle, both older. Now it is quite hard for them to travel."

"Ah. Well, thank you for coming so quickly. Perhaps you could sign these releases, standard information releases so that we can legally speak with you. You will notice your brother's signature here on this one."

They looked pretty standard to Yvonne, so she signed them without looking very closely. "Why exactly is he here? The nurse who called me wouldn't say."

"Schizophrenia, most likely," Weatherly said. "Of course it will take some time to confirm the diagnosis but for now it's the most likely candidate. His delusions and hallucinations point towards a paranoid type, from which full recovery is, I am sad to say, quite rare. But rest assured we are on the leading edge of treatment and we shall do all we can."

"Why did this happen?" Yvonne asked.

"We can't say, of course. Even just a few years ago we would have asked some personal and intrusive questions about your mother. These days we speculate there must be some biological reason, genetic most likely."

"So you'd like to ask some intrusive and personal questions about both my parents."

"In a nutshell, yes," he laughed.

"In that case you should tell me your name."

"Weatherly. Doctor Weatherly."

"No," she said, "you told me that already. Your first name. I'm Yvonne."

"Very well. It's Charles. Delighted. Well, except for the circumstances."

For the next hour she answered questions about her family history, essentially confirming the account Walter had already given over the past several days.

When that was done, they let her see Walter in a small private room by the exit. He looked gaunt and haunted, eyes sunken, hair disheveled. He had on light-blue scrubs and a tag on his left wrist. The room didn't look much better: plastic chairs, big table with a Formica top scattered with cigarette ashes, blue tile floor with more ashes.

"You need a haircut," Yvonne told her brother.

"You're probably right," he said. "You always took good care of me. Did the doctor say how long I have to stay here?"

"Not really," Yvonne replied. "I doubt it will be for very long, though."

"Just a blip."

"Yes, just a blip."

"Yvonne? I'm afraid," Walter said, looking at her shoes.

"Oh, don't be afraid, dear. What is there to be afraid of?"

"That they won't let me go. Mostly that they won't let me go. Or sometimes that they will. I mean, what if all these drugs actually work? That means that I'm crazy, doesn't it? And I'll be crazy forever."

There was not much to say to that.

After a long silence, Yvonne asked, "Can I bring you anything?"

"My math homework," Walter asked at once. "The term started without me. Imagine that. I'd really like to be able to think I wasn't getting too far behind."

"That sounds hopeful. I'll ask Doctor Weatherly if they will let me bring your assignments. Perhaps I'll send your friends with it. Would you like if they came to visit?"

"Well, yes and no. I mean, I'd love to see them, but I don't want them to see me like this."

"From what I hear," offered Yvonne, "they've already seen you at your worst. I'll talk to them, shall I?"

"Yeah."

"Anything else?"

"Yeah," he repeated. "Something to read. All they have here is back issues of National Geographic, and they were boring when they were printed fifteen years ago."

Yvonne laughed. "I still have all your books. Anything in particular?"

"Isaac Asimov," he said.

***

Yvonne rode the bus across town to Walter's school. She could as easily call but Hugo and Peter would not be easy to reach at the dorms in any event. Washington D.C. in the fall was cleaner and more picturesque than New York City. The bus was hot and noisy, rattling over the road like a casket of bones. The windows were dirty inside, smoke everywhere.

The bus was almost full. People wore the least they could get away with. Men in suits had their jackets over one arm, their shirt collars open under loose ties. People had briefcases and handbags, paper sacks of groceries, all the accoutrements of normal life.

Yvonne sat on one of the side-facing seats near the front. An older woman sat next to her, clunky shoes marking her out as some sort of domestic or menial worker. Housekeeping, maybe. Across from her were two men who might have had any job at all, really, but for their dirty boots. Outdoor workers. Also across from her was a young girl of perhaps eleven, no parents visible.

Suddenly the bus entered a tunnel and the darkness turned all the windows into mirrors. For a second the glass in front of Yvonne seemed to hold Valery's reflection. She gasped, blinked, and the illusion was gone. Just her, Yvonne, same old Yvonne in her beige overcoat, green blouse, khaki skirt to her knees.

Valery was gone but it was no surprise she saw him everywhere. It had been nine months now, not even a year, not remotely enough time for her husband to leave her life sufficiently that she did not have daily, hourly, almost moment-by-moment reminders of his absence.

The tunnel was short. Light returned to the world and the bus came to a noisy stop. The men in front of her got out. Some women with little children got on, flashed bus passes, sat down across from her. She waved at the babies, forced a smile she could not feel. Then it was her turn to get off.

The school was beautiful but Yvonne did not notice. Her heels tapped out her sadness as she walked, echoing back and forth between the buildings. She went to the administrative offices first, stood in line behind some young people for a while. When it was her turn, the middle-aged woman behind the desk waved her forwards.

"How can I help you?" she said kindly.

"My brother..." Yvonne unexpectedly choked up, had to stop talking for a moment and gather her energy. "My brother is sick. I need to arrange for his homework to be sent to the hospital."

"Oh, I'm sorry, Miss. We wouldn't handle that here. Maybe you can give me his name, and I can send you on to his professors?"

"Walter. Walter Bradbury."

"Wait one moment, please," the secretary said, and zipped away on her wheeled chair. Behind her were racks of files on tracks in the floor and ceiling, tens of thousands of individual records all organized in brown cardboard shrouds.

After more than a moment, the woman came back with a piece of lined yellow paper full of names and room numbers. "Good luck," she said, and waved up the next person cheerfully. Yvonne felt dismissed without feeling demeaned and inwardly congratulated the secretary on her manner.

Then it was a long, sweaty walk across the campus, eighty degrees and swampy, buffeted by crowds of young people in the first flush of their adult freedom. *I remember how it was to be young*, she thought. Her own first days of college had been nineteen years ago, nineteen fifty-two. Boom years. Medicine had seemed an infinite horizon then, like they could do anything, become gods. Triumph even over death itself.

Nearly twenty years later she had discovered the limits of such aspirations. And now it should be her baby brother, born nineteen years after her, walking across this quad full of optimism and boundless hope. Just like all these other people.

Inside the big brick building the cold was like a wall between the front doors, air conditioners making life possible in this hot, muggy place. People were everywhere, talking, laughing, a group of three young men standing on chairs and singing. Yvonne consulted her list, looked around for some sign of where she might be.

"Help you, miss?" said a voice from her right. "You look lost." It was a young man, barely twenty if not a teenager. Black jeans, yellow shirt, slim and handsome.

"Oh, yes, thank you. I need to find this room, Professor Moldavie. Some sort of math class."

"Your first term?" the fellow asked, pointing towards a stairwell and walking alongside her. "Moldavie's pretty tough but you'll be OK if you just ask for help when you get stuck."

"Oh, no, no. I'm not a student, I'm... well, I'm a doctor. I'm old."

He looked at her again, closer. "You sure? Huh. Go figure. Well, what does an old doctor need with a math prof anyway?"

"It's for my brother," Yvonne said. "He's sick. I need to collect his homework." They walked up the stairs together, the young guy stealing glances at her when he could. Down the hall a little way was the lecture room, and her timing was just right. Students streamed steadily by, all clutching books or bags of books, chatting amiably, complaining about Moldavie or praising him to one another.

Yvonne pushed her way in when the crowd abated. Moldavie turned out to be a corpulent man in his fifties with smooth skin and eyes as grey as his hair. "Be brief," he said, not unkindly. "Have to run across campus for another lecture and as you can see I'm not made for running."

"Oh, sorry to trouble you. Do you know my little brother? Walter Bradbury?"

"Walter? Oh, I have so many students, I'm sorry..."

"You'd remember him, I think. Only nineteen, been in college two years already. Working on... I don't remember, something about prime numbers."

"Does he have a pair of young friends, all came in together?" Moldavie wondered.

"That's him. Peter and Hugo. Been friends forever."

"Can we walk and talk? Yes? Good. Um, yes, I think I remember him. How can I help?"

"I just need to collect any assignments so he can continue his work. He's in the hospital right now." Every time she said it, it got a little easier.

"Oh, sorry to hear it. Here, write down the particulars and I'll have everything sent over." He stopped, gave her the back of a brown cardboard folder to write on.

"Thanks so much," she said, scrawled the information. Luckily she had never managed the art of writing like a doctor: her cursive was neat and legible. "He'll really appreciate this."

The professor took the note gently, took his pen back just as gently, and then hurried off. "Tell him we're thinking of him," he called over one meaty shoulder.

Outside the lecture hall, the young fellow waited for her. "Get what you needed?"

"Yes, thank you so much. Only now I have to visit all these other people, and you must have a class to get to."

"Not as much as you'd think," he said. "I'm a graduate student with the physics department. They've sort of sent me to look out for lost-looking people and help them find their way around. Let me help you some more."

"Oh, you don't have to..." she started to protest. At the same time, she wondered how young he had started graduate school. Was he older than she thought?

"But I want to. My name is Timothy, by the way. Say, do old doctors like to drink coffee?"

***

"What would you say were your goals for treatment?" Doctor Weatherly asked. The office had a big conference table in the middle. There were two nurses, one of them male. There was a doctor in a white lab coat with a stethoscope around his neck like a badge or rank. There was a social worker named Marnie.

"Well, I guess I just want to get back to school, Doc. If you would let me have my work so I didn't get too far behind..."

Weatherly took a long pull off his pipe, set it down on the table. Smoke eddied about his head like his neck was on fire. "The team is not so certain the stress of study would be good for you at this time. You should try to rest and relax, give your mind and your brain time to recover, if recovery is in the cards. We don't know that much about what is happening to you right now, what predicts wellness and what predicts ongoing illness, but we think rest is best."

"Here's the thing, Doc. I'm bored. You know, I go to the groups and I exercise in the yard and I eat what you say and I take the pills, but I'm bored. It's driving me crazy. Well, to coin a phrase."

Amused looks shot back and forth across the table. "Not very surprising you don't find the environment restful. Personally I think the psych ward is the last place we should keep people who are experiencing psychological difficulties. But it is the best we have. What else might help you to rest?"

"Honestly, my work helps me rest. You don't understand. It takes more work for me to not do my mathematics than it does to keep up with it. I don't do mathematics, I am a mathematician. Math is life. Well, from where I'm sitting. Hey, you said you don't really know anything, right? So how about an experiment? Give me my work and see if I get better or worse. Or if it doesn't change anything at all, right? I mean, we have a two in three chance of winning."

"He has a point," offered Marnie. "And our directive is to move towards a patient-centered approach."

"All right, we'll give it a try, then. But let's not expect any miracles, shall we? Good. Next order of business. Walter, tell me about the red-haired girl. Have you seen her lately?"

Walter visibly hesitated. Weatherly wondered if Walter knew he should say *no*. Regardless, the young man said, "I still see her. Her teeth aren't as sharp as they were before, that's the best I can say. She's outside right now, by the fence outside the exercise yard. But she hasn't bothered me yet."

"You said before she only watches."

"Yeah, that's so. She doesn't say anything. I don't know if she *could* say anything. She's just a picture in my head, right? Only she watches and that makes me scared."

"How's your appetite?" asked the man with the stethoscope.

"Not so good, but I eat anyway. Actually maybe the kitchen could send up a little less on my plate. I'm starting to gain weight."

"You're still a bit under where you were when you came in," said Weatherly, "but weight gain is a side effect of some of your medicines. It is a good idea to keep track. Any other problems?"

"Just boredom. And anxiety, I guess. I'm restless as Hell, if you'll pardon my French. You know, I feel like my life is going on out there without me. Like I'm missing it."

The nurses were nodding. "We can certainly sympathize with that," Weatherly offered, trying to hold Walter's attention. "For the meantime, though, we are stuck with what we have. Perhaps you'll leave us to chat for a while now, and I will have the orderlies bring you your schoolwork."

"All right, thanks, Doc." Walter left by the side door, sort of slinked off.

"That seemed to go quite well," Weatherly announced when Walter was gone.

"I'm still very concerned," said the head nurse.

"I don't think he's telling us the worst of it," agreed Marnie.

"You may be right. On the plus side," Weatherly said, "we successfully deflected him about going home. He'll settle for having his homework for the time being."

"All of physics is either impossible or trivial. It is impossible until you understand it and then it becomes trivial."

Ernest Rutherford.

Four

"Doctor Jiminez, you're needed in admissions. Doctor Jiminez."

"Who the Hell is Jiminez?" asked Gertie, looking at the speaker as though the answer was there.

"You're the charge nurse," Yvonne replied, clamping a tube so she could remove the IV from her patient. "If you don't know, nobody knows." She mopped up the little trickle of blood coming from the IV entry wound, covered it with a cotton ball held in place with a Band Aid.

"They charge us for those," Gertie said. "No sense wasting them. Bob's just going to wash her in his sink anyway."

"They only charge the patients who are alive and have insurance," Yvonne said. "Besides, dying is undignified enough. I'll save my parsimony for Accounts Receivable." She pulled an extra sheet out of the cabinet behind her, covered the patient gently. "Be a dear?"

"Oh, you haven't signed the TOD yet."

"Oops." Yvonne grabbed the chart from the end of the bed, flipped to the last page. Mrs. Heinlein had been terminal for days, so the relevant paperwork was prepared. There was a final note already, though, detailing time and cause of death so the pathologist could do up a certificate.

"Is this some sort of joke?" Yvonne asked.

"What?"

"I think I found your Doctor Jiminez. Look here. Whoever it is already did the care note for Roberta's death."

"What? Give it here." Gertie took the chart, flipped to the last page. "I don't see anything."

"Hm?"

"The last note is mine. See? We forced fluids this morning, switched to IV morphine when she couldn't wake up to take a pill. Nothing after that."

"That's..." Yvonne was about to say impossible, but now she was looking at the chart again, and what she had seen was plainly no longer there.

"Not funny, Yvonne."

"No, I don't think so either. I'm sorry. Maybe the stress is getting to me. Here, I'll walk her down myself, get a cup of coffee or something."

"Go ahead. Won't be any more excitement here tonight."

The patient's personal effects were already bagged and tagged ready for the morgue. Yvonne usually avoided the place, even though this was her hospital, not the one uptown where she had identified Valery. But she knew the way. Everyone lost patients sometimes.

There was a service elevator in the back exactly so the patients never needed to see the handful of corpses that made the trip every day. Sometimes they used the front elevator anyway and just treated the patient as though they were sleeping and nobody was any the wiser. The back elevator could have sort of a spooky feeling to it. It was old, full of rattles and shakes and groans, with a mesh front and a half-door of unfinished wood. Everything had to be opened and closed manually.

The outside door was like a clamshell. You took hold of a strap in the middle and pulled down. The steel half on top went up and the wood half on bottom went down. Yvonne did that, pushing the bottom part down the last couple of inches with her foot. Then she pulled aside the mesh screen and stepped inside. Pulled the rolling bed in after her. Pulled up the outside door. As the plywood rose up the steel half came down to meet it. Then she closed the inner mesh, stabbed with a finger at the button marked B2.

The elevator lurched and groaned and started to descend. The air cooled perceptibly as it sank down to ground level and then below. A minute later, the little bell in the corner chirped to announce arrival, and the whole thing shuddered to a stop. Then came the procedure with the doors again, opening and dragging the bed out and closing them behind her.

"Another customer?" said Bob Wilson, the pathologist.

"Roberta Heinlein, down from oncology," said Yvonne.

"Yvonne?"

"Yes, Robert?"

"Huh. For a second I had the funniest feeling..."

"You know, everyone says that lately. Is this some type of big practical joke? Because it is starting to annoy me."

Bob came and took the bed, wheeled it over by the human-sized steel sink where he would wash and begin to prepare the body. Checked the paperwork attached to the bed. "No autopsy, this one says. I'll just clean her up, then, and call the county coroner. No next of kin?"

"No, Bob. She was homeless. I didn't think we let our old people be homeless in New York City in nineteen seventy-six." Yvonne made use of the department's sink, and liberally applied antibacterial soap to her hands, lathered, scrubbed under her nails with the little brush provided for that purpose. "You mind if I borrow a cup of coffee?"

"So long as you promise not to return it after you drink it."

"Thanks, Bob." She got a little styrofoam cup, poured coffee from the pot in the little glass cubicle that, at least according to regs, separated food and drink from dead bodies. A little sugar - no, a lot of sugar, let's face it - and she was on her way. The elevator groaned to life behind her, rising to pick up another rider. Hopefully not another customer for pathology. "Maybe I'll take the stairs."

***

"We're giving the position to Jenssen," Michaels said. He was a tidy man: big plastic glasses, fringe of short dark hair above his ears, immaculate white lab coat over a gray suit.

"Jenssen only has one ER rotation and three less years on oncology and was the bottom of his class." Yvonne blew on her coffee. The cafeteria was no place for this kind of conversation - probably why Michaels had chosen it. She'd be less likely to make a scene.

"We're going with Jenssen. He is more careful with the resources, costs us less money. We need a man who can -"

"You need a man. I'm sick of this glass ceiling crap, Carl. You're promoting him because he's a white guy who went to the right school, like all the other staffers you promoted because they're white guys who went to the right schools."

"A man who can keep the costs in line and not take everything personally. You're far too emotional, *Doctor* Leskov. You worry about every case far beyond the point of reason. You can't save everyone."

"But Carl-" she interrupted, setting down her coffee too hard, sloshing it over the side and over her hand.

"I'm your friend, Doctor Leskov. As your friend, I'm telling you: you have to let him go. There was nothing you could have done and there isn't anything you can do, and you won't break through the glass ceiling ignoring directives and instigating cost overruns. This is the new world, Doc... Yvonne. The new world is about cost control, keeping the bottom line healthy. You want to move up? Be a team player."

Yvonne looked around, saw the place was more or less empty. It was the middle of the night. An elderly couple shuffled around looking at slices of pie in the chiller.

"You have no right to say that to me, *Doctor* Michaels. One psych rotation doesn't make you my damn psychoanalyst."

"Have it your way. But have it your way in your current position. Look, you're gifted. We all get that. But right now your gifts are for saving lives, not saving money. When you're ready to use those talents in the bigger world, the forest and not the trees, come back and see me. We'll make it happen. I'll write a job just for you. Until then, have yourself a good night. I've got to hit the ER. Full moon. Going to be busy."

Yvonne held her tongue, all the profanity in her mind better left there. Michaels would be off to the ER to count beans (in the form of sutures, gauze pads, surgical tape), not to stitch people up. A night of making sure nobody closed a wound with four stitches when three would do it.

"Thanks," she eventually said to the air where he had been sitting. "Guess I'll go save some lives instead of saving money."

***

For his part, Michaels left the room with a profound sense of disconnection. All the reasons he had given Leskov were really rationalizations. Truthfully, he hadn't seen her application. They had hired Jenssen because the only other option - Jiminez - was far too new. They had hired Jiminez after Leskov had died in that car accident two years ago.

Only there was no Jiminez and the more he thought about her the less he could recall. And Yvonne had survived the accident. Hell, he'd just sat with her over coffee and post-hocked her, back-rationalized a decision they hadn't made. It beat the hell out of admitting they'd never seen her application. What kind of hospital loses track of its own staff?

The place was sure getting weird. All the attention to costs, dollar amounts. That was one thing. The new suits sitting on all the boards were another, probably driving the first. But Yvonne was the weirdest.

I went to her funeral, Michaels thought to himself, riding the elevator down to the main floor. *I buried her, shook hands with her husband, gave a dry commiseration. I remember it.* But the funeral was like Doctor Jiminez: the more he thought about it, the harder it was to remember. *Was it her funeral? Or was it her husband's after all?*

The ER was busy, as expected. Full moons always meant busy. Busy ERs full of drunks and stab wounds and crazy traffic accidents. Busy neonatal units, three or even four women laboring at one time. Some nights they ran out of little plastic cribs in the newborn viewing room.

He was in the ER by now. There were two guys who had been in a traffic accident. One had gone through his windshield after T-boning a convertible, smashed into the passenger. The night was mostly about pulling the two guys out of one another and stitching them up.

"Scrub in, Carl, we're gonna need you," the charge doctor said.

I knew I should have worn my old suit, he thought.

"Mathematicians deal with large numbers sometimes, but never in their income."

Isaac Asimov, Prelude to Foundation

Five

The ping-pong table was noisy. That meant it was Christmas.

Walter had quickly learned how to measure the passing of the seasons on the unit. It was evident in the weather, obviously, but also in the moods of the other patients: some were increasingly frantic to get out, while one guy who had never had a family Christmas always seemed to get himself moved here. There were presents and eggnog and music, the best Christmas Clarke would ever have.

Some guys got really depressed. Walter could sympathize. Christmas was sort of depressing when you thought about it too hard. He would not see any family. Only his sister was out there in the world anymore. His friends wouldn't drop by - they were headed home for the holidays. It would be pretty lonely here.

But one thing that happened every year about Christmas time was one of the staff members bought new paddles and balls for the table.

Walter tried to concentrate on his math books. He was repeating complex function theory. But the noise was incessant. *Click-tock, click-tock, click-tock.* He looked up. Clarke was there, playing table tennis with Arthur. Walter briefly wondered who Clarke had punched in the face to get his transfer this time. Then he saw Clarke had a partner helping him: the red haired girl. Everything Clarke missed, she caught, until the beleaguered Arthur missed.

"Double bounce!" Arthur was yelling. "My point!"

The red haired girl turned her attention to Walter, smiled her toothy smile while the men sorted out the score. Then the ball was moving again, and she was all over it.

Maybe I'll study elsewhere.

Walter gathered up his books, papers, the little golf pencils the nurses let him have. In the common room, a bunch of guys were watching The Muppet Show. The two old guys in the balcony complained about how bad Gonzo's comedy was. The red haired girl watched with the guys and it never occurred to Walter to wonder how she had gotten here from the game room so fast. She flashed her sharp teeth at him as he went past.

Obviously no peace was to be had here, so he checked into the big communal bedroom they all shared. Too busy in there, too. Two men smoked weed behind the lockers and Benny was raping Thad. Not a good place to get math work done.

The library was down past the nurses' station that doubled as a conference room. They were talking about him in there.

"Could it be a Charlie Brown thing?" Marnie was asking, the social worker. She was a pasty blonde woman, wrinkled at thirty-five, too thin.

"As in Peanuts?" asked Doctor Guy, fiddling with his stethoscope.

"Yeah, Peanuts. Chuck Schultz."

"Interesting idea," said Weatherly. "What brings us to this suspicion?"

"Well, all the delusions are based on something real, aren't they? You're the one who always says we don't have any more Napoleons here because Napoleon isn't in our minds any more. Now people worry about the government, the CIA, the police."

"Yes, conceded, by why Peanuts?"

"Not much. Just the way he says it. The red-haired girl. Not the redhead, not the girl with red hair. Just that phrase." Marnie put her hand over Guy's to stop his fidgeting.

"Fair enough. Refresh my memory. What about the red-haired girl and Charlie Brown?"

"Wasn't she always the *little* red-haired girl?" wondered Guy.

"Yeah," said Marnie. "And Charlie was always obsessed with her, but too scared to do anything about it. He saw her all over the place, ball games and school and so on. But he never worked up the guts to talk to her. I think it's about shame and self-esteem. Charlie Brown doesn't have the confidence, can't exploit an opportunity. He's ashamed of himself for even liking her, because he doesn't deserve anything back."

"Thin," said Weatherly.

"Not sure what we stand to gain by psychoanalyzing Chuck Schultz by proxy, actually..." Guy offered.

"All true," said Marnie.

"But maybe a starting point. And the girl has yet to threaten him, which is unusual for a paranoid schizophrenic with such hallucinations. No violent episodes for a few weeks. What caused the last one?"

"Someone messed with his math book," the nurse said.

The unit alarm buzzed, a claxon with flashing red lights, and everyone with less education than a master's degree piled out of the nurses' station to see where the trouble was. "In the dorm," called an orderly, and that's where everyone went, probably to tackle Benny. If nobody did anything to get tackled in the course of a day sometimes the orderlies would make something happen.

Two orderlies ran past Walter as he passed the station. Around the corner and into the library. Nobody was in there. In Walter's opinion, most of the people here were pretty much meat-heads and low-lifes. They wouldn't be caught dead in a library. The trouble was, it was usually locked. Today it was open - someone had forgotten to lock it. Probably the two guys who had just run by. They would be back this way soon: the hall outside was lined with seclusion and restraint rooms.

The best thing was, the red-haired girl never came back here. Once he laid on the couch, there was nowhere else to sit. Books took up three walls, the couch most of the fourth. At last, peace.

He opened his books, each to the marked page, opened his notebook, and started to write.

After a while, when his wrist was starting to hurt from scribbling his formulae and he was starting to think about peeing, someone knocked on the door. "How'd you get in here?" Marnie asked, kindly.

"It was open. I like it in here. I like the books, and the quiet."

"Well, you might as well stay. You have a visitor."

"A visitor?" Walter repeated. "But, my work..."

"It will still be here later, Walter. How often do you get a visitor?"

He frowned, thought about it. "Well, who is it?"

"I'll bring him in," Marnie said, without answering the question.

A minute later, she showed in a tall, gangling man dressed in slacks and a sweater over a dress shirt and tie. He had on wire-rim glasses and wore a little beard, just on his chin.

"Timothy!" Walter said, his work forgotten for a moment.

"Hello, Walter. Your sister asked me to send her love." Timothy had a package behind his back which he brought out as Walter came over to hug him. Walter seemed very small next to Timothy, indeed had never been a large man and seemed to be shrinking year over year.

"Is this for me? I bet it's another book."

"Your favorite," said Timothy.

And it was: a science fiction anthology with introductions written by Isaac Asimov. When Walter pulled off the brown paper and let it fall to the floor, tears filled his eyes. Then he opened the front cover and saw that the book was signed by Asimov himself. Walter's face could not decide whether to smile or weep for joy, so he just stood there, thunderstruck for a minute.

"How?" he said finally, and there was more to the question but it wouldn't come out through the lump in his throat.

But Timothy knew what the whole question was. "Well, Yvonne just sent him the book, with a return envelope and return postage and a nice letter, and he kindly signed it and returned it. The letter he wrote in return is in the back. It's to your sister, but she thought it would mean more to you than to her. For her it's just a reminder."

"Of Valery," Walter said. "He liked science fiction, too."

"Yes. Quite a man, if your sister is to be believed."

"He was nice. But his sister had red hair. Uh, here, sit down. Tell me how you're doing."

Timothy took one end of the couch, a brown leather thing with little tears in the arms and scuffed wooden legs. It belonged in a thrift shop. He said so. "This couch belongs in a thrift shop. And I should know: I'm a mathematician. All my milk-crate furniture comes from thrift shops."

"You're a physicist," Walter said. "Surely that's more lucrative."

"Depends on the kind of physics you're doing, I suppose. I mostly do basic research, abstract stuff. Cosmology. I'll never invent a bigger, flatter television or a better mousetrap. I hear Sagan is going to do a show on physics. But I'm happy getting chalk on my pants. Anyway, how the hell are *you?*"

"At least as good as you'd think," Walter said, and his face had volumes written in his expression. "It's not so bad here as you might expect. I get to do my work and I don't have to earn a living. I miss being in the world, but at the same time, I'm not sure I'm ready to go back into it. It's pretty scary out there. The other inmates, they're really the hard part. And the food is pretty uneven. The cherry pie isn't bad, or the fried chicken, but most of the food really blows."

"Maybe that explains why you're so skinny."

"Everyone says that," Walter said.

"It's true. You're wasting away. Well, a little asceticism might be good for the soul. How is your math coming? I hear you're redoing some advanced theory work."
Actually, Walter was always redoing that class, over and over, and never seemed to notice. They just photostatted

the same homework like it was new. At the start of the course he knew he was repeating it, he thought for the first time. By the end he had forgotten.

"It's harder than I thought. The medicine they give me, it slows me down."

"Can I take a look?"

"Well, I'd rather just keep it private."

"That's all right. You'll call me about any big breakthroughs though, right?"

"You'll be the second to know."

"Hey, now. Who's going to be first?"

"That would be me," Walter giggled, and it was a wholesome sound, incongruous and delightful in this unwholesome place. Even the library smelled vaguely of urine.

"You want me to tell your sister anything for you?"

"No, I'll call her tomorrow," Walter said. That's what Walter always said. But tomorrow he would have his head buried in his notes. There would come a time, perhaps, when even an Asimov book would fail to occupy his mind.

"Well, I should get going. You want I should come visit again in a week or so?"

"Can you?"

"Sure. I'll bring some Burger King. See if we can put some waist back under your waistband."

***

Walter laughed, and it was hard for Timothy not to ruffle his hair like Walter was his kid brother, ten years old ten years ago. But Walter was a grown man. They said their goodbyes, then Timothy found Marnie to get let off the unit. It was always a little disconcerting to visit Walter here. Timothy wondered whether he would come on the unit one day and be mistaken for a patient and never allowed to leave. Today was not that day, though.

He went out the big door, flirted with Marnie just a little even though she was not his type, and headed down the stairs. There were rabbits out in the parking lot. Reputedly they would eat the insulation off the wires in your car if you left it out there too long, leaving you stranded. Since he didn't have a car, that was hardly a worry. He walked out to the main road and sat in a bus shelter. Grief pressed against his eyelids, against his sinuses. He hadn't known Walter when he was well, but he had been visiting every few weeks since he had met Yvonne two years before. And Walter was going downhill fast.

Back at home, he called Yvonne.

"I'm sorry to say, I think he's worse. I mean, from here, it doesn't look like he's ever going to recover." The Bakelite phone felt heavy, smelled distinctive. It was easier to think about that than how Yvonne might be feeling in this moment.

"Did he like his book, at least?"

"That seems to be a way to reach him, yeah. He got out of his head for a few minutes, even smiled and laughed a little. You could still see the strain, though. That place... It might be the best you can do, but I'm sorry, it isn't a good place. Not at all a good place."

"I don't know what else to do," Yvonne said, her voice small and remote over the telephone.

"That's the worst thing. I don't think there is anything to do. He sort of has to fight this battle on his own, and it seems like he's going to lose. Or he has already lost. I've been doing some reading on the subject, and it doesn't seem like most folks who stay florid this long ever really come back from it." Timothy sighed, rubbed his temples.

"Well, thanks for going to visit. Your visits mean a lot to him. I'll call him again later this week. Can I call you, too? Is there anything I can help you with?"

"I'm doing OK, Yvonne. Thanks for asking. Those letters you wrote really helped. I'm starting as associate professor come spring and I can live on grants until then. You've really been a darling."

"All right, Timothy. Now you call if I can help you any more. Happy Christmas."

"Merry Christmas, Yvonne," he said back, and listened to the distant, obscure *click* on the line that signified her absence.

Timothy sat down in his chair, one of a handful of furniture pieces in his little apartment. It was brown leather with a box frame underneath and rolled on castors. A real thrift-store find. There was a little tear in the upholstery but Timothy had taken the leather off the chair, sewn the tear shut with needle and thread, and reattached it.

The other furniture included a folding card table, a typewriter, and a bookshelf. He owned a rug but left it rolled up in the corner because it made it hard to roll around on his chair. There was a mattress on a box spring on the floor in the bedroom and a radio on the kitchen counter. Timothy owned nothing else of any value, except for his books.

There was no light in the room, only the overheads in the open-plan kitchen. He had his eye on a hanging lamp at the second-hand shop. It was a big orange glass thing that looked like it should be hanging off the back of a pirate ship, with a faux bronze chain that disguised the electrical cord and allowed one to hang it from the ceiling. But for now he had to read in the kitchen.

Today's project was to wonder if some of the strange quantum behaviors of photons and electrons might be reproduced at a larger scale. Say, at the level of an atom or even a molecule. Just as he had all his books open to the right pages, the phone rang again.

"Hello?" he said, shoving the receiver into the space between his head and shoulder, trapping it there with his ear.

"Timothy?"

He did not recognize the voice. "Yes. Who's speaking?"

A burst of static confused the answer. He was sure he heard the name of an unfamiliar woman. Then the rest came in clear. "Are you there? I'm sorry to bother you again, but..."

"Yvonne?"

"Yes, it's me."

"That's funny," Timothy said. "For a moment I thought it was someone else."

"Who?"

"I don't know, there was static on the line. Just my imagination, probably."

"I don't think so," said Yvonne in that tinny, tiny voice, far away. "That's why I'm calling back. I've been so nervous to tell anyone about this, but if I can't tell you, who can I tell?"

"Tell me what?"

"I think I was supposed to die in that accident, Timothy."

"Oh, you can't know that," Timothy said. "There is no such thing as determinism at the middle scale."

"I know, I know all that. You know, those days of hanging around smoking weed, I learned so much from you, and it did a great deal to help me with losing Valery. I feel so close to you. If I was only your age, we might have married."

"But you were old then and older now," Timothy laughed.

"Yes," Yvonne agreed, and Timothy could hear a strained smile. "But something is going on right now, and I need help to understand it. Wherever I go I am not expected. Someone has been there ahead of me, living my life and having my relationships. Sometimes I see Valery's reflection in glass or in mirrors and at first I thought it was just my imagination, wishful thinking, but now I'm sure I'm seeing something real. And some other doctor... people remember her when I'm not around and forget her when I show up. She has a name, and I can't remember it. I wrote it down but the writing disappeared.

"Timmy, Timothy, I'm frightened. Something very strange is going on around me."

"You know how you sound, don't you?"

"Yes," Yvonne said. "I sound crazy."

"You sound scared," Timothy corrected. "Hey, do you have any time off coming? Maybe after Christmas?"

The holiday season was always busy at the hospital and Yvonne preferred to work, giving other people time with their families. "New Year's?"

"Fine, fine. Do you want to come visit? Stay with me a few days, I'll make room somehow. Visit your brother a little, and tell me more about what's going on. I'll do some reading between now and then, see what I come up with."

"All right, Timothy. I'll think about it. Hey, thanks for listening."

"You got it," he said, and listened as she disappeared from the line for a second time.

Timothy looked back at his work, at the nearest open book. *Wheeler, however, does not endorse the hypothesis that the state of the photons is affected by the observation prior to the observation but, rather, that any sort of measurement annihilates the photon itself. As we know, measurement affects the particles being measured, a well-known observation effect sometimes confused with the Heisenberg uncertainty principle. Equations for the wave form instability...*

Those were the equations he wanted, useful even though the book that contained them was written for undergraduate students. "An introduction to quantum uncertainty," was the title.

Something about that passage tickled in the light of the phone call. A simple coincidence? Anxiety?

"No middle-scale determinism," Timothy reminded himself. But somehow his own voice echoing off the bare walls in this drab, lonely apartment was more unsettling than comforting.

***

"What would you say were the funding potentials of a project like this, Doctor Card?"

Timothy was still not used to being addressed as "Doctor." The ink was not exactly wet on his degree certificate, but he was sure he could smudge it if he tried.

"Uh, well, this is pretty basic-research sort of stuff." Basic research meant the opposite of applied research: no better televisions, no nastier weapons, no prettier, sleeker automobiles. Just more knowledge about the universe. "But it's not completely worthless. I mean, I've heard from some non-profit foundations that are interested in the work."

"To the tune of how much, roughly?" asked his supervisor, Doctor Trant.

"Well, if all the money came through, it would add up to on the order of fifty."

"That won't support a staff," Trant said.

"It will more than pay my salary, though, and truthfully I don't need much of a staff. I could get by with a research assistant and we can pay him in college credits."

"True, true. You anticipate this work taking up most of your time? Large-scale wave function anomalies?"

"Most," Timothy said, feeling defensive. "Not all, to be sure. You have something else in mind?"

"Well, as the new kid in the department, so to speak, there will be some scutwork to do from other projects. Especially fundraising, especially as your project is not well-funded. The more you can publish the less nasty that will be, of course, and tenure would help you out tremendously. But there is a defense project, high-energy particle measurement..."

"What would be the defense applications of measuring cosmic radiation?"

"Gamma rays."

"Oh." Timothy thought for a bit. "We'd want to get some students in on this one, right?"

"If possible. The more our students can publish before they fly off into the larger world, the better our institution looks, and the less time they have between college and career." Trant sat down in his big chair, black leather behind a giant steel desk, leaving Timothy standing.

"Well, Doctor Trant, it actually sounds like a good fit. It's not exactly what I'm working on now but just close enough we'll likely see some synergy between the projects."

"My thoughts exactly," said Trant, steepling his fingers.

That seemed to end the interview, so Timothy headed out of the small office and out of the department. He wasn't exactly being paid to come in and have these conversations, but luckily the department respected his time by keeping them short. Not that Timothy had very much else to do before the school term started.

The bus ride back to his neighborhood was short but cold. The bus was dirty and the windows fogged, obscuring the beauty of D.C. in the wintertime. He felt at home on the bus, though: everybody looked homeless in the winter, by his estimation, and he was one missed check from homeless himself.

His apartment building was a few blocks from the bus stop. There was nothing so dramatic as snow to slog through but D.C. was usually so hot that the just-above-freezing temperatures felt much colder. The humidity was nearly unbearable, too, giving the cold long, intrusive fingers to reach through layers of clothing. Other people were out walking on various errands. A lady with a sack of groceries in a brown paper bag. Some kids with Grizzly Adams and Happy Days lunchboxes. A couple of old guys, more sauntering than walking, smoking pipes.

There was his building, up on the right. *It looks like a slum*, he thought, *but at least it's authentic*.

The elevator was out. Had been since he moved in. His neighbors could not reliably remember a day when it operated. So Timothy climbed stairs, flight by flight. Twelve flights in all to go up six floors. How many stairs? Twelve per flight: if you counted the floor at the bottom as zero going up and one going down, and the opposite for the floor at the top, twelve. Otherwise thirteen. So one-hundred forty-four, or one hundred fifty-six.

Is this step a stair? he thought, on the landing at the bottom of the last flight of stairs.

Does it matter?

It did not seem to, so he forgot about it.

"Those who are not shocked when they first come across quantum mechanics cannot possible have understood it."
Niels Bohr

<u>Six</u>

Yvonne slept. Her covers were tangled up between her legs, under one arm, her shift stuck to her with sweat, though the room was cold. In the walls, a rat scratched unnoticed.

Her bed was high off the floor, four dark wood posts in Queen Anne style rising over her. A clock ticked relentlessly on the nightstand by her head, its numbers faintly luminous thanks to radium paint. "Big Ben" was inscribed on the faceplate.

Her dream was so real, so crystal clear, that it was unreal. She was Valery, the night of the crash. The plow hit the passenger side and Yvonne died, just as she should have. The blade of the plow smashed through the door, caved in the roof, and she was just crushed. There was no escape from such an accident.

Valery climbed through the shattered windscreen on his hands and knees, getting glass shards in his palms, in his knees, his pants shredded.

Mister, you all right?

Yeah, I'm fine - but you killed my wife.

An ambulance ride but no injuries. Incredulity all around. So familiar, only she was Valery, not herself. There she was, his wife, just thirty-six. He would never have another birthday absent tears for her, absent the absolute rending loss of her. She was on the steel table, covered by an antiseptic white sheet except for her poor face. The doctors had tried to hide the worst of the damage to her skull but it was too extensive.

A day in the hospital, more incredulous doctors. *It happens sometimes*, they said. But it didn't, it never happened. Nobody walked away with nothing at all, not a single scrape or bruise. It was impossible.

What am I supposed to do now? What can I do without her? And why should I?

Back to his job with the law firm, researching precedents on environmental cases. Writing checks to care for his brother-in-law, fading away in some hospital down in D.C.. Passed over for partner. Lonely, so, so lonely. And he saw her everywhere, saw his lost Yvonne where his own reflection should be, sometimes. For a while, that was oddly comforting. But then people started to lose track of him, forget him if he wasn't around. He'd catch little hints of another man living parts of his life: forms signed at work that he should have signed, but the signatures disappeared in a moment, and he soon forgot each incident but remembered them all as a sense of wrongness.

This wasn't supposed to happen, not like this. She wasn't supposed to die.

Valery had gone to school with a chess prodigy from Russia - the only man he knew who did not make fun of his name. The chess guy, Gergiev, knew a math guy who knew a physics guy who... who what?

Yvonne woke up with tears on her cheeks, her nose full of snot. It was hard to breathe - that was what had wakened her. And now she sat in bed, crying and aching, not quite sure who she was. *Am I crying for Yvonne or for Valery? What have I lost?*

Everything. I've lost Valery, and I've lost my self.

***

Yvonne sat at the typewriter in her study. The neighbors might complain as it was barely morning and the typewriter was pretty loud, but let them. She typed:

Gergiev chess prodigy high school

Russian

Then she looked at the sheet of paper next to the typewriter. The name she had typed there the other day had faded away, like invisible ink. But she remembered typing the name if not the name itself. Whatever was happening, the effect was growing stronger.

There was a phone by the typewriter, a modern thing made to look antique in cream and gold plastic. It had push-buttons in a circle like a dial. She pressed just one of them: 0.

"Operator," came the remote voice. Yvonne pictured a woman her own age, hair in a bun, in a little cubicle. One wall would be lined with little sockets and she'd have patch cords all around her.

"Yes. Good morning. I wonder if you have a listing for Gergiev."

"One moment please." Obscure sounds filled up the moments as the operator looked through her reference material. "Sixty-three listings for Gergiev. Do you have a street address, Miss? Or a first name?"

"Oh. So many? No, that's all I have right now. I'm sorry."

"Anything else I can help you with?"

"No, no thanks. Have a nice day."

The operator clicked off the line. Yvonne dialed Timothy. He answered on the first ring.

"Timothy?"

"Oh, Hi, Yvonne. I was just about to make a call. What's new?"

"I want you to try to remember something for me. Write it down. Do whatever you have to."

"What is it?" he said gamely.

"Gergiev." Yvonne spelled it for him.

"Wait. I think I know a Gergiev. In the math department at Princeton. Works on game logic, systems programming or something."

"He doesn't play chess at all, does he?"

"No, why?" asked Timothy.

"Valery knew a Gergiev, or I dreamed he did. Chess prodigy. Must not be the guy. Just try to remember his name?" Yvonne knew it was too good to be true. There was no way that could be a reasonable coincidence.

"Slow down," Timothy said. "I didn't say he never played, I said he *doesn't* play. He retired from the chess circuit ten years ago. As a grand master. To make money in computing."

Yvonne said a word that her mother wouldn't have approved of. "Not possible."

"Likely, actually. Math and physics are crossover disciplines, and they're both pretty small. Everyone knows everyone through someone. Gergiev was my advisor's advisor. He actually did some notes for me on my dissertation. Smart guy. A bit... temperamental? But smart as a whip. You'd like him."

"Can you introduce me?"

"Yeah," Timothy said. "Sure. I'll take the bus up there in the morning, see you tomorrow night?"

"All right."

They talked a few more minutes, hung up the line. Then Yvonne made one more call.

"Michaels," came the reply after a few rings.

"I need some time off," Yvonne said shortly.

"Who's calling, please?"

"It's Yvonne. I work there. Take a minute to remember."

Silence on the line. "That's funny. You're right. I did need a minute... What's going on here?"

"I don't know, but by God I'm going to find out. I need some time off."

"It's Christmas," Michaels said. "You usually cover it..."

"Not this year. Something's come up. Hey, you owe me, Carl. I need to work this out while I remember there is something to work out. I know how it sounds. In fact, call it some mental health days."

"All right, Yvonne," he said at last. "Call me when you're ready to come back to work."

"Hey - don't hang up yet," she interjected suddenly. When she was sure he was still on the line, she asked, "When I called, I bet you were thinking I was someone else, someone you've never met but for a minute you thought she worked for you. Whenever I'm not around, you get to forgetting me and remembering her. I need her name."

"Jiminez," Michaels said without hesitation. "How did you-"

"Thanks," she said, and put the phone back in its cradle. Then she put a fresh sheet of paper in the typewriter, fiddled with the knobs for a minute, typed:

Jiminez, doctor, female.

"Operator? Do you have a listing for Jiminez? Doctor Jiminez?"

***

I can't do this before breakfast, Yvonne thought to herself. She went to the kitchen and fixed coffee first. Once Mr. Coffee was purring contentedly she put on eggs, toast, bacon.

Don't forget. Ten minutes went by as the bacon sizzled. It was hard to keep the name in mind. *Jiminez. Her name is Jiminez.* The paper gave up its ink to the universe and the bacon burned a little as she re-copied the words with a blue ball-point, freshening the name and phone number. She did it again as she was eating. Luckily, she liked her bacon a little blackened.

The greasy food left her stomach churning. Maybe before breakfast would have been better after all. Then Yvonne washed up the dishes, carefully copying the information twice more between tasks. *I'm stalling now,* she thought.

Yvonne went back into the study, picked up the phone. Dialed the number. Waited as the phone rang on the other end.

"Good morning?"

Yvonne had expected a Hispanic voice but there was no trace of accent. "Hi," she said, then found she had run out of words.

"Hello? Who's calling, please?"

"Um..." Nothing left to do but hang up like a crazy person or take the plunge. "Um, you don't know me, at least I think you don't, but I have to ask you a weird question. Um, have strange things been happening to you? Like you remember things that haven't happened, or you feel like you're sometimes in the wrong life?"

"Who is this? Is this some crazy religious thing?"

"My name is Yvonne. Doctor Leskov."

"Oh my God," Jiminez said. "Really? Are you... is this a prank? Am I on the radio?"

"I'm right, aren't I? These things happen to me, too, and it's not our imagination. You think sometimes you work at Manhattan General. But you don't. You even know the names of the people there, unless you think too hard about it. Then you forget and your real life comes back to you."

"Yes," Jiminez said simply. "What's going on, Yvonne?"

"I don't know, but now at least I know something really is."

"We should meet, I think."

"All right, Doctor Jiminez. When and where? Can it be in two or three days?"

"It's Rosie. And that would be fine. You'll bring some explanations, won't you?"

"I'll bring more questions," Yvonne said. "Here, take down my telephone number. And watch out - it's going to keep fading away on you. One more thing: Do you know any mathematicians? Or physicists?"

"I'd better," Rosie said. "I'm married to one. The other Doctor Jiminez is a nuclear physicist."

"In the beginning there was nothing, which exploded."
Terry Pratchett

Seven

Walter paced the unit. It was two hundred and seven steps from end to end. At one end was the door to the staff offices, a hallway Walter had never seen. With your back to that door there was another exit door to the left, leading to a stairwell and the world. To the right, the library. From there he walked straight ahead, passing the visiting room to the right and then the nurses' station, the seclusion and restraint rooms to the left and then the dining table and what passed for a kitchen. Then a dogleg right and left again, past the common room with the big TV set and crummy couches. Then another long hallway, with open-plan rooms left and right. At the end of that hallway, there was a multi-purpose room that opened off the hall, with the ping-pong table and some folding tables and chairs. Finally, at the ultimate end of the hallway, there was one more exit door leading to a stairwell down. Again, Walter had never been through that door and most likely never would.

There he turned around and set to pacing back to the other end.

Sometimes one of the animals who lived here would follow him, ape him, for a little while. One day last year he had lead a procession of eight or nine guys, all giggling and making stupid jokes about him. Most of them were gone now and he was still here. Walter had so much practice by now at ignoring the red-haired girl that ignoring real people was second nature, so they never bothered him.

Walter arrived where he had started, at the staff door, touched it with one finger, said, "One." Then he turned and started another lap.

Thus was the time measured: in soft footfalls on cheap tile, footfalls that echoed off bland paint and outlasted everyone.

Walter had no time for such thoughts, though. He was working on a problem. The most serious problem in all of mathematics. It would change the world one day, open the way to free energy, to immortality, and to world peace. There would be no more war and no need for nuclear weapons. It was the idea to end all ideas, and nothing else mattered. But he had to work out the equations, the formula.

So as he paced off time on the unit, he muttered softly under his breath the numbers and characters needed to work out the problem, desperate to finish his laps so he could get back to his notebooks.

Walter had gained about twenty pounds. His face was fleshy and he wore scrub pants from the unit closet because his waist was too big for his own jeans any more. It was the drugs, mostly. That and the food, the greasy, fatty, hi-carbohydrate diet. And the boredom. But mostly the drugs.

The only way to combat the lethargy was to get up and move, force himself to action, so that's what he did. Day after day. Twenty laps, which he figured equaled about two miles. And then as many push-ups as he could handle (he was up to about fifteen good ones), then sit-ups, then his daily shower. He didn't like doing it, feeling so exposed and leaving his notes so vulnerable, but if he didn't shower regularly the staff got on his case.

The drugs. They left him foggy, apathetic, fatigued, hungry, nauseated, and agitated. He twitched and spasmed his way through each day and thought about his math. His sister said he had to be careful of his weight and so he was, and also careful to keep his heart strong: the meds messed with something called the Q-T interval, something about the timing of heartbeats. As if he didn't have enough to worry about.

"You OK, Walter?" asked Marcus from the staff table. He was the lead orderly today.

"Fine, Marcus," Walter said, without stopping.

When Walter passed the staff table again, Marcus prodded a little more: "Anything you want to talk about today, buddy?"

"No," Walter replied, and kept going.

"You see the girl today?" as he passed once more.

"No," he lied. And that was the totality of his psychiatric care for the day. Marcus recorded the exchange in the big black book with Walter's name on the spine that Walter was not allowed to read. Later Walter would take a fistful of pills.

Later still, at last, he touched the door and said, "Twenty." A little bit out of breath, his pulse washing through his heart, Walter hit the showers. His problem weighed heavily on his thoughts.

***

Proofs were Hugo's favorite part of mathematics. They were the hardest thing to do, in his opinion, requiring rigid adherence to logic and formality, but also insight and creativity. All science derived from the logical rules of mathematical proofs.

"This one might be too hard for me," Peter said.

"Well, we're coming to the end of the program," Hugo replied. "Time to separate the men from the boys. As it were."

"You don't think that's a little sexist?"

"You see any girls in our classes?"

"Touché. Still, I'm not sure I can handle this problem. I've been knocking my head up against it all morning, and I can't find an entry point," Peter said. "I bet Walter could've handled it, though. He was always the best of us."

"Yeah, maybe. He'd have probably graduated by now if not for... Well, you know. But he's gone and we're still here. You know, what we need is a break. Like you said, we've been at this for hours now. Sometimes you just have to step away and clear your head."

"But it's due tomorrow," Peter protested.

"All the more reason to get it right," Hugo said. "Let's take a break, get the rest of this done tonight."

"Well..."

"We can go to the candy store, look at comic books. Or maybe the bookstore. You know what? I just finished November's *Fantasy and Science Fiction*. It's got a bit by Asimov in it, a list of his essays. You know who'd like that."

Peter smiled. "OK, bub, you talked me into it."

The two men tied sneakers onto their feet, grabbed coats and wallets and keychains, and left the dorm room behind them. The hallway was redolent with smoke (not all of it from tobacco) and with music. Hendrix wafted out from behind this door, The Doors from that one, Cream from the last door before the stairwell:

Hugo sang in a horrible falsetto as they went down the stairs, and Peter didn't know if he was making fun of Eric Clapton and company or thought he sounded just like him. "Dawn-light smiles on you leaving, my contentment. I'll wait in this place, where the Sun never shines... Wait in this place, where the shadows run from themselves..."

"Knock it off," Peter said. "You're terrible. Get a day job and don't quit it." Hugo laughed. "Besides," Peter continued, "seems a little creepy considering where we're going."

"Nothing wrong with the nuthatch," Hugo said. "Those guys're just guys, like us, like any other meatheads."

"Seriously, we're not guys like other guys, so that's really not a point in their favor."

"There you go," Hugo said. "We're as nutty as them. Who else would think about proofs all morning? Isn't math a kind of insanity, a removal from the world of concrete reality into a special abstract world with its own rules? I mean, what's the difference between our proofs and Walt's red-haired girl he sees everywhere?"

"When you put it that way it sounds..."

"Great?"

"Not what I was thinking, but close enough."

***

"Visitors?" Walter repeated.

"Yeah, visitors. Peter. Hugo. They've been here a dozen times since you arrived. You always seem so surprised. Go. Library. They're waiting."

"Thanks, Marcus," Walter said, and set off down the hallway.

In the library, Hugo took up two thirds of the couch, leaving Peter squashed into the remaining third. "Walt!" Hugo said, loud. "Hey, man - you look like crap. What are they feeding you here?"

Walter smiled vaguely, a fey, phantom thing that flitted across his face and was gone. "It's the drugs."

"I bet. Hey, it's the seventies. Everyone's on drugs these days. I was just telling Peter, we're all about the same here. Your roomies here don't think about anything weirder than the rest of us do."

"I guess." Walter's eyes flitted away from his visitors to his stack of notebooks under the table next to the couch. It didn't look like they had been touched at all.

"Come on, buddy. Don't let me hog the couch," Peter said, standing up. "Here, I'll stand over here. This room isn't too big at all, is it?"

There was hardly room next to Hugo, but Walter squeezed in.

"Not much to say, huh? Well, it's good to see you anyway. Hey, I brought you this mag." Hugo pulled the rolled up Fantasy and Science Fiction from his coat pocket.

"Thanks," Walter said, a little light finally back in his eyes. He flipped straight to the Asimov pages. "We don't get magazines in here. Well, not good ones. Old National Geographics. And they tear pages out of those. Anything that might be too exciting."

"Walt?" Pete opened. "You still a whiz with proofs?"

"The drugs, they make it hard to focus. And I'm working on... on..."

"Foundational formulae?" Hugo offered.

"Yeah." He had been about to reveal his secret, but if he did, his friends might steal it, or let it slip to the wrong person, who would steal it. It was hard enough to keep it from the guards, who all worked for the Red-Haired Girl.

"I'm really stuck on a proof, buddy. We're taking a break from them for now. We were hoping a little head space would help us start fresh later. You know how it is."

"Yeah," Walter said, but what he was really thinking was how hard it was not to look at his notebooks right now and give it all away.

"You wouldn't believe how crazy these problems are getting. Like, out of control complex. No chance you've ever heard of the Jiminez problem?" Peter asked.

"Jiminez? No. What is it about?"

"Translating four-dimensional objects into three-dimensional spheres."

"I wouldn't know about that," Walter said. "I mean, unless by forth dimensional you mean like a hypercube, in which case it would convert to a three dimensional sphere by using the same equations you'd use to translate the cube into a sphere, only extended along the dimension lines using imaginary numbers. I mean, the fourth dimension would be imaginary to begin with, so imaginary numbers would be necessary. I think."

Peter's mouth dropped open. "Holy sh... crap. You're right. That's what I was missing. The numbers you would need for the fourth dimensional translation don't work in three. You need an imaginary number. Walter, you've saved my life. Or at least a bunch of hours later tonight."

"Can you go now?" Walter asked, quietly. "I don't feel so hot. I need to lay down for a bit."

"Sure, Walt," Hugo said, getting up and taking Peter by the arm. "Come on, Petie. Let's give the man his space. Walt, don't you go changing. We love you, man. I know you can't hear that right now, just try to remember it, OK?"

Walter was already laying down with an arm across his eyes. "I'll try," he said, mostly to get rid of them.

In the stairwell, Peter said, "I shouldn't have asked, I guess. It seems like math is poison for his mind or something."

"He's still got it, but he can't use it. Such a waste. You know, I'm going to work twice as hard from here out. It should have been him, he should have been with us this whole way. Who knows what he could have discovered? So I'm going to discover twice as much. We've lost him, we can't lose his work, too."

"Yeah," Peter said. "Yeah, maybe you're right. But we don't have to lose him. We just have to work harder to accept who he is, even as we work harder to try to cover his missing brilliance."

"Maybe," Hugo said.

"It is often stated that of all the theories proposed in this century, the silliest is quantum theory. In fact, some say that the only thing that quantum theory has going for it is that it is unquestionably correct."

Michio Kaku

Eight

"So glad to see you, Timothy," Yvonne said, hugging him tightly. People flowed around them like a stream past a sunken log. The bus station smelled of burned diesel fuel, of urine, of damp wool and coffee and trash, of New York City in the morning.

"Try to keep me away," Timothy said. "I have this fetish for old ladies..."

"Be serious."

"I am serious. Anyway, I did as you said. I wrote down the name. Gergiev." Yvonne was leading him by the arm, slowly out of the stream of traffic and towards the parking lot. "Then the damnedest thing happened. I lost the note. Or I thought I lost it: I looked all over my little place and all I could find was a blank bit of torn-off note paper. So I wrote it again - it was hard to remember - and then, later, it was gone again.

"It faded right off the page. Anything else I wrote stayed, but Gergiev's name kept fading away."

Yvonne only nodded. They were at her car now, an old silver Mercury, sleek and low.

"You know, I expected more of a reaction," Timothy said, a sly smile hinted around the corners of his mouth.

"It's normal for me now," Yvonne said. "Ink fading selectively from paper has become an ordinary element of reality. That's almost the least weird thing I've heard today."

"Well, at least now I'm sure you're not crazy."

"I love you, Timothy. Thanks for coming."

"All right, I take it back. At least now I'm sure you're crazy - but you aren't wrong. Some weird stuff is definitely localized around you," Timothy said.

"What do you think about ghosts?" Yvonne asked.

"I think there are too many movies about ghosts. And demons, devils, aliens, and the Foreign Legion. The universe is weird enough without recourse to the supernatural. I mean, the natural is super enough."

"That's what I thought you'd say," Yvonne smiled.

"What, word for word? Anyway, why would ghosts fly through the world erasing peoples' names? There's got to be a physical explanation. Although, for the moment, one escapes me."

"I can't imagine what natural phenomena would steal certain names from paper in different parts of the world."

Timothy steepled his finger and intoned, "Just because one cannot imagine a thing, does not mean that thing does not exist."

"You talk to your students that way?"

"Haven't decided. Haven't met a student yet. Do you think I should?"

Yvonne just laughed at him, started negotiating the car into the correct lane for the bridge across the river into New Jersey.

***

"I didn't know Princeton was a castle," Yvonne said, cruising around the big, empty parking lot.

"Neither did I. But it's pretty cool. I think I saw that bridge over there painted on the side of a van," Timothy said.

"There should be Orcs crossing it, and Frodo and Sam hiding underneath."

They both had a good laugh, a delighted laugh that broke some of Yvonne's tension. It was as though she hadn't realized she was holding her breath, and finally let it out.

"What's Gergiev doing here, anyway? It looks like everyone else is sensibly at home enjoying winter break."

Timothy shrugged. "I phoned him up and this is where he wanted to meet. I don't guess he goes home much. Even when the students aren't here, he keeps his lab ticking over."

They parked, walked across some grass that was better cared for than most people's kids. The inside matched the outside, "collegiate gothic," the style was called. But Gergiev's office was way in the back, in a less ornate part of the campus behind the facade.

Gergiev himself rose from a small metal desk that looked army surplus, put out a hand like a bear paw minus talons. Timothy shook his hand with enthusiasm, Yvonne more cautiously. Gergiev looked her up and down while he talked with Timothy - nice to see you after so long, how did you solve the vanishing number series problem, what are you doing now. Yvonne was prim in a long skirt, turtleneck sweater and tweed jacket. Gergiev had on a charcoal grey suit with a turtleneck but it looked like he had slept in it, perhaps been woken from hibernation in it. He had a mound of fuzzy grey beard, a nose like Karl Malden (lumpy, full of broken blood vessels perhaps from too much drinking), gray eyes that seemed unfocused except when they trailed across Yvonne's calves.

Formalities completed, Gergiev finally made eye contact with her. "So what can I do for such a lovely visitor this morning?" His Russian accent was slight but definite.

"I believe you knew my husband," Yvonne said.

"Valery Leskov. A good man. Timothy told me what happened to him. Very sad, very sad. He was too good for this world, as he frequently told me."

"The thing is, and this is going to sound strange, I think he wants me to talk to you. And someone else wants me not to." Yvonne looked at her shoes as she said this, not sure how the scientist would receive such information. Computers were coldly logical and this was the man who taught them to be so.

"Americans are always ready to believe in supernatural things. Bigfoot and ghosts and possession." He chuckled a little, making his belly wobble. Yvonne was suddenly put in the mind of Hemingway. "But Russians, we invented the science of the paranormal. Remote viewing and Uri

Geller. We have more UFO reportings than the rest of the world combined. The world is strange place. So, what makes you think he is talking from beyond the world of the living?"

Yvonne told him about her dream, and about the other weird occurrences. "Something is definitely wrong here. Timothy says there must be an explanation, but I see an intelligence at work here..."

"Did you know my first degree was in psychology?" the bear-man said, reclining back in his chair. It was soft, creaky leather to the cheap plastic Yvonne and Timothy graced with their weight, but Gergiev would never have fit in one of these tiny modern contrivances. "Of course you did not. You knew nothing about me. I studied psychology to get better at chess. But you did not know that, and you did not know about projection."

"I did a psych rotation in the fifties. Projection is attributing another person with your own thoughts, feelings or motives."

"Yes, good. Splendid. People see patterns in things, agency in things, when really there is just randomness and order. Sometimes the recognition of a mind in a mindless thing is an eerie sensation. Like making eye contact with yourself in a mirror when you are home by yourself. You recognize the intelligence in the image but it is only that: an image in a piece of glass backed by a silver pane. Your flesh dimples with fear and awe, the presence of someone, but there is only something."

"Is this helpful?" Yvonne asked.

"Perhaps yes, perhaps no," the big man rumbled. "But you are here, and we don't know what that means yet."

"Perhaps if you clarified what it is that you do..."

"I develop microchip architecture to miniaturize computer processors. Silicon chips embed logic systems into hardware so that those processes can be exploited by software. The better the hardware, the better the potential software.

"It is like your body. Your mind cannot conceive of anything for which you do not have the neural architecture. For which you need the appropriate genetic codes. Every thought you have is enabled by genetic code expressed as proteins in your brain."

"I understand. What I don't understand is why my dead husband would send me here to discover this."

Gergiev shifted in his seat, causing it to groan uncomfortably beneath him. "I don't suppose he would," he said. "But I will think about this and perhaps little else. You story is extraordinary."

"No," said Yvonne, "I doubt that you will. I think you will forget that we ever had this conversation."

"Yes?"

"Yes, and I will, too. It will be as though I was never here."

Timothy started to speak then, but held his tongue. The beginnings of a thought had tickled his mind, gently, like unseen cobwebs in the dark. But the thought was gone now.

"I hope that is not true," Gergiev rumbled. "It has been a delight to look at you. Valery was a good man but married far above his station. It explains why he never introduced us. The marriage could not have survived such a meeting. I would have been compelled to steal you from him."

Yvonne blushed, started to think and therefore say something indignant, but suddenly changed her mind. "Is this some old world flattery routine?" she asked instead.

"Not at all," said Gergiev, clearly meaning yes. He stood, and she stood, and he took her hand again. This time rather than shake it he kissed her gently on the knuckles, his wiry beard brushing her fingertips. "All of life is a dream that we forget when we die. Whether I forget you or not, it was worth the time I knew you. But I think I will remember you on this side of the grave dirt."

"I didn't tell you," Timothy chimed in. "Vitali has an eidetic memory."

***

It was a long, quiet drive back to New York City.

It was getting dark before Timothy broke the silence. "Do you see any kind of a picture forming?" he asked, thumbing through a notebook that seemed emptier than it should.

"It's hard with all the information disappearing," Yvonne said. "Whenever I get a grip on things, I forget why it's important."

"I know what you mean. You know, you seem almost ghostly at times. To me. I mean, I don't know what I mean. I've been sitting next to you in this car for an hour and every once in a while it was like I was waking up, even though I was always awake, coming to consciousness in this situation with you. As though before that we weren't really here."

"Don't you think life is creepy enough without such thoughts?" Yvonne said, then immediately took it back: "No, no, maybe that's another piece of the puzzle. Turning away from stuff won't help. Will it?"

"I don't know," said Timothy.

"Will you stay with me?"

"I'll try," he said, "but it's hard. Some force, whatever is causing information to be deleted from the world, just keeps zoning me out."

"No, I mean tonight. Stay with me tonight. I miss you. And I don't want to be alone."

"Oh." It was Timothy's turn to blush. "Of course I'll stay with you. You think I drove all this way just to chat with that old bear in his castle? Although, if your husband is watching over you..."

It was the wrong thing to say. Yvonne said nothing. Indeed, after a little while she *thought* nothing, just drove the car.

After a while, Timothy said, "Maybe this forgetfulness thing can work in our favor."

"How so?"

"You could forget the last thing I said. It was insensitive. Stupid. I mean..."

"What was it you said again?" Yvonne asked sweetly.

"Thanks," Timothy said. "Does this mean I still get to stay with you, or have you forgotten that, too?"

***

The telephone rang a little after dawn. Yvonne threw a bathrobe over her shoulders and padded across the apartment to the office. She got the phone on the third ring, her breath visible as vapor as she said, "Hello?" into the receiver.

"Good morning. It's Rosie."

"Rosie? Rosie who?" Yvonne asked.

"Jiminez. You called me."

"Oh. Oh! Yes, I did. I'm so sorry. I told you this would happen, didn't I? That we would tend to forget all about one another?"

"Honestly I don't remember," said Rosie.

"Neither do I." They both laughed nervously. "Let's sit down for a cup of coffee and go over what we know."

"I'll bring my husband."

"If you like. Why, though, if you don't mind my asking?"

Rosie said, "I don't know. It seems like you were interested in physicists."

"Is he one?"

"Nuclear," Rosie replied.

"Oh. Interesting. The universe seems to be shoving scientists at me left and right. I'll explain later."

They set a time and place, and Yvonne put up the phone. Timothy was up by now. She could hear him puttering in the kitchen, putting on a pot of coffee. Yvonne was down to a few cups a day but he still had his graduate-student caffeine habit to contend with, at least a pot a day.

"I'll be in the shower," she called to him, and went off to soap up. After a few minutes standing in the swirling steam, hoping the apartment heat would kick on before she had to get out, Yvonne heard Timothy come into the room.

"Do you want privacy?" he asked.

"No," she said simply.

Timothy stripped off his shorts and climbed in with her, precariously because the shower was really a bathtub with a showerhead attached by rubber hoses, and slippery. "Good morning."

"Getting better," Yvonne said. She washed him and he washed her, and they kissed a little. "Are you going back today?"

"I can stay another day. If you want."

"I do. But don't put your whole life on hold for me. I'll come down to visit in January, just like we planned."

"All right. I'll stay anyway," he said. "It's lonely in D.C. without you."

The heat did not kick on. Yvonne dried and dressed hurriedly when they were done, shivering and puckering. Timothy seemed not to be too troubled by the cold even though his breath was a visible as hers. "I'm going to meet another puzzle piece," Yvonne said. "She's bringing a husband. Will you come with me, even out the numbers?"

"If you like."

"There's coffee involved."

"Well, that does a little something for my enthusiasm."

They laughed and joked for a while like it was old times while Yvonne finished getting ready. Timothy was already ready, having thrown on his pants and sweater and yesterday's underwear. But Yvonne was a woman, and that meant an involved morning ritual. Clothes, hair, make-up, jewelry, shoes, purse.

Finally they were out the door and on their way downtown.

"We were on our way to an Agatha Christie Club meeting," Yvonne said, halfway there. "It was Valery's birthday, and he didn't want to go. I was going to make it up to him. I so loved the mystery book meetings. We pretended we were in her novels. One of the fellows even made up mysteries about us. It was fun. After that night, though, I never really went back. Just once, to say goodbye. And they didn't know who I was. It was the first clue, really."

Timothy had nothing to say, so he just put a hand on her knee, comforting.

"It was just there where it happened, right in that cross street." Timothy could see she was shaking now but there was nothing he could do or say. "My life ended there," she went on. "It ended but I'm still here, still creeping along. Without him."

"You're about to wonder why," Timothy said then. "To say something like, it's not worth it without him. But I think you maybe shouldn't. You wouldn't really mean it, and it would cheapen what we have."

Yvonne was quiet as they waited their turn to clear the intersection. Soon enough it was behind them, and their destination started to edge closer.

"You might be right," Yvonne said eventually. "I'm sorry. You are worth knowing. And loving. I hope you can understand how a person can have all the love they can get and still feel lonely."

"It doesn't add up - but people are not logical. We obey different rules than numbers do."

Yvonne parked the car, then they went inside the little bistro Rosie and she had chosen. Inside, a few couples sat across from each other at little wooden tables with tiled tops. Two people looked up as they came in, obviously waiting for someone.

"Rosie?" Yvonne asked. The two Doctors Jiminez stood, and there were greetings all around.

Soon there was hot coffee steaming in tall, slender ceramic cups, and pastry, and easy friendship.

"You're obviously a medical doctor," Yvonne said to Rosie.

"Yes, at the teaching hospital," Rosie replied. "But sometimes I find myself driving to your place instead. I've been late five times this year because of this. It is very disturbing."

"I bet if we compared calendars, those would be the days I was late and we were on the same shift. When was the last one?"

"Last week," said Rosie. "Thursday."

"Swing shift. There was traffic on ninety-second street and I had to stop for gas. I was about fifteen minutes late."

"I was half into my drive before I realized, I don't work there, I work at the campus."

Yvonne said, "It's my fault. My fault somehow."

"I don't know what you're talking about," said the other Doctor Jiminez. He was dark where Rosie was fair, short and stout to her tall and slender. "Coincidences happen all the time. Whose fault is a random intersection?" He had just the trace of an accent, maybe Cuban.

"Write down my name," Yvonne challenged him. "Here, on this napkin. Tomorrow there will be nothing on it - if you can find it, if you can even remember to look for it."

"Well, for the sake of science..."

"What does a nuclear physicist do, exactly?" Yvonne asked him next.

"I try to work out what is inside of atoms."

"OK. So I'm aware of positrons, neutrons, protons, electrons. Timothy says there are more exotic things out there too, smaller things..."

"Quarks, bosons, muons, lots of stuff. I've read Tim's papers. He works along more mathematical lines, but I stick to what is observable. Smash things together, see what comes out."

"Not strictly true, Doc," said Timothy, entering the conversation for the first time. "You have some higher-dimension translations. I had to get past them for my undergraduate studies."

"My first doctorate was in a math field," the physicist replied. "And call me Raul. We are all doctors here, it will save some confusion.

"Timothy, who do we have involved in this right now?" Yvonne asked.

He referred to a notebook, re-wrote some missing words. "Well, It looks like you and Rosie, Raul, who'd we visit yesterday? Gergiev, that's right. Your brother appears to be in the middle of things. Why? You said you saw your husband's reflection when you were going to see Walter. He's going to radiate out through all sorts of math guys."

"Did you say Gergiev?" Raul said.

"Yes, Grigori Gergiev."

"I knew him. I know him. I was in his chess club in high school. Now he helps with the chip logic for our electron collider, measuring particle emanations."

"I'll be darned," Timothy said.

"Wait. My dream. It had Gergiev, a math guy, and a physics guy," Yvonne said.

"We used to waste time with Brian Moldavie," Raul said. He did not play chess. He snuck into pool halls underage, sometimes we went with him but we did not look old enough. He liked the geometry."

"I know Moldavie," Yvonne said. "Is it possible? He's at George Washington. He was Walter's teacher before... before."

"Possible?" said Raul. "Yes, but unlikely. Very, very unlikely. Rosie? Is it true what she says, about the forgetting?"

"Yes," Rosie said. "Absolutely true."

"Then we need a way to remember. If there is something here to be known and not just hysteria, superstition and coincidence, we need a record that is permanent."

"You believe us, then?" asked Timothy. "You didn't write down Yvonne's name on the napkin."

"No, but I wrote it on this business card last night," Raul said, reaching into his pocket. "Aha. Sure enough, today, nothing. But these particle trajectories, I wrote them as a control. And they remain."

"How did you know to do that?" Yvonne asked.

"Rosie told me to. She's the clever one here. I am just good at math."

"So how can we achieve a permanent record if everyone is affected by this memory changing phenomenon?" Timothy asked.

"Maybe not everyone is," Yvonne said.

"I remember discussions with Bohr which went through many hours till very late at night and ended almost in despair; and when at the end of the discussion I went alone for a walk in the neighbouring park I repeated to myself again and again the question: Can nature possibly be so absurd as it seemed to us in these atomic experiments?"

Werner Heisenberg

Nine

Someone knocked on the door. Walter started, shocked out of the world and into the library where his world resided, couched in piles of glue-bound notebooks. He tried to ignore the sound, focus on his numbers, but whoever it was knocked again, then pushed into the room.

"Walter. You have a phone call, man."

It was Riley. Riley was new, a black man who wore nurses' scrubs and a black longshoreman's cap. Walter didn't like Riley. The red-haired girl was always nearby - though she still wouldn't come into the library. There were always new people here: nobody lasted very long. Well, almost nobody.

"Walter, Earth to Walter, nanu-nanu. Come get the phone, man."

"Who is it?" he asked at last.

"What am I, your secretatry? Come talk to her yourself."

Her? he thought. *Can't be the red-haired girl. She doesn't have a voice. How could she make a phone call? But if it is her, maybe she will say what she wants.* All this time, he still had no idea what she wanted.

Walter stood up, stretched, padded across the library. Down the hall, ignoring the shouts and hammering from the guy in the seclusion room. If Benny didn't settle down soon the staff would strap him to the metal restraint bed, which was probably what Benny wanted, but all that was nothing to Walter. He only knew who Benny was because the big, soft-headed guy had tried to fondle him in the toilet.

The phone booth was by the bathroom door, between the dining table and the common area. The phone sat on the little shelf in there, black and foreboding, its silver cord not long enough to quite reach the shelf and thus not quite long enough for anyone to hang themselves with.

He sat in there, impervious to the stench of all the dirty, sweaty men who had sat in there before him, and put the phone to his ear.

"Hello?" he said, almost whispering.

"Walter! Hi! I wasn't sure you were going to come to the phone."

"Who's this?" he asked, suspicious.

"It's Yvonne. Has it really been that long you don't remember my voice?"

"I guess not."

"Walter, are you doing all right? I mean, the best you can?"

"I guess so," he said, thinking mostly about getting back to his notebooks. The Problem rolled around in his mind and the red-haired girl was there at the dining table eating watermelon with the animals who lived here. If he thought about The Problem out here where she could see, she would get to the answer first, and then everything would fall apart.

"Listen, Walt, Waltie, I need to know. When we start talking, am I ever anyone else?"

"Why would you be? Did the doctor ask you to ask me that?"

"No, no. I know your life is strange right now, but mine is getting pretty strange too, and you might be the one person I know who... I don't know. It's just you've never seemed to be affected. Like you're immune."

"Immune to what?" he asked, staring at the red-haired girl.

"Can I tell you some things, and ask you about them tomorrow?"

"I don't know. I don't like to be interrupted. I have a lot to do," he said.

"I know that, Walter. Please, though? It would be a big favor."

"I guess so. Can this be quick? She's watching me right now, and I don't know how long I can keep it a secret."

Yvonne took a deep breath, started reading off a list, freshly typed, on the typewriter in front of her. "Gergiev, Jiminez, Moldavie. Do you think you could remember those names?"

"I know Moldavie. He's my math teacher. Sure, I can remember those names. Can I go now?"

"Yes, Walter. I love you, so much..." She said some more, but now she was talking to the dial tone. Walter was already gone.

Riley tried to get him to sit at the dining table with the other guys but Walter wasn't about to do that. He'd been exposed long enough. It was time to retreat back to the library. "Here, at least take a plate with you," Riley said, and put a Saran-wrapped dish of ham and potatoes and gravy into his hands. That was not the first time Walter took his food to the library, by a long shot, but he would almost never eat in public again.

"Hey," Marcus said, "We try not to let him eat back there. We need to encourage socialization."

"I get what you're saying," Riley said, "but if that cat eats anything, anywhere, I'll be happy."

"If he's ever going to get out of here-"

"He ain't," Riley retorted. "I've been doing this ten years and I know the look. That boy's a lifer. Best we can do is help him be comfortable."

The words faded behind Walter as he retreated.

***

"Hello, Jean," Doctor Weatherly said. "First case conference?"

"First with my own license on the line," Jean said. She had replaced Marnie a week ago after a long internship. Jean was tall and heavy-set with silver-black hair and a big hooked nose.

"Well, not to worry. Walter is an easy client. Never gives us many problems. Nice fellow, really, with an old story. Was a math prodigy, all set for a fast-track to fame and fortune, a genius. Psychosis overtook him in college at about the age psychosis usually takes its victims for the first time. Sometimes they get better but Walter never really did."

"Even with all the new drugs we have available, is there nothing we can do?" Jean asked.

"You know, when we take him off the Clozapine he becomes disorganized. Not very, just enough to hold him back. And every time he gets close to discharge, then he becomes disorganized, too. He really has us over a bit of a barrel. Unless we wanted to try electroshock our hands are really tied." Weatherly lit his pipe, assumed his most grandfatherly posture. Walter would arrive momentarily.

"In school they told us psychosis was solved," Jean said.

"Not by a long shot," said Fiona, the charge nurse. "Most of these guys never get any better."

"Well, we have a biased sample," Weatherly said. "We only get the most severe cases, and the most violent at that. Overall, though, the Rule of Thirds seems to apply."

Jean looked a question at him, but it was Fiona who answered. "A third get better with meds, a third get better but need to take the meds forever to stay that way, a third never get better no matter what."

"Yes," said the doctor, "although 'better' is arguably vague. I mean, imagine what Walter might be like without any medication. He might be substantially worse."

"Walt's here," Marcus called from the door. "You all ready for him?"

"Send him in," said Weatherly. Walter came and sat in his appointed spot as he had done every third month for years now. "Cigarette?" Weatherly offered.

"I don't smoke," Walter replied, as he always did.

"Of course not. Where is my memory? Walter, how are you today?"

"Good," he said, looking at the floor.

"Is that all?"

"Yes."

"Walter, have you met Jean? She will be your social worker from now on. Marnie moved on to greener pastures."

"OK."

"Hi, Walter," Jean said. "We met the other day. Do you remember?"

Walter said nothing.

"Walter, I wonder if you have any goals for the next quarter."

"No," he said.

"Hey, doc, Walter has a call," Riley said from the side door, barging in. "Can he come take it, or do you need him?"

"Walter, would you like to take your call?" Weatherly asked. "You've been patient with us over the years, we can wait for you."

"No," Walter replied. "Just tell her Gergiev, Moldavie, Jiminez."

"What am I, your-"

"Just tell her," Walter said, and looked up to make eye contact. "She knows what it means."

"Go ahead," the Doctor said, and that was that. Orderlies did what the psychiatrist said, at least as long as he was looking. That didn't mean there would be no recriminations later, but Walter didn't think about that. He only thought about The Problem. "So, perhaps some goals?"

"No," Walter replied.

"Would you mind if we suggested some?"

"No."

"Very well. Marcus, what do you think Walter could accomplish this quarter?"

"Not hitting would be a start," Marcus said kindly.

"Remember all behavior goals must be positive. Dead men can not hit. And besides, Walter is our least aggressive patient. What can Walter do, affirmatively, rather than not do?"

"I don't know, Doc. Get along with the other guys?"

"Good. We'll start there. Anything else? Jean?"

"Are we looking for an outside placement?"

"I don't think so," Weatherly said. Walter shook his head fractionally at the suggestion.

"Walter's done a good job with his weight," Fiona said. "He could safely lose about five more pounds, and then maintaining under one-eighty would be good, for his height. If he lost a lot more than that, we'd worry."

"Good, good. Walter, that will do for now, don't you think? I sense you're anxious to be away?" Weatherly suggested.

"Yes."

"Marcus, perhaps you will let Walter out?" When Walter was gone, Weatherly continued, "No real problem for us, as you can see. Walter is the sort who internalizes his struggles. His psychomotor activity is depressed rather than agitated as in some of the other men. His psychosis remains florid, most likely, although there is not much overt behavior to signify it - unless you intrude on his delusions. Storing his notebooks is going to be a problem eventually. We tried to throw some of them out a year ago and he became extremely combative. Won't even let us store them."

"You see him ever getting back to his life?" Riley said, coming in and taking a seat at the conference table. One of his patients was up next.

"No, no, sadly not," Weatherly said. "We won't give up on him, of course, but our goals for him are more maintenance than repair at this time. Help him accustom to the fact that his life is here now. Unless they invent some new treatment or medicine in the coming years, Walter is one of us."

Riley looked meaningfully at Marcus, who just shrugged and went out to watch the unit.

***

Walter took the day off from working on The Problem.

He couldn't really afford it. He'd have to work twice as hard on it tomorrow, and work even harder to keep it from the red-haired girl. But at this moment, he had another problem to work on: his sister was as crazy as he was.

The red-haired girl was stalking him, so Walter sat in one of the seclusion rooms. There was a video camera, best kept at his back so it couldn't see what he was writing. That put his back to the door, and Walter was sure she would be standing there, watching. But that put her eyes on his back, too, blocking her view of his notebook as effectively as the camera's.

The red-haired girl was his crazy problem. The doctors told him it was true but, then again, the pills didn't make her go away - so they were lying. If he told them about his sister's crazy problem they might give her pills, too - but that wouldn't make the problem go away any more than they helped with his. She would just get locked up someplace with the problem, unable to run or even hide very well. So he did what she wanted instead.

He wrote down all the names she had told him, all the events she could remember although she was already forgetting them the way people forgot weird dreams the mind was not structured to hold. The thing was, he remembered all his dreams. They made about as much sense as much of reality these days.

He was in there an hour or so before one of the staff bothered him. Walter didn't even bother to turn around when they asked what he was doing.

"I need some time to calm down," he said, not really lying.

"Oh. Good job, Walter. If we need the room for someone we'll have to move you, OK? But otherwise take all the time you need."

Whoever it was left full of pride at Walter's insight and self-regulation. He kept writing.

When it was done, he had more than a few notebook pages. They would need to be hidden. If someone came looking, they couldn't search his other notebooks, or they would learn The Problem and maybe beat him to the solution. They would have to be someplace his sister could find but the animals who lived here wouldn't ever look.

A book.

He grabbed one of the hardbacks his friends had brought - The Gods Themselves, an Asimov novel - and started tearing pages carefully out of the notebook. He interleaved them with the novel pages. Then he put the novel back among the other books. Nobody would ever touch it again except him, when he had occasion to put more pages inside. No other hand would touch it. At least, as long as he lived.

"Physics isn't the most important thing. Love is."
Richard P. Feynman

Ten

He proposed to her during the end credits of Raiders of
the Lost Ark, in the dark, with people sidling past them to
get out of the seating row and into the flow of people
leaving the theater. The lights were up by the time she had
understood what was going on and managed to say, "Yes,
you idiot, of course I will."

Peter had never been happier.

"You're my life now, Ursula," he told her. And he felt
at that moment that it was true.

"No, I'm not," she said, pushing her glasses higher up
on her nose. They were big square panes in brown plastic.
Her dirty-blond hair was styled high on her head. Peter
saw none of that, nor the way the colors of her clothes
clashed in the growing post-movie light of the cinema.
"Math is everything to you. Or nearly everything. That's all
right, though. You're a good man, and I love you, and I'll
take whatever's left."

They walked out of the theater together, arm in arm,
awkward. Neither had much experience with love. "I don't
want you to be right," Peter said. "Maybe you are. But I
want you to be everything."

"I couldn't stand that," Ursula said. "If I were the Yoko
Ono that broke up the math group? No, I won't have that.
If I had all of you, minus the math and the movies and the
comic books, I wouldn't really have you, would I?"

"I don't get it," Peter said.

"Well, imagine I'm Wonder Woman, and I get you in
my Lasso of Truth. Then I ask you questions and you
answer them honestly. Does that mean you're an honest
man?"

"I guess I hadn't really thought of that," he said.

"If I had all of you, I'd only have the parts of you that
needed me and wanted to be with me, not the parts that
were brilliant and abstract and infuriating. I wouldn't have
you at all. Only the uninteresting part that didn't love math

or nerdy things." She sighed. "I don't know if that makes any sense."

"A little," Peter replied. "So I guess I shouldn't ask you to give up electrical engineering periodicals for me, either. Although I do sorta wish you wouldn't read them when we have dinner someplace romantic."

"That I'll agree to," Ursula said. She smiled, and that was all Peter saw.

***

"I can't take this anymore," Gilda said. She didn't shout it, but her tone was like a shout. "I'm going. Don't call me, don't look for me, and leave my friends alone."

"Crap," Hugo muttered without much real passion. The apartment stank of old Chinese food. There were piles of books around him, all sorts of math and a few flavors of philosophy. Cigarettes. A busted ashtray from the latest fight. "Crap," he repeated, louder, and threw a book at the wall. It was unsatisfying.

Hugo dragged himself up out of the recliner, reflecting that his belly was getting too big. He retrieved his book, marked the page, set it gently on top of a stack that made sense in his mind but nowhere else. "Another satisfied customer," he said, and felt in his pockets until he found his smokes. Camel, unfiltered, extra wide. Live fast, die young.

Then Gilda stormed back in. "I can't believe you let me leave like that, you insensitive, logical, useless prick. I give you everything and can't even look up over the edge of your goddamned books to notice. I was on my *knees* for you." Then she lashed out at the books, at the pile where Hugo had just set *Quantum math: multiplex solutions for multiplex problems*, scattering two dozen books across the cheap carpet. She slapped him across the face, hard, her mood ring leaving a shallow gouge across his cheek.

This time when she stormed out she stayed gone.

"Crap," Hugo said once more, and stepped over the chaos of books on the floor to get to the kitchen. There was a bottle of cheap vodka in a plastic bottle in the freezer and a finger of that might make the problem seem more amenable to reason, or at least less urgent, but then the telephone rang.

He knocked over another pile when he tripped on a Lovecraft he had been meaning to get rid of - there was no time for science fiction and fantasy stuff anymore - but he found the telephone before the caller gave up. It was a beige twelve dollar K-Mart thing.

"Speak to me," he said flatly.

"She said yes," Peter said, obviously joyful.

"Congratulations." Hugo tried to sound happy. This was his best friend, after all. At the same time, all that was keeping Hugo going right now was the immutable fact that he was too poor to buy a pistol and a bullet to off himself.

"Will you come to the wedding? I mean, don't just come, be the Best Man. The only man, really. The groom's side is going to be pretty bare. Without you there it wouldn't mean much..."

"California?" Hugo muttered, mostly to himself.

"It'll be fun," Peter said. "Sand, surf, maybe a shot at repairing your broken love life. If you're over Bella yet, that is."

"How did you know Bella left?"

"They always leave, chum."

Hugo wanted to swear at him but Peter was right, too right. They always left. "I'm not getting over Bella anymore," he said instead. "I'm getting over Gilda, who I picked up on the rebound from Rhonda."

"Hugo, you have to come visit. Come on, man, before you wreck yourself."

"I'll see what I can do."

They chatted a little longer, old friends apart too long, and finally Hugo said goodbye, hung up the phone, set it back on the floor between a book on gradient calculus and one on Anton Lavay's principles of ethics. The vodka sounded even better now than it had a half hour ago, but he was tired. Bone-tired. So he lay down on the couch with about a dozen books, two slide-rules and a giant Texas Instruments calculator, and fell into an unsatisfying sleep.

He dreamed of Walter.

***

"I can't marry you," Yvonne said.

"You can, but you don't want to."

"All right, Timothy. I don't want to. You know I love you. So much, I love you. I love you so much I won't do that to you."

"Do what to me?" Timothy said, knowing the answer already. It was an old argument by now.

"I'm forty-three. You're not even thirty. There's what, sixteen years between us?"

"That and two cups of cold coffee." They were at a little wrought-iron table outside a deli, enjoying the few nice spring days in D.C.. It was no longer despairingly cold outside and not yet the grinding, muggy hot that would plague the city until fall and people were outside everywhere.

"Come on, you're a math guy, do the math. When you're forty, I'll be fifty six. An old lady while you're just hitting your stride. When you're fifty I'll be sixty-six, ready to retire."

"Just numbers," Timothy said. "Math isn't real. Don't reify the abstract. I'm a physicist, anyway, and I know something else: some particles attract and there's nothing we can do about it. I want to be with you. You want to be with me. What could be simpler? Do it. Take the ring."

"I can't," Yvonne said, and a tear worked its way out of her left eye to die on her cheek, soaking into her foundation.

"You could."

"No, I can't."

"Is it Valery?"

"Yes."

Timothy just sighed, leaned back in the metal chair. A breeze came along at that moment, snatched away the little cocktail napkins that came with the coffee. Neither of them noticed the napkins leaving.

"Would he want you to give up the rest of your life for him?" Timothy asked after a long pause. "To mourn him forever?"

"I can't mourn him," Yvonne replied. "He isn't dead. I can only search for him, find him in still moments and odd reflections and unlived parts of life. I dream of him, of *being* him, and I know he was supposed to survive the crash, not me. He's with me all the time, trapped between the possible and the real.

"I can't marry you. I have to get him back. I have to bring him back out of the possible and into the actual."

Timothy had forgotten about all the strangenesses but remembered again now, remembered forgetting a hundred times and being reminded a hundred times and promising over and over to help find the answers.

"I forgot," he said now, feeling stupid. "Can you forgive me for the umpteenth time?"

"Yes."

"If I could remember this for more than a few hours, I could help. I know I could help."

"You are helping," Yvonne said.

"I am? How?"

"Your work is the work he needs done."

Timothy thought about that for a little while. Wave-function anomalies in one department, cosmic radiation measurement in another. What was the connection? Certainly there was more than a casual connection between the two problem sets, but how did these relate - if at all - to Yvonne's strange experiences?

Yvonne let him think a while, then interrupted. "You said once, back when you were studying for your doctorate, that quantum physics was preposterous but also true. The preposterous nature of it comes mostly from trying to apply the laws of large-scale reality to small-scale phenomena. Thinking, for example, of elementary particles as objects, which they fundamentally are not.

"That's the problem here. Two truths are co-existent at once. Valery died in that accident, but he also didn't. For some reason, there is a whole reality around his having survived the accident and it is intruding on this reality. Your work will help us find out why, and it isn't a coincidence. Gergiev's work is going to help, too, and so is Jimenez'."

"Every other time we've talked about this, you were sure it was his ghost guiding events. What changed your mind?" Timothy wondered out loud.

"If you believe in ghosts," Yvonne said, "you have to believe in everything else. That means bigfoot, UFOs, Heaven and Hell... there's just no way to sort any of it out. On the other hand, cosmic inflation was proposed last year, and it offers an explanation."

"Huh? Here's an unexpected turn. What does that have to do with it?"

Yvonne took a deep breath. Timothy knew she was smart, never condescended to her, but physics was his thing - and physics was still a man's game. "Look, if inflation turns out to be true, there's no reason to suppose it only happened once. There was a singularity, and then there was space. The space itself is something, and it grew between objects at an incredible rate, and that's the universe.

"Now, every time we look for something smaller, we find it. Under atoms we have protons and neutrons and electrons. Under them, muons and quarks and bosons. And every time we look for something bigger, we find that, too. The Earth used to be the center of the universe, then it was the Sun, then the Milky Way was the whole universe, now we know there are other galaxies. I think we'll keep finding them, new galaxies all the time.

"Now we have cosmic inflation. If it happened once, it could happen all the time. The universe is going to shrink - become one of many universes.

"Once that happens, we'll find there is plenty of room for other dimensions of reality, that every possibility is real somewhere. Every choice unmade *is* made somewhere, and whole lines of possibility exist that aren't real here.

"In one of those, or some of those, or every line but this one, Valery is alive. This one is wrong, goofed up somehow, and we need to reach across to one of the lines where he still exists, put it to rights."

"That's crazy," Timothy said.

"I know it is," Yvonne replied, crying now in earnest.

"No, no, I mean Starobinsky and Linde are each working on these ideas but they're not at all ready to say anything like you're saying - at least not in public. But you wait and see: everything you just said is going to be totally mainstream in twenty years. What you're saying isn't crazy at all - the fact *that* you're saying it is crazy.

"But this stuff is best left for college guys smoking weed in their dorms. Application is hard to imagine."

"So," said Yvonne, "imagine it."

"I've changed my mind. I don't want you to marry me anymore. Other guys' wives want them to mow the lawn and patch the roof and stamp on spiders. You want me to merge elements of multiple universes to bring back your dead husband."

They laughed together for a while, then walked off towards the National Mall arm in arm.

"Among all the occurrences possible in the universe the a priori probability of any particular one of them verges upon zero. Yet the universe exists; particular events must take place in it, the probability of which (before the event) was infinitesimal."

Jacques Monod

Eleven

Vitali Gergiev marched through the hallway with an intense look of pride on his face. Another piece of the puzzle had fallen into place today, one more bit of chip logic. Today, it would become possible for central units to coordinate multiple inputs. Or at least with fractionally more ease than had been possible yesterday. Computing was not a matter of huge breakthroughs but cumulative incremental steps.

Thus was Moore's Law born in 1975, and computer speed doubled every eighteen months or so.

"Got the cream, did we, Gergiev?" said Yancey as Gergiev strutted into the faculty office.

"I should say so. Another step forward in processing power."

"And another year of continued departmental funding."

"Don't be jealous, my friend. Plenty of wealth to go around." Gergiev stepped into his own office, took a seat. The pain started then but he ignored it. Kilroy, the department head, followed him in and took one of the student seats in front of the desk.

"Congratulations," he said.

"Good news travels fast."

"Not as fast as bad news. Jenkins' law. But fast enough, quite right. The Solid State rep will be by tomorrow," Kilroy said cheerfully.

"We can't sign with Solid State. Chip Logic has been our backer for years."

"You know how it is. Loyalty is old fashioned. It's all the bottom line now."

"I won't do it," Gergiev said. He was starting to sweat but put it down to anger, and never mind that he did not habitually sweat because of anger.

"Well, it's up to you, but he's coming and you have to meet with him. And be seen meeting with him. Anyway, think of it as a bit of a Hammerstock Maneuver."

"Hammerstock? I don't think I'm familiar," Gergiev said.

"You should be. Hammerstock played you in sixty-eight."

"I remember now. He wasn't that good. Had no place in the finals. Certainly not good enough to have moves named after him."

"Well," Kilroy went on, "not strictly a strategy involving the movement of the pieces so much as their placement. The chap he beat before you was a bit obsessive. A lot obsessive, in fact. So Hammerstock set up all his own pieces off-center in their squares. Miller asked him to center them but Hammerstock refused."

"Not cheating, strictly speaking."

"Not honorable either, really. And there you have it."

"I see," said Gergiev, and he did. "When Chip Logic shows up, Johns will be worried about Solid State. But he won't be able to ask any questions, that would reveal he has a source in the department. Can't touch another player's pieces, after all. I hate to shake them down for more money, though..."

"Don't worry so much about it. They'll make a hundred million dollars off your work alone, and the whole department is working on bits and pieces for them. We just need our share."

"You know, I feel unwell," Gergiev said. He was sweating heavily now, and a certain amount of pain was starting to radiate out from his arm. He made to stand up, failed, plopped back into his seat heavily.

"What's wrong, Vitali?"

"I don't know. I think it might be my heart."

"I call a doctor immediately. Bruce!" Kilroy grabbed Gergiev's phone, dialed an outside line and 9-1-1. But it was too late.

Gergiev clutched his chest, slid lower down in his chair, and left the world.

**

"There is only one elementary particle in the universe, that we know of currently, that can experience all four fundemental forces. What are those forces? Yes, Morris?"

"Professor, they are the strong and weak nuclear forces, electromagnetism, and gravity. But some people wonder if gravity is really an elementary force because it is so weak."

"Good," said Doctor Jiminez. "And what is the particle?"

A young woman in the back row put up her hand and, although several other people also raised their hands, Jiminez picked her.

"Quarks?"

"Is that a question, Hanks?"

"No, Professor. Quarks."

"Good," he said. But her hand was still up. "Yes, Hanks?"

"Does that mean hadrons experience all four forces at once?"

Some of the students tittered. Jiminez frowned at them. "If you don't ask, you can't know," Jiminez said. "And I bet she wasn't the only one wondering. On the other hand, she's smarter than half of you, so maybe she was. Who knows the answer? Hale?"

"Hadrons are strongly interacting, therefore experiencing the strong nuclear force."

"Don't gloat, Hale. That's right, though. Next week we'll cover where all the other forces go when quarks are joined together into hadrons. Any other questions?" A few hands went up. "Questions you could not answer for yourself by looking at the syllabus?" All but one went down. "And not about the problem set I told you I wouldn't be answering any questions about? Ah, good. Then see you next week."

Jiminez packed up his books and pens and chalks, headed out of the lecture hall while his assistants worked on wiping down the boards. Across campus, at the lab, Rosie waited with a paper bag. "Lunch, dear?"

"Don't mind if I do." They sat in his office.

"Did you think about what I said?" Rosie asked.

"Yes," Raul said, "and I think you're right. There were sixty-two men in the lecture today and three women. The gentlemen were quite abrasive towards the females. I think science is observably biased against the ladies. I don't know how treating them differently can profit us but, on the other hand, we're already treating them differently.

"Did you know seventeen women applied for the program, and only four were accepted? The acceptance rate is half that for men. Given that, maybe I should make sure the three we have get the best chance of passing."

"I was hoping you'd say that," said Rosie. "Here. I brought you a Twinkie."

"You know," said Raul through a mouthful of whatever white substance graced the inside of Twinkies, "I've been meaning to ask what brought all this on. I mean, of course the problem is endemic, and anyone open to objective study can see sexism is a big problem in the hard sciences. But you never mentioned it before this year."

"It's that damned hospital administrator position," Rosie said. "Every year I apply, and every year I get nothing back. After six years of working there I at least deserve a courtesy interview."

"At Teachers?"

"At where?"

"Teachers. You work at Teacher's hospital."

"I do?" said Rosie, then her frown dissipated and her eyes went wide. "I *do*. Why would I think I work at Manhattan General?"

"I don't... wait, yes, I do know. What was her name? We had coffee..."

"Yvonne. My God. How did we forget? All of it? It was so strange, I thought I'd remember it always."

Raul chuckled. "No, we did experiments, remember? The information won't stay in this universe. It evaporates from paper and leaks from brains without constant maintenance. Ah, that reminds me: I have a big experiment finishing up this week, and I must remember to think of the results in terms of this problem."

"What are you doing?" Rosie asked.

"Colliding protons to observe anti-neutrons," Raul replied.

"Like Cork?"

"Yes, only we can observe the results with a bit more accuracy. I think the various anti-particles point to a sort of symmetry to the universe that might be best explained by invisible dimensions of space and time."

"Well, I don't have time for all of that," Rosie said. "I thought I was on a lunch break from M.G., but I'm supposed to be leading rounds at Teachers. Love you, see you tonight."

"Yes, see you. Thanks for the Twinkie." Tomorrow, Raul would repay the favor. For now, though, there was a thornier problem: how to remember all this information when he could not even remember to try to remember.

***

"Cake, everyone eat cake, please! Don't make me take any home!"

General laughter followed. Brian sipped cola from a red Solo cup, imagining a lot of students would be drinking beer from the same sort of plastic-ware all over the country. And thinking, at the same time, that they were no longer his problem.

"Congratulations, Brian," said Gerry. "We'll be sorry to lose you."

"You'll be sorry to have to do your own lectures," Brian said cheerfully.

"That's true. I'm a dreadful lecturer, ask any student."

"I don't have to - they happily volunteer such information. On the other hand, you kept me out of the research side of things, so it all comes out in the wash. See you, Gerry. Don't be a stranger."

"Doctor Moldavie!"

He turned around to see who was talking and was surprised to see a young woman he knew. "Patricia? Why, I'm so glad to see you, but what are you doing at a faculty party?"

"I *am* faculty, starting this term. Don't you remember writing my recommendation?" She shook her head sadly but her smile was irrepressible.

"I suppose when I lost half my weight I lost half my mind, too," Brian said, patting his greatly-reduced stomach. "And I didn't have that much to lose."

"It's a myth that all math profs are absent-minded," Patricia said, reaching back to tie up her brown hair. "They're just present to the abstract and the unreal. I guess I should say, we're."

"Well, I was just leaving, but do feel free to call me if you need any help or advice. I'm going out to pasture but I can't help thinking I'm leaving behind the best part of my life."

"Happy retirement," Patricia said.

Brian shook a dozen more hands, hugged a few of his closest friends, and eventually made it out the door.

Patricia is right, Brian reflected once he was safely in his little brown Chevy Citation. *Math is a kind of insanity, a focus on the unreal*. That made him think suddenly of Walter, poor Walter, who had crossed fully into unreality. How long ago had that been? Seven years now? He knew Walter was still locked up in the psychiatric hospital because they sent for homework every few months, even though Walter hadn't sent back any work for years.

I shall have to phone Patricia, he thought, *and tell her about the arrangement*. She would need to make the photostats now and mail them over. Not that Walter was ever going to graduate anything. But it never hurt to be generous and there was precious little else anyone could do to help.

On a sudden impulse, Brian popped on his turn signal and jumped off the highway, leaving the path for home and instead getting on the path towards the hospital.

"Every valuable human being must be a radical and a rebel, for what he must aim at is to make things better than they are."

Henry Abraham Boorse and Lloyd Motz

Twelve

Walter was asleep.

He was dreaming about a web of numbers, and the numbers were possibilities, probabilities. They were interconnected, conjoined, oddly frightening.

The more he looked at the numbers, the more he saw the numbers were things in the world.

That mass of digits, changing around a constant as its molecules vibrated slowly, was a table. Those numbers atop it, the more chaotic ones, those were books. Hundreds of books, or at least dozens. Here was the couch he was sleeping on, less stable than the table. There were walls, the door, the door-handle made of metal and thus the most stable of all.

The objects were all joined together, dependent on one another. The floor accounted for some of this, and the molecules in the air (hard to see as they interacted, changed rapidly - here is a number encoding the location of an oxygen dyad, with another encoding its velocity, and yet more detailing its history).

There was Walter himself, asleep on the couch, seen from above in his own mind. There was so much data here that it was hard to see what Walter might be. The equations were so confusing and complex that they were like a kind of darkness, so much data causing an absence of information, nullity.

The numbers signifying the doorknob suddenly changed, in an orderly fashion: a rotational translation in three dimensions. "Walter?"

He woke up, blinking away the dream and settling back into his own body, his own perspective. The Problem still weighed on his mind, heavy but, he perceived suddenly, not massive: it was weighed down by consciousness but would be more easily lifted inside the chaotic system of dreaming.

"Walter, is this a bad time?"

He didn't recognize the man in the doorway. He was tall and sallow, with sagging jowls like a man who has lost a lot of weight. He had gray hair and white sideburns. For a second Walter wondered if it might be Isaac Asimov, but this man was much too wasted to be the Great One.

"Do you recognize me? We only met once or twice. I spoke to your sister more than to you in the end. I'm Professor Moldavie. Or just plain Brian now, I suppose."

"You have cake frosting on your chin," Walter said, and that was the longest sentence he had uttered in weeks.

"Oh, thank you," Brian said, fishing a handkerchief out of his jacket pocket. The jacket was a silly tweed thing with leather elbows. "Retirement party. As you can see, I eat less cake than I used to. Out of the habit."

Walter just stared at him. Through him, really. The dream had not entirely faded, and Walter saw equations swirling around Moldavie, passing through him, through the other dimensions of space and time all around him. Moldavie's presence bounced off of all the other things in the room, changing them, too.

"You have to go," Walter said. "You're messing up the books." And he was. Math swirled out from the man and infested the notebooks, mixing up the numbers inside the way the tie-dyer draws in swirls of soap and ink floating on water.

"I'm sorry. I shouldn't have intruded. I just had a sudden impulse to come and see you, see if you needed anything."

"You house is burning," Walter said out of nowhere, laying back down on the couch. Consciousness was killing his thinking: he needed to get back into the dream and that seemed possible. The numbers still mixed and collided and flickered. "Not your house here, the new one, in Rhode Island. Your wife is there."

"What? What are you saying?"

But Walter was snoring.

"Excuse me, nurse? I need a telephone, right away," Brian said, flustered. How could Walter even know he had a wife, let alone a house in Rhode Island? Mrs. Moldavie had won the state lottery last year, enabling his retirement, and a house out in the wind and rain had been her dream, so that was where they were going.

The nurse took him into the nurses' station, offered him a telephone, showed him how to dial out. He jabbed the buttons. He knew the line had been installed because he had talked to Janet last night. It started to purr now, a seductive noise, calming. Three times, four. Eight. Twelve. No answer.

That might mean nothing. Janet would be busy unpacking, or maybe had gone downtown for a spot of lunch. All the same, Brian hung up, dialed the outside line again, called the police department near the new house. *Thank God I work with numbers*, he thought. He remembered every telephone number he encountered with essentially no effort.

The local police answered quickly. "Hello?"

"Hi, My name is Brian Moldavie. I'm wondering if I could have you swing by my house for a welfare check? My wife is not answering the telephone right now. Yes, I'll hold..."

"Something wrong?" asked the nurse, a bearded man in his forties.

"Walter says my house in on fire."

"Surprised he told you anything. He barely speaks any more. Is that who you're calling? Checking on your house?"

"Yes," Brian said. "He only said two or three sentences, but each one was filled with things he couldn't have - Oh yes, I'm here."

"Give us the address, sir, and we'll see if we have someone in your neighborhood. Is there somewhere we can reach you?"

Brian had seen the first carphones, big things that sat in the console between the driver and the passenger. Only rich people could afford them so far - but now he was, essentially, a rich person, and he wished he had one. "No, don't bother. Do make the visit, please, but I'm on my way from D.C.. I shall be there to see for myself soon enough. Yes, that's fine, thank you. May I call back in a few hours? Thanks. Thanks very much."

"Well, good luck out there," said the nurse, a sardonic smile on his lips.

"Thanks," said Brian. He tried not to rush off the unit, out to his car, taking measured steps through a growing feeling of foreboding. *I ought not to have come this way.*

***

Raul walked through the mall. There was a toy store on the right that would be Hell come Christmastime but now was quiet, nearly deserted. Then he passed a shoe store that smelled of leather and polish, and a jeweler. Sparkling gems glittered inside glass cabinets with chrome fittings; the women there to sell the gems glowed nearly as brightly, the sexism in hiring here overt.

Finally he came to the pet shop, on the corner by the escalators. Puppies played in Plexiglas displays in the front window. One wall had small animals: rodents, birds, a few lizards. The opposite wall held fish tanks. The middle aisles were full of the equipment needed for keeping pets. And there in the open space just inside the store was what Raul needed.

Kittens lounged atop carpeted wooden boxes, or inside them, or played on the carpet. They were enclosed in a Plexiglas display case and were completely adorable, every last one. Raul did not need their cuteness, but he supposed that would be an added bonus.

He walked up to the cash register. A young woman was standing there, clad in jeans, a paisley shirt and a blue apron with yellow stitching. "I'd like a kitten," he said.

"Oh, sure. We have lots. Did you have one in mind?" The girl (*woman*, he corrected himself absently, thinking of his conversations with Rosie) smiled and chewed her gum at the same time, a strange effect.

"No, any kitten will do."

"Well, most people like to get to know one first. Is it a gift?"

"Yes," he said, appreciating the way out. "A gift." He hoped it would be.

The young woman stepped over to the case and opened it with a key, one whole wall swinging outwards. She kept the animals inside from escaping by blocking their progress with one foot and stepped inside with them. Kittens mobbed her for affection and, for a few moments, she seemed like the happiest kid Raul had ever known.

"Here, this one, we call him Sparkles, he's really friendly. Is it for a kid? He likes children, though most cats are wary of them."

"He'll do fine," Raul said, suddenly emotional. He couldn't quite put a finger on the emotion but it filled up his chest, watered his eyes a little, and muzzed up his voice.

"Okay, Mister. Give me just a minute..." She picked up the little guy, a black cat with white flashes on his face, ears, paws, and chest. Then she wrangled her way out of the case, expertly keeping all the mewing cuteness inside.

"You ever lose one?" Raul asked.

"Sure, just this morning one got away on Benny. We had to chase him all over the mall. A little girl caught him by the Macy's." She put the baby animal in a little cardboard box with the name of the store on the side and breathing holes in the top. The kitten mewed, sounding more mouse than cat. "That's twenty-eight fifty, Mister. Unless you need something else? Dishes, brushes, collars..."

"Yeah, I didn't think of all that. Let me have the whole set-up."

Eighty bucks later he walked out of the shop with the box in one hand and a bag of cat-wrangling gear in the other. The kitten mewed all the way home.

***

"A kitten!" Rosie said. Raul could not tell if she was excited or dismayed - both feelings rushed across her face and got all tangled up there. "What are we going to do with a kitten?"

"Keep it safe indoors, for one thing. He's not to go outside. He's much too important."

Rosie looked a question at him, but picked up the little animal and snuggled him in her arms. He was skinny and pathetic, just the size of her hand.

"Entanglement," Raul said.

"I still don't understand, dear. I know we've been married some time now, but things like this still take some explanation."

"Schrödinger's cat."

"Oh, you're just watching him for someone? How marvelous. Now you're making sense, at last. What's his name?"

"Schrödinger will do," Raul replied. "He's our cat but will partially replicate Schrödinger's experiments. I shall take him to work tomorrow, entangle some of the component atoms of his body with material at the lab, and he will serve as an information store. Whenever we see the cat, elementary reality will reassert itself. Never again will you drive to Manhattan General rather than Teacher's Hospital."

"Why would I want to go to Teacher's?"

Raul waited a minute.

"Oh. Oh yes, I remember. How can I keep forgetting something so simple? Hey, wait a minute, what does any of that have to do with the cat?"

"Part of the information leads to all of the information. I don't understand why. Maybe with eighty years of research we could understand it, but we haven't got that long. We can just know it. If I can encode some of the information somehow on the cat - because it's too simple to forget, because I can get subatomic information onto it that is not changed by whether Valery is dead or alive, whatever - then whenever we see the cat, we'll remember everything."

"I still don't quite understand," Rosie said, "but the kitty is sweet. Here, get down a dish and we'll give him some milk. Why use a cat, anyway? Wouldn't a bar of steel be simpler and safer and just as effective for doing whatever you're doing with subatomic particles?"

"I suppose," said Raul. "But you're the one who always complains physicists have no sense of humor."

"I don't see the joke."

"Just because it's highly compartmentalized does not mean it isn't funny," Raul said. "Besides, kittens are sure cuter than steel ingots. You're right about that much."

"Nothing happens until something moves."
Albert Einstein

Thirteen

Valery woke up, stretched, kicked the blankets onto the floor. He laced his hands behind his head and watched the light in the room grow by how much he could see the ceiling.

Life had become strange and stayed that way for a long time. He missed his wife, his first wife. It had been years now since Yvonne had died and the grief was still fresh, maintained by his constant encounters with her: in mirrors, in dreams, in implications. He was the one who should have died. He knew that now. Yvonne would haunt him until he found a way to repair whatever was broken, to reverse the events of that night in nineteen seventy-three.

When he could see the ceiling well enough to count the paint-drips that made the room acoustically acceptable, Valery rolled over onto his side, looked at his other wife, his second wife. She was pregnant and round and radiant. Any day now he would be a father.

Yvonne should be the mother, he thought, for the hundredth time or the thousandth.

Valery collected the blankets from the floor, covered Sheila gently so as not to wake her, and padded into the study where the typewriter sat next to the phone. Sheila wanted to replace it with an electric or even a word processor, but it was Yvonne's. It was so hard to part with anything of hers. And so hard to imagine how Sheila put up with it, with his insistence that life was skewed on some aberrant trajectory, away from truth and reality, away from the fact of Yvonne.

He picked up the telephone, dialed from memory.

It rang distantly a few times, and then a tired voice replied, "Yes?" It was a woman's voice so Valery almost hung up.

"Gergiev," he said.

"This is she."

"Oh. I didn't realize he married. I mean Doctor Gergiev. The chess master."

"Oh." He detected something in the voice, some pain or reluctance. "Who is it? Who's calling?"

"It's Yvonne," she said. "We met at the funeral, Mrs. Gergiev. I just wanted to be sure you were all right. Nothing we could do for you?"

Silence for a moment. "Yvonne? There isn't a man there with you, on another line?"

"No, why?"

"I would swear this is not how the conversation started. There was a man, asking after my husband..."

Yvonne shuddered, turned to face the mirror on the closet door. There was Valery, naked as the day he was born, facing her across the semi-dark study. She needed to blink to clear the sudden tears from her eyes, but she knew if she did that, he would be gone. She put down the phone for the time being, half-listening to the buzz of Mrs. Gergiev talking now to empty space, reached out for the glass. Her fingers stretched out, almost touched -

And then he was gone, only her own reflection there, goosepimples over her naked skin.

Yvonne picked the telephone back up. "I'm sorry, Mrs. Gergiev. So sorry. I'll call back soon or maybe stop in to check on you. Can I bring you a casserole?"

"That would be lovely, dear."

They chatted a little longer but Yvonne's heart was not in it. The encounter with Valery had her aching and a little spooked. He had seen her as clearly as she had seen him, had reached out from the mirror...

She went back into the bedroom to grab some clothes, saw a strange woman sleeping in her bed, a pregnant woman. Just for a moment, long enough to gasp and step back and blink, and then gone, everything back in its proper place. Her bed was empty, the way it was supposed to be. The way she remembered it.

I'm losing it for real now, she thought, and went to sit on the toilet. Only once she was there all she could do was cry.

***

"Mrs. Gergiev, would you like eggs or a muffin this morning?" Mathilda moved efficiently around the kitchen, one eye on her charge and the other eye on the water she was boiling for coffee.

"What, dear? Oh, just coffee."

"You have to eat something, Ma'am. Or the medicine will upset your stomach."

"Oh, I'm not hungry, dear."

Some days, Mrs. Gergiev did not understand. She was off in her own world, recollections maybe, or just imaginings. But Mathilda was patient. She started work on a batch of muffins. Mrs. Gergiev liked muffins. The smell would arouse her appetite and she would forget all about not being hungry.

The water came to a boil. Mathilda set up the percolator, listened to it drip and bubble, smelled it brewing. Wonderful. When it was ready, she poured two cups, set one in front of her patient.

"Oh, thank you, dear. I was just thinking about Vitali. Not fair of him to leave me, so young. I remember a day in Pittsburgh, where we met. Must've been forty-six, forty-seven. There was a flower shop..." She trailed off into her own reminiscences, melancholy but not really unhappy.

She was just fifty-six, but the senility had already been at work on her for two years, burning through her memories like wildfire. And, since Vitali had died, there was no-one else to take care of her. The children had emigrated to Australia years ago. There was just Mathilda, working on contract from the home healthcare service. Mathilda was nearly Ruth's age.

Good days and not-so-good days. This one was shaping up to be about average. By midmorning, Mrs. Gergiev had taken her pills and eaten a muffin. A cup of coffee brought her back somewhat to the world. Mathilda set to work on the laundry, with a shopping list next on the agenda.

Downstairs, folding laundry next to an ironing board, Mathilda heard Ruth creeping carefully down the stairs. As her mind wandered off into wherever it was going it seemed to be taking her body with it, withering her, making her frail. Ruth came into the basement room and started folding socks. Mathilda let her: such work was good for her, kept her attached to the world.

"He's not dead, you know," Mrs. Gergiev said after a while.

"Yes, Mrs. Gergiev," Mathilda replied. It was pointless and perhaps unkind to try to correct someone in Ruth's state.

"Oh, don't patronize me," Ruth said. "I know my Vitali has passed. I mean Valery."

"Valery? Who's she?"

"He. He called me this morning, only that's impossible. Then he was Yvonne. But he was Valery first. Old friend of Vitali's. If only Vitali could still be alive, too. But he never took very good care of his heart."

Mathilda stopped listening now. At first Ruth had seemed cogent, but this was clearly just more of the delusional thought of senility. Mathilda shivered, thinking about the mere handful of years between them. *God save me from this, whatever this is.*

***

The lab was more of a super-clean warehouse floor. Big bits of equipment littered the floor in a way that might look haphazard to non-initiates. Indeed the first reaction of most graduate students was to wonder how the essential order of the universe could be found in such a messy, disorganized place.

Raul fiddled with a laser, calibrating it. "Here, Ms. Hanks. Just the tiniest action on this screw, here. This moves the crystal, you can see the alignment exactly on this readout."

Jill took the tiny screwdriver, very gently maneuvered it into the slot, turned it fractionally. "Too much?"

"Just right, but too fast," Raul said. "Take your time, be careful. Do you drive, Ms. Hanks?"

"What sort of question is that?" she asked, shaking the hair out of her eyes.

"An impertinent one, perhaps. Manual transmission?"

"Yeah?"

"Well, have you ever tried to work the brakes with your left foot? Unnatural, yes? The car jerks to a halt with the slightest pressure. But your right foot know just how much to apply. You'll have to do many such calibrations to get that sense in your fingers. Fortunately, you will have many opportunities."

She put the tool down, looked Doctor Jiminez in the eye. "Why are you being so good to me?" she asked, frowning.

"Why wouldn't I?" he replied.

"It's just that... well, you hear stories. If you're a girl in a math or science department, you hear about profs who are interested in something besides science from you. Is that what's going on here?"

Raul laughed, a friendly sound. "I'm sorry it's like that. No, I really am. But no, that's not what's going on here. My wife, Mrs. Doctor Jiminez, she pointed out how few females were in my classes, in the field. She said I had to make sure you got a fair shot. From where I sit, a fair shot means special attention - not because you aren't smart enough, but because you are going to get passed over for so many opportunities."

"I'm not sure I like that," Jill said. "It sounds vaguely inappropriate."

"I don't like it either," Raul said back. "But there it is. Look at it this way: every professor picks out a few students he thinks is worthy of some special attention, some extra mentoring. They are never, ever women except, as you say, unless he has some other need to satisfy. So if I pick you because you are a woman, to redress the balance somewhat, can you think badly of me?"

"Well..."

"Look, don't get me in trouble with my wife. Let's get back to work."

She laughed now, the tension broken as if it were never there. "Why are we pointing this thing at that box of smoke to begin with?" Jill asked.

"You know about cesium beam clocks?"

"Oh, wow - is this one?"

"Almost. There is a cesium atom in there, and we're going to measure it constantly. We won't count the vibrations, though, not for the sake of time. We are measuring its vibrations so we know it's still cesium."

"Is it entangled?" she asked.

"Good job, yes, yes it is. What leads you to that conclusion?"

"Could it decay if it were entangled with another atom that decayed? If you had entangled a subatomic particle, say a quark, with one of the quarks in the cesium atom, if it changed some characteristic then the other would change to match, the hadron would change in some way, the atom would lose one neutron or positron. Then it would no longer be cesium, would vibrate at a different rate."

"Brilliant," Raul said.

"Just one problem: how do you entangle quarks?"

"Not published yet. Probably not ever. This is a secret, a great secret. When this is all up and running, it will get more complicated. A lot more complicated. The last thing we need to do is irradiate a cat."

"Tell me," she said.

"I will. Just as soon as I figure it all out. For now, let's get this laser calibrated."

Jill picked up the little screwdriver again, wondering at how much it was like the one she used to fix her glasses when the screw worked its way out of the hinge that held the arm to the frame. Such a mundane item to be part of so weird an experiment.

"Wait a second," she said suddenly. "If it isn't going to be published, what's the point of it? What happened to publish or perish?"

"There's more to life," Raul said, "than trying not to perish."

"You don't need to predict the future. Just choose a future -- a good future, a useful future -- and make the kind of prediction that will alter human emotions and reactions in such a way that the future you predicted will be brought about. Better to make a good future than predict a bad one."

Asimov

Fourteen

"Some party," Jenssen said. The conference room was bare and only a few doctors stood around the table. "Couldn't even come up with more than twenty bucks for his own farewell."

"Or nobody likes him well enough to kiss his backside if they're getting nothing in return," Yvonne said. "He'll be gone tomorrow. No more favors to get from Michaels."

"That statement defines a particularly psychopathic relationship style," Jenssen said.

"Feel free to tell me I'm wrong any time, Jim, but the higher Carl moves up the organizational structure, the more psychopathic we get. Did you know the emergency room is on divert because too many black kids come in with gunshot wounds they can't afford to get stitched up? Did you know three young Black men died last week because the ambulance had to go an extra thirty miles north to get them treated? I mean, how do you define psychopathic?"

Jim just laughed, a sound with no joy in it. "Yvonne, that kind of talk will get you sent to the reconditioning camps. You know Carl Michaels is already President of the United States of America. With Reagan at the helm, guys like him are going to rise like cream in the milk jug."

"Just let him rise the hell out of our way."

"I can't afford to do the job much different, you understand."

"Yeah," said Yvonne, "but at least you'll hate it."

Michaels himself showed up then and started slicing the sheet cake with a surgical saw. A dumb joke; he'd not done a surgery himself in six years, only wrote up other doctors for the way they did theirs. "Eat, drink and make merry," he said, and one of his cronies brought in two-liter bottles of fruit punch. "I'll keep this short. You're one helluva team, it's been my honor and privilege to point this hospital towards the new age. Special thanks to the board of directors" [none of whom were in evidence] "and I'd love to stay with you great people the rest of my life, but I've been made an offer I can't refuse. Thanks for four great years!"

There was a half-hearted cheer and then people ate cake and drank cheap punch. Most of the attendees had only come for the cake in the first place. Carl didn't even stick around to mingle - there was nobody in the room who could do him any favors so he bailed.

"He invite you to the real party?" Jim said.

"Why am I not surprised there's a real party? Let me guess: department heads with more than a million in grants, and board members."

"Not far off."

"No," Yvonne said, "obviously neither of us is invited. Wouldn't go if he asked me. Actually, I think I'm done here. Take one side of this cake, we'll take it to the waiting room downstairs. Carl would hate that he was giving freebies to patients."

Jim laughed and took one end, getting chocolate frosting on this thumbs. "Why so bitter?" he asked. "You're moving up one grade, too."

"And, like you, I'm going to hate it."

***

Nineteen eighty-two dawned with a day similar to any other year before it on the psychiatric ward. Most of the guys had stayed up to watch the Times Square ball drop on the television, listened to Dick Clark wish them all a happy new year, and then gone to bed.

Walter hadn't bothered with any of that, hadn't even noticed dinner was special that night. He'd absently spooned Cherries Jubilee into his mouth while scribbling in his notebooks back in the library. And now he was doing the same with leftovers: a ham sandwich and more cherries. A new golf pencil, a fresh notebook.

There was no longer room under the couch table for the old ones. And his locker was starting to fill up. But he felt no closer to a solution. Still, he kept scribbling, could do nothing else.

He did not notice the natural light of day dimming, turning yellow as it was replaced by the yellow light of interior bulbs. Someone brought food and he ate it. Someone else suggested he think about sleeping, and he said he would, but just kept writing. Soon the notebook was full and he opened the next one, started on it. He didn't notice a fight in the common room a world away, didn't notice a new day dawn. Someone brought breakfast and he ate it, and kept writing.

Eventually Walter slept on the couch. Staff came to wake him, touched his shoulder, and he fought wakefulness. Things made more sense asleep. But the Staff wanted him to get up, go somewhere. And there wasn't any fight left in him now.

He really needed to pee, so he did that, and Staff waited for him, asked him if he'd washed his hands, sent him back into the toilet to wash and brush his teeth. Then Staff escorted him into the office.

There were new people and old people in there waiting for him, but they were all just Staff in his mind. All the same. Same face, same demands, same irrelevance. The red-haired girl was at the table, smiling, and he barely even noticed her. Only The Problem mattered now, and he could feel time running out.

"Walter, welcome. We'd like to try something a little different today."

Walter said nothing.

"Linda is your new social worker," the voice said, and Walter was not sure who was talking. "She's heard of a new approach to problems such as yours. It's called 'psychosocial rehab,' and it involves moving back into the community, working. We'd like to know what sort of work might interest you."

Walter said nothing.

"I don't think he's listening," said a different voice, but it was just Staff to Walter. "Is he even lucid? Is he medicated down right now?"

"Best not to talk about Walter as though he's not here. Walter, do you remember when we changed your medications last month? Did it help with the feeling that everything was made of numbers?"

Walter remained silent. It was hard to see how the questions being asked might concern him in any way. The Problem nagged, and it occurred to him that the red-haired girl might be looking into his head. Funny. She had not aged at all. She was still about twelve, wearing the same Holly Hobby dress she always had. His mother had given him a Holly Hobby rag doll and Easy-Bake oven when he was five. Where did that doll wind up? He hadn't seen it in years and years. But there was still The Problem.

Staff were still talking, and he had a feeling it might have something to do with him, but Walter could not even pretend to be interested any more. He got up as though he weighed a thousand pounds, shuffled to the side door and let himself out. If anyone tried to stop him, he didn't notice.

He shuffled down the hall, getting lighter and lighter as he got farther from the prying gaze of the red-haired girl. Back in the library, safe, Walter picked up one of his notebooks, and fell asleep on the couch again.

***

"I understand your point," Weatherly said, "but I just don't think he's a good candidate. Poor Walter is completely dependent. Nothing we have ever tried has done more than take the edge off his hallucinations. He's on a mild sedative now after some manic behavior a few months ago, and that doesn't seem to be very helpful."

"We have half the funding we had last year," Linda said. "And we have more urgent cases that need the beds. Walter's going to have to go somewhere, and soon."

"He can't fend for himself. You'd be killing him."

"He can do more than you think. They all can. They're helpless because they're coddled here. Places without hospitals have the same rates of schizophrenia but less invasive symptoms - because people are needed and therefore useful." Linda put her hands carefully on the desk in front of her, relaxing her fists, calming herself.

"He's not going," Weatherly said, "and that's final. Get rid of someone else, someone more appropriate for jail. You know as well as I do that that's where these men will end up if you toss them out."

"If that's what it takes for them to learn self-reliance, that's what we have to do," Linda said.

"I've been here a long time," said Roger. "Twenty years in. I got most of these gray hairs up at Wilford Hall. All this time I never seen anything that says a guy like Walter is secretly competent. He wouldn't cut it. And a guy like Benny, he's damned dangerous."

"But some of them could make it," Shane said. She was new. "Steve and Thad, for example. Thad's main problem is he's black."

Roger looked sidelong at her. "Best you explain that one," he said.

"I mean, if he weren't black, staff down on the acute team wouldn't have been scared of him and sent him up here to the chronic and dangerous team. He never hit anyone or even threatened anyone. He's just tall and black. He's scared silly up here, poor guy. No reason he couldn't make it in a halfway house."

"We're not here to debate the merits of psychosocial rehab," said Weatherly. "We have our directives from on high. But we cannot afford to apply directives in a sightless, blanket fashion. Very dangerous to do so. I am the unit psychiatrist and I say Walter stays. The way things are right now, my word is final. Let's move on to the next case."

Linda smiled with her face, turned the page on her notepad, and thought about power structures. "The next one is George's," she said. "You don't need me for this." The side door beckoned and her egress was not notable. She passed George in the hall, smiled "hello" at him.

Linda stepped off the unit via the door to the staff offices, but she wasn't going to her office. She went around the corner to the right, down the stairs. Visitors would head out the doors to the left from here, but she went right, down the long hallway that lead to the administrative wing.

Five minutes later, she knocked on a nondescript office door.

"Ms. Hale, nice to see you. Come in, sit down."

"Thank you, Doctor Michaels."

"Please, call me Carl."

***

Timothy started up his car, an old Citroen a bit like the one Peter Falk drove in Columbo. It wasn't a Cadillac, but Timothy reflected that he was at least moving up in the world. His breath stuck to the inside of the windshield and he had to wait for the blower to do its work, which meant waiting for the engine to warm.

In another neighborhood, he might have left the car idling and gone inside to wait. Here, though, even this old junker was subject to theft. Best to wait right here.

A brown bag sat on the passenger seat (a ham and cheese sandwich inside, along with a bag of potato chips) and a briefcase on the floor in front. Some candy-bar wrappers in the back seat told a story of a man with a sweet-tooth and not much down-time.

But this was down time. Timothy wandered into his mind for a while, rolling problem sets backward and forward.

Something about steps. How many are there? Do you count the floor? It had been bugging him for years now and it seemed relevant to high-energy measurement, but he couldn't quite slot together how...

His reverie was interrupted by someone tapping at his window. Timothy looked up, startled, and saw a police officer standing there. Red and blue lights flashed in his rearview. *That's what I get for daydreaming with my eyes shut*, he thought. He rolled down the window.

"You sleeping in there, Chief?" the officer asked. He had gray hair and laughing eyes. The badge on his chest said his name was Daniels.

"No, no, just waiting for the engine to warm up enough to keep the window clear."

"Your doors locked?"

"No. Should they be?"

Daniels nodded. "We've had two highjackings in this neighborhood this season so far. Victims are guys just like you: running the engine while sitting still, waiting for the engine to warm up. Keep your doors locked."

"Thanks for the warning," Timothy said, locking his door. "You know who's behind it?"

"In general, yeah. Crazy guys. Budget cuts."

That didn't add up to anything for Timothy. "What do you mean?"

"The hospitals. Normally the hobos go there when it's cold. No money for that any more so they do what they have to."

"Oh."

"Well, have a nice day, and be careful," Daniels said.

By now the engine was warm. Timothy reached over and checked the other door was locked, and started the drive in to school. He saw two bums wrapped up in blankets on the street corner at the end of the next block. A guy tried to squeegie his window when he stopped at a light under a bridge downtown. Now that he was aware of them, bums and hobos crept into his vision everywhere.

When did D.C. develop such a homeless problem? Timothy thought.

"Rather than ask why something happened (i.e. what caused it), Jung asked: What did it happen for? This same tendency appears in physics: Many modern physicists are now looking more for "connections" in nature than for causal laws (determinism)."

von Franz

Fifteen

"Yvonne is asleep," Valery said.

"I certainly won't wake her," Vitali said.

"You seem to be dead."

"So. In the same boat, are we?"

"No," said Valery. "Not exactly the same. Nobody is trying to save your life in an alternate dimension." He could still smell Yvonne's perfume on the mouthpiece of the telephone, though it had been nearly a decade since she'd put on her musk oil in the morning. That smell drove him wild, always had, made him curiously hungry and horny at the same time.

"Ruth must not love me so much as Yvonne loves you," Vitali responded.

"Not that at all, only that I wasn't supposed to die in her world or she in mine. You probably shouldn't be alive in either one, drinking the way you do and eating what you eat."

"Pah," the older man said. "There is no should, you know this. There is only what is. And here, now, this morning, I am still alive. At least for as long as your wife stays asleep, yes?"

"That's how it seems to be. When she wakes, when she's fully aware and not daydreaming, reality slips sideways. This space we occupy..."

"Is not real."

Valery stroked his own cheek. "Hard to grasp, right? Sounds crazy?"

"On the basis of your recollections alone? Oh yes, ungraspable. But still I work on the systems logic."

"When?"

"Soon, my friend. Soon enough, I hope."

Valery looked down at the phone, feeling strange, stretched out and faded. The body of the telephone was there on the table, and the receiver appeared to be there too, neatly in its cradle. Simultaneously, it was at his ear. Both conditions existed at once.

"She's waking up," Valery said.

"I understand. Go to her while you can."

Valery hung up gently, quietly, walked back into the bedroom. There were two women in the bed, partially occupying the same spaces where their arms and legs crossed. Yvonne had put green sheets on the bed, and they coexisted with the cream-colored set his other wife had picked out. Yvonne's eyes opened and reality slipped sideways, her version of events becoming real. She was alone in the bed now, moving to sit up, scrubbing sleep out of her eyes with the heels of her hands.

Valery watched as long as he could, yearning to reach out, touch her, sit with her, kiss her lips, yearning to be, exist. Yearning was not enough. By the time Yvonne's eyes were open, there was nothing new to see.

On the way to the bathroom, Yvonne caught a scent. Her husband. Valery's aftershave. Hai Karate, a ridiculous affectation that she had never liked. It seemed stronger the more she approached the office. She started to daydream in there, standing by the phone, imagining him standing there with the phone in the crook of his neck, making a dinner reservation and smiling.

"I miss you," she said. "I miss you, Valery, so much. I want you back, Valery."

There was no answer, but she had not expected one. So Yvonne wiped away tears like she had scrubbed out sleep moments before and went back into the bedroom. Slid open the closet door that was also a mirror, pulled out a dress for the day, slip the door closed again.

There, in the middle of the glass, was a hand print. A man's hand print.

"Valery," Yvonne breathed.

**

She stood there for a time, just breathing, listening to her heart pound in her chest. Sometimes she could visualize it, nestled down in its cavity between the lungs, but not now. Now all she could think of was Valery. He had been standing here. His smell, the sweet sweat underneath the cheap aftershave, lingered in the small space. She remembered the first time she had smelled him, close, intimately.

A dance. A school benefit. In the dark, young people shuffled around the room dancing slow to something instrumental. Their bodies were pressed together and that felt good, fine, perfect. Sweat trickled down her back, staining her dress. And she breathed him in, could do nothing else but sway to the music, clutch him as tightly as he held her, and breathe in the air that hung around his body.

A perfect night. Later he had driven her home, to her father's house where she still lived while getting her pre-med, kissed her tenderly on the doorstep. In another decade she might have lived alone, might have invited him inside. But it wasn't the eighties, and their urges had to wait on a different kind of propriety.

The bedroom. Now. She came back to the present to find her hand was touching his hand, or at least the print he had left on the glass. It was gone now, whether faded the way a breath does, normally, or through the vagaries of whatever strange phenomenon was taking place here. She couldn't say which. Didn't care.

Yvonne got down on her knees, put her face close to the spot the handprint had been, her breath tickling the glass so that fog waxed and waned on the mirror. She moved her hand to the side, leaned in, put one soft kiss right there, there where Valery had touched. The glass was cold, hard, nothing like the lips she yearned for. She wanted her man back, wanted him to breathe into her mouth as he leaned close, wanted to smell that horrible cheap aftershave.

Her lips had left a little mark, a damp print that did not fade away like the handprint or her breath.

Didn't fade.

The bathroom. She uncapped a brownish-red lipstick, her favorite. It brought out the deep brown of her eyes. She applied it liberally, using the mirror by habit even though a shower would eliminate any mistakes a few minutes from now.

Back to the mirror. Another kiss, this time an obvious one at face-height.

More.

The lipstick became chalk, the mirror the blackboard. "I love you," she wrote. "I can see you sometimes. Tell me you are real."

Lipstick was not meant for writing messages. It had been low already and now was out. That would have to do.

Work seemed a futile interruption, pointless in the light of what was happening, but she went back into the bathroom to get ready.

***

"I'm sorry, do I know you?" Timothy said into the telephone. He had been on his way out the door, his brown bag in one hand still, briefcase on the floor between his feet.

"Sometimes," the voice said. "Other times I need to remind you. My name is Raul. Raul Jiminez. Do you need a second?"

"I'm sorry, Raul, I'm late for..." He trailed off as memories started to creep and then collide and then flood into being, strange truths that were somehow forgotten over and over again.

"You're late, so I'll be brief. One of my students was helping me an experiment in quantum entanglement. We got an unexpected result and elaborated the experiment to attempt to reproduce the effect. In short, we were measuring the oscillations of a cesium atom, and that atom contained, as one of its constituent components, a single quark entangled with a quark in a separate area. We altered a property of that quark with a high-energy laser, causing the entangled quark to also change states, and the cesium atom to degrade into xenon.

"The trouble is this." Timothy had only one ear on this long description, still reeling under the weight of new/old memories that shed new light on his entire existence. But Raul went on. "Cesium makes an excellent clock. We can count the oscillations, and indeed that is just what we were doing, because cesium oscillates at a different rate than xenon.

"The cesium degraded before we altered the state of the quark, Timothy. We expected, hoped for the atomic-level entanglement. But *the results preceded the cause.*"

"That's impossible," Timothy said. "It's all impossible."

"It's not impossible. We have replicated the results six times."

"Why do you remember, but I don't?"

"My cat. I encoded quantum information, this encoding resulted in a mild radio-decay event, and the cat became mildly irradiated at a non-harmful level. The cat lived. Had it died, I would have needed to try again until one lived. Now whenever I see the cat, I am reminded of the quantum encoding, and everything else. The whole strange mess. Part of the information cannot exist without all of the information, so all the information returns to being."

"That's crazy," Timothy said.

"So hang up. Except you know it's not crazy. You have been helping Yvonne through this for years now. And I do remember, crazy cat experiment or not. That's not important now. What is important is that the effect preceded the cause."

"Meaning what, exactly?"

Raul spoke quickly, immediately, barely waiting for Timothy to finish the question. "Everything that is happening, all the strangeness, we caused it to happen. In the future."

"Mathematics is the cheapest science. Unlike physics or chemistry, it does not require any expensive equipment. All one needs for mathematics is a pencil and paper."
Pólya

Sixteen

It was a strange realization, a science fiction story. And it was hard to keep hold of. When he came into being, he remembered everything as though he had always existed, even though he only existed for short periods of time. And those memories made it hard to remember the truth: he had just emerged into being and had limited time in which to work.

Valery sat across a desk from Vitali Gergiev, trying to imagine how he could explain this whole mess. Unlike Valery, Vitali forgot everything each time he emerged into being. He existed because Valery existed, somehow.

"Solipsism," Valery said aloud without realizing it.

"I love you, old friend, but our time is short."

"I understand," Valery said. Their time was indeed short, but Vitali thought it was because of a meeting.

"I need whatever you have," Valery said.

"The equations are nothing like completed. It is like boiling water. If you take a spoon out before the water is boiled, that isn't boiled water. None of it is ready until all of it is ready."

"That's all right. I still need what you're working in. To preserve it."

Vitali sighed. "Why do I do these things for you? Is it because you are crazy? In Russia, the madman is holy, closer to God. These mad thoughts of yours, tell me, do they come to you from Heaven?"

"I wish that were true," Valery said. "But only my parents were Russian. I'm an American. Here we just lock our mad people away." He was thinking of his poor brother-in-law. Since Yvonne had died, Valery was all he had left in the world. How long since he had paid a visit? He remembered a bus in nineteen seventy eight. Had it been four years? "If I really am crazy, you're going to have to deliver all that logic to the madhouse."

"Such would seem like home," Vitali said. "I will have my secretary photostat the first few pages, the material I am comfortable with, and mail it to your apartment. Will this satisfy you for a while?"

"Yes. I am grateful. I know you're humoring me..."

"Yes, my friend, without too much condescension, I hope. Grief is hard, and the best thing to do is to let it be hard for a while. When its work is done, it fades into the background, leaving you sad but not shattered. And a sad man is a wise man, one who makes his decisions in the light of grief and hurt but not under the weight of them."

Valery stood, waiting for the Earth to shake and change and delete him. In a moment, he would not exist again for a time, but he would remember existing as though he had. He would remember going to work, driving home, maybe taking a day off. *Yes*, he thought. *It's time I visited Walter. The apartment is empty.*

A lipstick message on the closet door had convinced his wife that there was another woman, perhaps a vengeful one, and she was gone, his child with her. His explanations seemed empty. Later, when the message had faded from the glass and she couldn't remember what they had been fighting about, she still remembered being angry, and filled in the blanks with imagination.

"Thanks, Vitali. You have always been a good friend."

"Be well, my friend," Vitali said, heaving up and edging his way around the desk. He had lost a few pounds, given up smoking, but he still looked too big to live. Impossible. Ten years ago nobody cared about health and now everyone counted calories but Vitali was too far behind the trends, had lived too vibrantly. Much larger than life and not long for it.

They parted ways, or at least Valery remembered doing it later. Because the gap between that event and the next was impossible, could not have happened, and so either his mind or the universe filled in the gaps.

***

Raul came into the study with a tray loaded with cups, saucers, a coffee urn, cookies. He set it on the small table off to one side.

"Thanks," said Rosie. "Not too long ago, he'd have his secretary do that."

Timothy felt his face flush. There was some old argument here and it felt like an intrusion for him to witness this little corner of it.

But Raul just laughed. "You set me straight, dear, and I'm glad of it. I'd never have found Jill Hanks, otherwise."

"Your student?" Timothy asked, begging the universe to let the answer be yes.

"Of course. She's brilliant, really. Maybe a touch rough around the edges, but aren't most good physicists?"

Schrödinger wandered into the room, drawn by the sound of voices. He wrapped himself around Timothy's legs but scuttled away when he tried to pet him. Then he rubbed his face on the table with the coffee service on it, causing the whole thing to rattle and wobble.

"Perhaps I should pour the coffee before the cat does it for us?" Timothy said, and set to.

"So, the list," Raul said. "Before the coffee, there was the list. My work. I think we can produce a high-energy event. Brian Moldavie. He can work out the translations, the math for higher-dimensional interactions. If we make anything that is transient in our sort of reality, I want to be able to track it. Gergiev, he was working on chip logic. We will need some custom hardware including custom chips to put this all together. You, Timothy, are on high energy particles and measurement. We are going to need measurement for the entanglement to work."

"But Gergiev is dead and this whole plan is crazy," Timothy said.

"That does present a wrinkle," Rosie said. "He wasn't training a replacement, didn't have an intern, any notes?"

"No," said Raul.

"Timothy passed out coffee, sat down, sipped. It was good. Dark, strong, hot. "So, what you want to do is... Smash energetic particles to attain higher levels of entanglement? To what end, ultimately?"

"I don't know yet," said Raul. "I just know I did it, in the future, and somehow all of this weirdness is a result."

"The pieces seem to fit," Timothy said. "But that doesn't mean it's the only way they could be assembled. I do agree our association is not a coincidence. So... Who's going to call Moldavie?"

"We thought you should do it," Rosie said. "You went to his school. Some of his classes even."

"All right. I'll set to work tracking him down."

***

"That was a weird call," Brian said.

"Who was it?" Janet asked.

"Former student. From Washington," he added, although he had never taught anywhere else.

"Come back to bed."

A long weekend in bed. *I might be older now, Janet too, but we know how to live*, he thought to himself. He went to the kitchen first, brought back cartons of Chinese from last night.

"Hey, you'll mess up the sheets!"

"We'll get new ones," he said. "We're rich now, remember?"

"We won't be for long if we keep spending money like water."

"That's true," he said. "So we'll be careful."

They weren't careful, though, not very. He put a movie in the Betamax player, a sci-fi movie. They ate, giggled, cuddled, eventually loved. "This is living," he said later.

"I like Rhode Island," Janet said. "I like the rain."

They stopped and listened to it for a while, rattling against the windows. A custom bay window opened onto a view of the Atlantic Ocean, now just a gray blur through the rain that beat at the glass.

"You know, the fire was a blessing in a way."

"How do you figure?" Brian said.

"Well, if this wing hadn't burned down, we'd have lived with the original windows. Since we got to rebuild the wing, we got to build these big windows in. They didn't have good glass when the house was first built. So these big windows were impossible."

"I guess," said Brian. "It was expensive, though."

"Yeah, that's all true. Remind me again how much I won?"

"Enough to buy new sheets every day for a thousand years," Brian said. "Let ruin these ones some more."

"Soy sauce?"

"Not what I had in mind."

"To succeed, planning alone is insufficient. One must improvise as well."

Asimov

Seventeen

Yvonne left the hospital after another long shift. Her scrubs were in the hospital laundry and she was in her street clothes: a blue track suit that simulated crushed velvet, neon pink tennis shoes. Over one shoulder was a gym bag, black with a neon blue sports logo. Her hair was tied in a neat bun.

Morning in downtown New York meant a noisy walk to the subway. Yvonne usually drove but today she had a stop to make and the train was more convenient. So her ears were exposed to the auditory melee of car horns, truck engines, people talking. The hot-dog vendor was just setting up for the day, as were the construction crews.

The crews meant the sounds of jackhammers were imminent, and cement mixers, and all sorts of other nonsense. They also meant catcalls.

Part of the reality of life as a woman was the interest of men, and that that interest would be made known in an inappropriate fashion. Yvonne tried to ignore it. Some of the insults (and no matter how they were phrased, she heard them as such) were shockingly direct.

Maybe I should have driven, she thought.

There were other women walking to or from the subway, some with men on their arms, some in close crowds, the single ones especially vulnerable to verbal predation. Like her, they had their heads up and shoulders back, trying to be impervious.

Then came the relative safety of the subway. She could feel heads turning behind her, men watching her from behind, and tried to ignore the sensation. The subway smelled of mud, must, disinfectants. In places it smelled oddly like a clean restroom. Downstairs things got crowded, no more people than up in the air but far less space.

Her train came just a few minutes later. Yvonne looked in the windows hoping to see Valery reflected there, but it was just her, shabby and tired-looking.

The train shook and rattled and rumbled its way along its given track, unvarying, as it did all day, every day. Before long, Yvonne was back up in the street, missing the way the noise of the train made it impossible to hear anything or anyone else in the environment. This wasn't downtown but men still looked even when they were quiet.

I wonder if they will not look any more when I'm old and gray - or if I'm stuck with this forever?

The camera store was partway down the block. A young man in a white shirt and black, skinny tie was rattling up the cage as she approached. "Go on in," he told her when he saw her waiting. "I'll be with you in a second, ma'am."

Ma'am? When did I become a ma'am?

She ducked under the raising metal cage, stepped through the open glass door. Inside were arrays of cameras of all sorts. Professional gear mostly on one wall, big blocky units and the giant lenses that would attach to them. Casual stuff on the opposite wall. These were smaller cameras, the size of a TV remote, some smaller and costlier. There were rotating cases of disposable flashes for these units.

"Morning, ma'am," said the young man, letting the door swing closed and straightening his tie at the same time. "What are you in the market for this morning?" He blushed a little, realizing he had said "morning" twice in two sentences.

"I need a camera. A Polaroid."

"Great, you're in the right place. Now do you mean Polaroid as in the name brand, or Polaroid as in any camera that prints its own pictures, and you don't have to take the film to a developer?"

"The latter," Yvonne said. "Other people make those?"

"Sure. Mainly Polaroid and Fujifilm. Is cost an issue? This one is the better camera all around, cleaner pictures, takes a few seconds longer but if you want quality, what's a few seconds? This guy right here, well, it's made for the mass market, does the job, most people would never notice the quality difference. It's mostly the film, to be honest. But they made these so the films wouldn't be interchangeable."

"I want the quality," Yvonne said. "I don't want any ambiguity."

"All right. This guy has an integrated flash, so you won't need that. Comes with this handsome carrying case, shoulder strap. Pretty big, made for a man's hands really, but... I'm sorry, I didn't leave myself anywhere to go with that."

"You're not as awkward as you think," Yvonne assured him, fishing her wallet out of the purse in the big gym bag. "Just relax. Don't worry so much about the script. Talk to people, not customers."

"Yes ma'am," he grinned, putting the camera in a giant plastic bag. The camera was big and so it came in a box that was even bigger, shrouded inside by white Styrofoam packaging, compartments for each component.

Yvonne didn't hear the catcalls or feel the looks as she went down the stairs back into the subway system. Her mind was focused: the next time Valery manifested in her apartment, she would have the means to catch the evidence.

***

"It's time to go to work," Staff said.

Walter said nothing, just kept scribbling in his notebook.

"Come on, Walt. You'll make us late."

Eventually they left without him. That's how it usually went. Once, they had talked him into walking down the stairs, across the soccer field, into the rehab building. They wanted him to fold boxes into shape, or put instructions inside dog toys. They said they would pay him, but what would he do with money? And all the time he sat there watching the other men work, she was there too, putting batteries in hearing aids and watching him out of the corner of her eye. If he looked away from her she stared at him until he looked back at her, then she pretended she wasn't watching.

The library was safe. Notebooks were piled up all around the space, years and years of work. Soon, he could start to reduce his findings to general principles, reduce all the pages of notes to a few equations that said something important, that solved The Problem.

Walter felt edgy, nervous, but didn't know he felt that way. His feet tapped of their own accord, unnoticed. He wrote faster but less of any importance. The numbers flowed. His heart ticked along too fast.

There was someone at the door. They didn't knock, just stood there. Walter tried to ignore her, but soon the distraction was too much. His numbers required all his concentration. Mistakes started to show up in the work. So he got up from the couch, quiet as possible, and dropped down to his hands and knees to peer under the door.

Two feet. Brown boots, Victorian era, with heels. He couldn't see any more than that.

"Go away," he said, his voice chalky from disuse. He sounded strange to his own ears - old, querulous. The girl didn't go away, just continued to stand there. Walter got back up, put a hand on the door handle-

And the door opened, knocking him backwards onto his tailbone. His head hit the couch, luckily the cushioned part. He lay there a minute, not really caring who was there, before he remembered that it was the Red Haired Girl and he needed to panic.

"Walter. I don't have much time."

That was definitely not her. He looked up, saw a strange man standing there. Maybe he was Staff. Staff changed all the time without really changing. Staff always wanted you to do things: take your meds, go to bed, go to work, brush your teeth, sign these forms, agree to these objectives.

"I've got something for you. I brought you a book."

"I don't read any more," Walter said, his voice surprising him. He usually ignored Staff as much as was practical.

"It's James Blish. I don't know how much you keep up with Blish. This is Star Trek: Thirteen."

Walter looked at the pile of books that made up the "library." The last Blish book was there, the twelfth Star Trek book. It had his wife's name on it because he died halfway through writing it.

"He's dead," Walter said. "There is no thirteen."

"No, there's a thirteen and a fourteen and up to twenty-one."

"He died in nineteen-seventy-five." Walter remembered that year. He wasn't sure what year it was now, but he remembered seventy-five.

"That's true. He died here, in this place, in seventy-five. Where I come from he's still alive, still writing books. Where I'm from, I'm still alive too."

"Am I still crazy?" Walter asked.

"Yeah, Walt. Yeah, you live here in my world. I'm sorry. Some things can't be changed."

"That's OK."

"Are you happy, Walt?" the visitor asked.

"I guess. What is happy, anyway? I'm close to solving something. I can't tell you about it..."

"No, I suppose you can't. We don't have much time, buddy. I just wanted to say hello, make contact, make sure you know I love you. We love you. There are people out here, in the world, and we love you, Walter. I hope that matters to you."

Walter didn't say anything. But he took the book, flipped through it. On the back was a picture of Blish, looking gray but hale, like Doctor Weatherly. When Walter looked up, he was alone.

He put the book on the pile in the library, realized he needed to pee. Peered out into the hallway, edged around the corner and peered down the longer hall that lead to the office, the lunch table, the toilet. No red-haired girl. Safe.

He padded down to the men's room. When he came out, he expected to see her sitting at the table, maybe drinking milk from one of those little half-pint cartons they gave kids in school, but she wasn't there.

Rather than run back into the library, he went into the communal bedroom, put on shorts and sneakers and a tee-shirt, started walking his laps. He hadn't done that in years and he was quickly tired. And he watched for her, but she wasn't there.

The ping-pong table sat unused - it wasn't Christmas time so there were no balls and only one paddle, with half the rubber ripped off. Nobody played. A guy sat down there reading a comic book. She wasn't there. In the common room, a couple of guys sat on fake leather furniture watching The Dukes of Hazard. She wasn't there. She wasn't in any of the seclusion rooms, outside the exit door window.

Walter finished a lap, touched the door with one finger, and smiled.

***

The emergency room was almost empty as Hugo staggered in holding his head. A waifish woman guided him to one of the cheap blue plastic seats in the waiting room. An elderly woman watched them come in and sit down.

Hugo was laughing. Not just giggling or chuckling, but full-on belly laughing. The more he laughed, the more his head hurt - and the more it hurt the more he laughed. It felt like all the hangovers he had ever had rolled into one and multiplied by a thousand. It felt like the blood in his brain had been flash-boiled, like he been stabbed in the back of the head with a nuclear weapon.

The pain was so absurdly, outrageously unbearable that it was also hilarious. So he laughed.

"Are you all right?" Ruth asked for about the ninetieth time. "Be careful, I think you must be having an aneurism."

She was first-year pre-med. And she wasn't reassuring. "It's not an aneurism," Hugo growled out through teeth suddenly clenched. Sitting still made the pain just a tiny percentage better. His mind tried to quantify it exactly but that was futile. "Go get the clipboard."

Ruth came back a minute later with a clipboard and a nurse. "What seems to be the problem?" he asked.

"I seem to have all the headaches in all the world," Hugo said, now laughing again. Tears were crawling down his cheeks.

"Sudden onset? Or how long has it been going on?"

"Uh, sudden. Really sudden."

"What were you... what was going on when it started?" he said, pulling out a pen light and peering into Hugo's eyes one by one. Ruth blushed and pulled her bathrobe tight about her. They each had on their nightclothes, bathrobes, and sneakers.

"We were, let's say, exercising."

"Wait here," the nurse said needlessly. He went into the nursing station, pushed a button on a control panel, muttered some words into the tiny microphone next to the speaker. A minute later two burly men and a tiny woman came out with a gurney. They were all dressed in institutional white and Hugo wondered inanely whether he was off to visit Walter, and the laughter swept over him once more. How since they had been roommates? Ruth tried to go back with him, but the nurse stopped her, thrust the clipboard into her hands. "Paperwork," he said.

Hugo was swept into one of those rooms made of fabric: walls that were really sheets hung around a steel bar in the ceiling by shower-curtain hooks. There was a little brown nightstand to make the place seem like a real room, and everything else was on wheels, including the institutional-blue work surfaces. The orderlies or nurses or whatever they were helped Hugo off the gurney and into the bed, which was softer than it looked and not at all wider.

It seemed like a Nascar pit crew descended on him then, taking his blood pressure and clamping one of his fingers with something, drilling an IV line into his wrist, doing at least six things he would not even remember later. Then they all disappeared, leaving him alone with things that dripped, beeped, or periodically chirped.

"Hugo? What are you doing in DC?" Yvonne said a minute later, appearing from between two sheets that were walls.

"Yvonne? Walter's big sister?"

"Not so big," she said, patting her little belly. "Forty was a rough year for diets."

"I didn't mean..."

"Of course not," Yvonne said. "I shouldn't treat you, but I sent the other doctors home. Not enough customers to justify staying open. What's up?"

"Headache," he said. "Like all the headaches in the world welded together."

"Williams said it came on during sex."

"Let's say exercise," Hugo repeated, flushing slightly. Somehow he couldn't talk about this plainly with Yvonne, even though he hadn't seen her since high school graduation.

"All right, then," she smiled. "And were you near the finish line?"

"Uh... yeah?"

"All right," Yvonne said. "This happens from time to time. It's a sex headache. I'll give you some propanolol for the time being. I want to do a quick neuro work-up, rule out aneurism - I wouldn't worry too much about that. Is your vision blurry?"

"Well, yes. But Ruth has my glasses, I think."

"Blurrier than usual? Foggy?"

"No."

"So, probably not an aneurism. We should also check out your ticker. This problem can mean some sort of arterial problem." Then she pointed at his belly. "That's the probably culprit though, all things considered."

"I'm too fat?"

"In a nutshell. Usually when a man loses a bit of weight, these headaches stop punishing them. What do you weigh right now? Two-fifty? I'd say a twenty pound loss would help you in so many ways. You won't have this kind of headache again, your heart will work more easily, you'll have more stamina."

"All right, doc," Hugo said. "How long do I need to stay here?"

"You just got here," she said.

"I feel better already."

"It's the distraction. And maybe the morphine in the drip bag. Kidding. It's just a saline drip but hydration is going to help. I'd say we run those panels, won't take long as we've not much else to do right now. Get you out of here by sunrise? I have to go make some rounds, but I'll come back soon and we'll chat, if you like."

"Sure," said Hugo. "I'd like that."

"Give me a place to stand, a lever long enough and a fulcrum, and I can move the Earth."
Archimedes

Eighteen

Yvonne went home later that morning, full of coffee but knowing she needed to sleep so she could work again that night. The place was empty, felt empty. Her footfalls echoed through the small apartment the way footfalls always echoed through empty places.

She put on a kettle, knowing tea would not help her sleep but wanting it anyway. Her tummy felt sour. Maybe a bit of bread, or toast. But first, she wanted a shower and a change of clothes.

Yvonne went through the bedroom without seeing it, into the little bathroom. Her clothes went on the floor while the water was warming. The hot water felt wonderful - even a slow night at the ER was a tense night, and it was good to wash the stress down into the drain. Even though the coffee should have kept her charged, fatigue worked its way with her, and Yvonne daydreamed standing there in the shower.

Almost an hour later, when the water was starting to run cold, she stepped out into the steamy room, wrapped herself in towels, and suddenly remembered the kettle. It had run dry while she showered and was starting to scorch, the blue flame of the fireplace licking it from underneath.

She cursed, refilled it, started over.

This time while it heated up she went to get dressed, snatching pajamas from the end of the bed where she had left them. When she turned to leave, her eyes raked the closet doors and caught there.

Letters, numbers, strange symbols covered the mirrored doors from top to bottom, the mathematical language she had seen Walter and his friends write in so many times without ever herself understanding. And she knew immediately how it had gotten there.

"Valery."

She grabbed the Polaroid camera from the nightstand, lined up a picture. Only so much would fit in the frame and still be legible, so it took four pictures to get it all. But what the devil did it all mean?

This time when the kettle squealed for attention she heard it, turned off the gas, made tea. And while she was doing that, she knew there were no coincidence left in her life. She went to the bathroom and dug a scrap of paper out of her trouser pocket. To the study, where she snatched up the phone and dialed the number on the paper.

"Hugo? Hope I didn't wake you. Yes, it's Yvonne. I need you to come over. Yes, right away. Why? Well, I could explain, but you'd just forget before you got here. No, I'll explain when you arrive."

***

"How's Ursula?" Hugo asked, shaking Peter's hand.

"She's good. Fantastic. I've never been so lucky. And she's wondering what's going on out here. I'd love to explain it, but I don't understand it." Peter tried to frown but wound up smiling.

"Math, buddy. Engineering, really, by the look at it, but math."

"Walt's sister? Did I hear you right over the phone?"

"Yeah," said Hugo. "I thought at first she might be crazy. You know, like Walter. But the math... it's so elegant."

They walked through the airport towards baggage claim. As they arrived, the horn sounded, a light flashed, and the baggage claim startled into life. Luggage started to slide out of a central hub down onto the aluminum plates that carried the suitcases and bags and duffels in an ellipse.

"Did you ever get to see what Walter was working on? The orderlies said it was pretty intense." Peter saw a black suitcase coming by, examined the tag, let it pass.

"No. But he couldn't pass undergraduate math courses any more. I don't think it's good."

"Are mathy and schizophrenic mutually exclusive?" Peter asked.

"Maybe. I guess we just don't know. Yvonne sure sounds pretty out of it. But then again she goes to work every day, runs a hospital department."

Peter picked up a suitcase, checked the tag, and this time kept it. "All right, where to?" Airports were not his strong suit.

"Train," Hugo said.

"Isn't there a taxi?"

"It would be about twenty bucks. The money train never rolled by my apartment..."

"I'll get it," Peter said. "No money train, but we do OK, and actual trains are more fun in the abstract, I find."

Hugo laughed. "Taxi's this way," he said. "Funny. I was always better at being in the world - you know, talking to people, find the way from one place to another? Buying clothes that fit?"

Peter laughed now, too. "I have to take Ursula when I need something, or else I forget to look at sizes or try things on."

"Remember that time your mom gave you eighty bucks and sent you to Penny's for school clothes?"

"Only did that once."

"I never had those problems. You were always more in your head, man. And now you're the one who's married and holding down a gig, and I'm the one not quite making it."

Peter laughed again. "You're too much for a woman," he said. "And it's just that your head has enough room for the world in it and mine doesn't." It was late and the line for cabs was short. A minute later they were riding in the back of a car, and old times took precedence over current problems.

****

"It's a little crowded," Yvonne said.

"We're OK if you are," Peter replied. "We've slept in tighter spots than this."

"That convention in seventy-nine," Hugo said. "There were eight of us in a room made for two. It smelled bad by the end but we didn't hang out in the room."

"I got thirteen autographs at that one."

"Walter was so happy," Yvonne said. "You got him that anthology, signed by everyone in it."

Hugo spread a blanket on the couch. Peter had drawn the floor and he made a nest there out of coats and a thick quilt to cover him. "You're sure you'll be all right?"

"Don't worry about us, Ma-- Yvonne," Hugo said. "We're all right if you are. You're the one whose privacy is at issue."

"It is a bit of an imposition, I'll grant you, but it will be worth it for someone else to witness what I see. Most days I feel like I've gone mad. And only Walter remembers anything I tell him."

"So why do the Polaroids not vanish?" Peter asked.

"I don't know. Something must have changed. Timothy called the other day, said something about a cat, but I couldn't understand any of it."

Hugo was going over the Polaroids again, comparing them with Yvonne's transcriptions and making corrections - she hadn't copied all the symbols just right because they weren't familiar to her. "What's this going to turn out to be? It's definitely some electrical engineering trip, but I've never seen anything like it before."

"I haven't the foggiest," Yvonne said. "I only know who wrote it, and he failed undergraduate calculus twice. He's copying it from somewhere for some reason."

"From who?" Peter said, "and why?"

"Something to do with what we're working on. I don't know exactly what we're working on, to be honest, but I know it's weird. Particle physics and entanglement, some multi-dimensional math - I don't even know what that is. Vitali Gergiev was supposed to be working on microchips, I don't know why-"

"That's it," said Hugo. "I'll bet you all the money in my bank account. I'll bet you all the money in Peter's. That's what this is, and that's why I've never seen it before. These are logic gates, for solid-state microcircuitry. I think. This is only the beginning, though. There would have to be more, much, much more, to have anything to go on. In fact, these first couple of sheets won't make sense without the rest. If they aren't ready yet, all these sheets could change."

"All right," said Yvonne. "So... what? What does it mean?"

"First, it means we have evidence of extradimensional communication. Second, the first thing is so incredible nothing else is really necessary. Third, we have to get this stuff to someone who can do something with it, make the chip. That's going to cost money and it's going to be hard to keep secret." Hugo shuffled the papers into order, set them aside.

"Well, I think I'm going to turn in, and see if I remember all this tomorrow," Yvonne said. The men watched her turn out all the lights, listened to her climb into her bed. It was hours more before they slept themselves.

"Photons have mass? I didn't even know they were Catholic."

Woody Allen

Nineteen

Brian looked incredulously at his bank balance. "Honey, have a look at this."

Janet came around the counter with its pens on ball chains and little slips of paper. "Is that right?" she asked.

"Well, I assume..."

"How can it be so much?"

"We haven't been spending enough?"

Janet laughed. "I've been doing some reading. Lottery winners usually quit their jobs, but have to go back to them within a few years. They didn't earn the money so they don't know how to look after it. We sure don't know how to."

"That's why we hired Geraldine," Brian said.

"So let's give her a call."

"Let's get a car-phone," Brian said. "Ever since the fire I've thought we should have one."

"Why were you in that hospital to begin with?" They were leaving the bank now, stepping out into Rhode Island sunshine from the dark-paneled interior. It felt strangely like the nineteen-sixties in there.

"I don't remember, really. I wanted to visit a former student. Came on me all of a sudden I should stop in and check on him. Hey, maybe I'm the psychic one." Brian held the car door open - a solid Ford LTD had replaced the old Citation, respectable but not luxurious. He shut the door behind her with a *thunk*. Walked for what felt like a mile around the hood, slipped into the drivers' seat.

"Well, we don't have a car-phone, so I suppose it can wait until after the christening."

"Nice of the Thompsons to invite us," Brian said.

"Very. Nice of them to help out after the fire, too."

"Makes me suspicious."

"That's because you're a bad person, dear," Janet said. He laughed. "Or you've studied too much game logic."

"One up, one down?"

"Zero sum. Life is not at all zero sum, dear. Maybe we should go to church more, and not just for baptisms and christenings. A little bit of humility might be good for us, a little faith in the human spirit..."

"I don't know," Brian said. "I like game logic."

"Math can't tell you one single thing about humanity," Janet said.

He drove on in silence.

***

"When you came in, you gave me more or less carte blanch," Geraldine said. "Do you remember?"

"Yes. We didn't expect our money to grow, though," Janet replied, "only to grow smaller more slowly."

"Well, that's an admirable goal, but you are rather young yet for asset protection to be your main strategy."

"Young?" Brian said, looking at his wife. She punched him playfully on the arm. "Oh, sorry, of course young," he corrected. "Only, I'm sixty."

"Which would of course be an issue if you didn't have much of a nest egg to begin with. But people with much money tend to live a long time, longer than younger people by far. And you have a great deal of money to manage. You could lose half this wealth and still have plenty to see you through. So I invested aggressively. One quarter in stocks, half in bonds, the remaining quarter in the highest-yield savings accounts I could manage. The interest on that last quarter is what you have been spending. If you'd like, I could take the dividends and put them back into your stock portfolio."

"What are we into?" Janet asked. "Nothing shady, I hope?"

"Is oil shady?"

"I shouldn't think so. Quite respectable," Brian said.

"Well, much of your money is in fossil fuels, a boom industry right now. You also got in near the ground floor on personal computers and compact disks. You're going to be rich."

"I thought we were already rich," Janet said.

Geraldine chuckled. "You were wealthy. Truthfully, not quite wealthy enough for the neighborhood you live in right now, but wealthy enough to keep up on the property taxes if not to be invited to the cocktail parties. This time next year, you'll look back on what you have now and laugh that you ever thought that was a lot of money. I promise."

"Aren't investments risky?" Brian wondered.

"Oh yes, individually. Not everything you have made money this quarter. But most of it will make money over the long term. Leave it with me. You'll be more than fine."

Later, in the car on the way home, Janet broke a long silence. "Don't you think if we're to be rich, actually mogul-level, cream-of-society rich, we should perhaps do something unselfish with our money? With our lives, even?"

"Yeah," said Brian. "But what? Charity? Poor children in Africa?"

"I don't know either," Janet said. "But we for sure should think more about it."

***

Vitali made sure his yarmulke was firmly in place - an ever-easier task as his hair thinned. He took a shawl from the rack, blessed and kissed it, put it on with the ease of long practice.

He took comfort from the sing-song ritual of a long service in Hebrew. This was an aging congregation, for the most part, and he knew everyone around him without knowing them outside of temple. He read along with the prayers, without really needing to. Stood on cue, sat when standing was not necessary. And at the end, he waited as everyone else filed out, back into their lives in the city, back into anonymity.

"Rabbi, do you have time for a word?" he asked, when he was alone with her.

"Of course. Doctor Gergiev, yes?"

"Yes, Rabbi Schultz. I was wondering. Do you think God keeps up with science?"

"I should think so," she said, a gentle smile playing across her lips.

"A reform rabbi with an old congregation."

"I have to be reform. Orthodoxy doesn't allow women to speak the word. I hear Russia in your voice."

"Yes, I came from there. I like it here," Vitali said.

"How do you come to be in a reform temple? Most Russians your age come later for the Orthodox services."

Vitali smiled, but it was a sad smile. "Sometimes we have to let go the past, or at least hold it loosely. In this world of microchips and easy money, rights for everyone, freedom and peace, orthodox teachings just do not seem so tenable as they once did. I need something more... flexible."

"Sounds good," Schultz said. "So what can we do for you? You didn't stay after the service to socialize, I think."

Vitali shook his head. "I've had this feeling..."

"Go on."

"My friend," he said, "his name is Valery. A fallen Jew, not even reform like us. I don't think he can even read Hebrew. Well, I think he's not well. He... says we do not really exist. That he died long ago, and I more recently, and none of that was meant to happen - but we live for short times while his wife is sleeping. Then we remember having existed, the gaps all filled in, although we did not."

Schultz rubbed the bridge of her nose with one finger. "Your friend seems to be going through some troubles. What is it you need from me? You said you had a feeling?"

"Yes, yes. Madness. Of course, he is speaking nonsense. And yet, I find myself sometimes losing faith, wondering if what he says might have some truth to it. What if I am not living, but remembering having lived? At my age, I suppose it must be somewhat normal to have such morbid thoughts, to start reflecting on one's past, trying to make sense of it all."

"What does it mean to live, rather than to have lived? Do you know?" She sat down next to him in the pew, took one of his hand in both of hers.

"I don't... No, I do, I do know. I would feel something here and now, I would remember having felt something in the moment when I reflect on the past. And I do, now, feel something. I feel real, substantial. Afraid to talk of all this, especially in this place where God can hear most clearly, afraid you shall think me foolish. But of earlier, nothing. I kissed my wife last night, I remember it, but as though I had read about it happening to someone else. Perhaps now I am real."

"Do you read?" Schultz asked him. When he raised an eyebrow in question, she went on, "Sartre? Camus?"

"No, no. No patience for French philosophy." He sank down a little into the seat, conscious of how much larger he was than the rabbi, wondering why she had sat down when she might have stood by him, maintained some small advantage in height.

She smiled again. "God made French philosophers and Russian mathematicians and American reform Jews all the same. Sartre tells us that life is without meaning, and our job is to live bravely in the face of meaninglessness, to embrace an empty life with courage."

"Nonsense," he rumbled. "Then meaninglessness becomes meaning and courage a virtue and Sartre has not at all embraced anything."

"And Camus suggests our greatest duty is to one another, that to live with courage means to embrace our feelings for one another even though those feelings might seem like they could crush us."

"I don't understand."

"That's all right, Doctor Gergiev. God understands. Do you love her?"

"God?"

Schultz laughed lightly, like the very distillation of mirth. "Your wife. Do you love her? Right now, this moment, do you love her?"

"With every splinter of every bone in my body," he replied.

"Then do that. Bravely. And next time you remember, remember that. What else matters, really, in the end, except that you loved her as best you could? Loved your God as best you could? Felt what you were able when you were able?"

Gergiev smiled now, not so fully as Rabbi Schultz but it felt good all the same. "Perhaps you are right. No, I know you are right. Such a bleak message to inspire so much comfort. What you are saying is what I have is all that I have, and that must therefore be enough."

"Yes. She's lucky to have you. And also that experience is sufficient evidence for experience. No proof that you exist is necessary except that you open your eyes and see the world around you."

"To be, or not to be..."

"Is not at all a reasonable question. You are, and have no other options. So be, and be as bravely as you can, with the help of God."

He stood then, freeing his hand gently from hers. "Thank you, Rabbi. I will return now to the work God has placed before me. If indeed I am dead in some alternate universe, He - She - must have some purpose for preserving me in this one. And if not, same answer."

"Go with God," Schultz said.

Vitali looked back once, saw her standing where he had left her, crying to herself. She did not seem to see him.

"It is change, continuing change, inevitable change, that is the dominant factor in society today. No sensible decision can be made any longer without taking into account not only the world as it is, but the world as it will be."

Isaac Asimov

Twenty

Valery got up early. Yvonne seemed to be working shifts at the moment, and he could not very well predict what shift she might be on each given day. So he rose at four, did a quick set of push-ups, grabbed the sheets Vitali had sent him. Crayon worked as well as lipstick, cleaned up easier (with the right chemicals), was cheaper.

By five, the mirrors were full of notations he did not understand. Some of the symbols were becoming more familiar. Today he was doing corrections: changes in the math on early sheets in the light of later sheets. A number in the upper right corner of the glass said this was sheet three, and he indicated the changed values or symbols with red boxes.

When that was done, he stepped into the shower, let the hot water turn on the rest of his brain. The more he awakened, the deeper his grief felt. Valery shaved there in the shower using his waterproof Norelco, and it seemed some of the grief went with the beard-stubble, as though sadness nestled in the wiry hairs on his chin.

He shut off the water, brushed his teeth, dried, then wrapped himself in a towel. He stepped through the little living area to the kitchen, drank some orange juice out of the carton, and then did a double-take back to the living room. "What the Hell?"

A tall man was spread out over the couch, covered in spare blankets from the linen closet. Another was getting up from a pile of coats on the floor, looking like he had slept in his clothes, a look of shock on his face. "I'm sorry," this man said. "We didn't know Yvonne had company..."

"Yvonne - You've seen her?"

"Yeah, she's right in... Crap... Are you Valery? It's been so long-"

"Peter?"

"Yeah, it's me. You haven't seen me since..." Peter trailed off, confused. Valery wasn't really there. Hugo sat up now, too, between Peter and Valery, only when Peter moved to get Valery back into his line of sight, it was Yvonne standing there. She was wrapped in a towel and looking as confused as Peter felt. "Yvonne?"

"Am I? Am I Yvonne? I was sure I was Valery. I dream sometimes I'm Valery."

"You were," Peter said.

"I was?"

"Valery. He was standing where you're standing. He talked to me. He saw me. He was surprised I was here."

"What did he say?" Yvonne said, stepping forward, leaning forward, reaching out with her hands.

"He said... Nothing really. My name. Your name. He wanted you. Then he was gone." Peter shrugged as if he could shrug off what was happening, return to sanity.

Hugo stood up then, went into the bedroom. "He was here, all right. Yvonne, you got that Polaroid? We'll need it. Man, this stuff is dense."

"He wanted me?" she said, and that seemed to console her but also make her hungrier, more avid. She rubbed her hands together like she was washing them, chewing her lower lip. "He's living like I'm living - he knows we were not meant to be separated. He's suffering like I'm suffering."

From the bedroom came the sounds of Polaroid film being exposed. "These look like corrections," Hugo said.

"You can't know that," Peter told Valery. "That he's suffering. You can't know he's suffering. He could be happy, or determined, or resolved, of he might not know anything is happening. Didn't you say you were forgetful? Maybe in ten minutes he'll have forgotten - wherever he is."

"You're right," Yvonne said, stepping into the bedroom, realizing for the first time she was immodestly covered. Hugo looked like he was done in there, just waiting for film to develop, so she said, "Do you mind? I need a minute."

"Oh. Oh! Yes, of course, sorry."

"You want to start some coffee?" she said to his back as he retreated.

"Do I ever."

***

"You know, it looks like high-energy measurement is going to take a lot of energy, in the long run?" Timothy paced in front of a chalk board about as tall as himself and twice as wide, one hand clutching a fistful of chalk in various colors, the other rubbing his face. He wouldn't realize his face was chalky until later that night.

There was nobody in the room with him but he figured talking to himself was, at this juncture, nearly the least of his worries.

One team imagined they could catch cosmic rays in heavy-water deep down in the Earth; if they interacted weakly with normal matter, the stillness down there where all other high-energy particles were filtered out would make any collisions necessarily weakly-interacting, massive particles, or WIMPs.

Timothy didn't think that was going to work. And it would be twenty to thirty years before the experiments were lined up to even try. That was why his blackboard was full of equations about magnetic fields, and why he was scratching his face and leaving chalk trails on his cheeks.

"I can't generate all this energy," he said. "If I could, I don't have the computing power to measure all the field interactions at once. We're going to miss something." Then he started to mutter, following the trail of a high-energy particle through an interlocking array of fields and counting how it would disrupt the fields just fractionally enough that a very sensitive magnetometer could pick up the change.

"Damnit, Gergiev, I need you right now."

The phone rang, startling Timothy. He dropped one of his bits of chalk. He picked up, half-expecting Gergiev to be impossibly on the line. But it was Brian Moldavie.

"What's happening, Brian?"

"I've been thinking," Brian said.

"Yeah? So have I. Hasn't done me any good yet. What's on your mind?"

"I want to fund some research programs."

"Congratulations. That's really great. How's Rhode Island?"

"You don't understand," Brian said. "I want to fund your research program. High-energy states and higher-dimensional math. I think it's worth exploring."

"Does this have anything to do with the fact that your name is on the Gergiev proof?" Timothy asked.

"Maybe a little. Hey, you can't fund everything. Although Janet and I, we want to make the world a better place. And we think knowing more about what's going on in the universe makes us better, all of us better. So, can you come out to Rhode Island and sign some paperwork? Do you need to bring a secretary or something? We'll have the foundation properly established by the end of the month."

"My boss with be delighted," Timothy said. "That's really generous. Most of the effect of that money will be to get him somewhat off my back, maybe a research assistant, maybe a smaller teaching load."

"Whatever works. So, could you come out in three weeks?"

"I'll arrange it," Timothy said.

When he went back to stare at the energy calculations some more, somehow everything seemed just a little more possible.

***

The doctor wouldn't tell Walter anything. He just asked questions. Have any pain? Any problems with daily activities? Does this hurt, or this? OK, now breathe in deeply. Whatever his findings were, they lurked in a file in a cabinet in an office somewhere.

On the way back Staff took Walter to a burger place. Walter ate a greasy hamburger out of a paper wrapper and felt alive for the first time in... well, as long as he could remember. He stuffed French fries into his mouth with such zeal that Staff ordered a second round, a big steaming basket of them, and Walter ate those, too.

"Haven't been off the grounds in a while, Walter. How are you doing?" Staff asked him.

"Pretty good," he said.

"Well, for you that's exceptional. You never even talk to me on the unit. So I'll take that as real progress. You need any more fries?"

He nodded, a big silly grin on his face. Staff signalled the guy at the counter and a minute later there was another basket of fries. Walter ate more slowly this time, noticing how the grease burned the ends of his fingers, how it made his chest feel hot as he swallowed. How the salt was so good it made his tongue hurt.

Their ride was an old Jeep from the motor pool. It was clunky and had bad shocks. Walter grinned all the way across town to the hospital, to home. He didn't even notice when they passed George Washington University. He just sort of basked in the sunlight and the smells of the old truck, the road, the grease on his fingers.

Back at the hospital, James pulled up by the stairs that would lead directly onto the unit, by the ping-pong tables. He got out and then let Walter out, opened the door for him, walked up behind him.

James used his key. When they were both inside, he made sure the door was secure behind him and went off to the office to turn in the paperwork.

Walter hit the toilet, and then went straight for the library. He smiled as he pushed open the door - it hadn't been locked for years now - and rushed in to pick up a notebook. His mind reeled with new ideas for The Problem and the red-haired girl had not bothered him all day.

But as he stepped into the room, Walter saw that his notebooks were missing. Nothing under the couch, under the tables. All gone.

He rushed back to the bunk room, went through his half of the closet he shared with Stukey. It was bare, as bare as the day they had brought him here. Nothing. No sheets on his bed, no shoes lined neatly underneath.

He tried to stay calm but Walter's heart hammered hard and sweat trickled down his back. His chest hurt from all the French fries he had eaten. He turned to run to the office but vomited instead, all over Stukey's bed. Then he was on his knees holding his head and screaming.

Next thing he really knew, Walter was in a seclusion room. There was a metal bed with fittings for restraints. They had let him have a mattress and a thin blanket. There was a window, heavily screened, with a view of the courtyard the patients below used for their smoke times now that smoking was banned inside the building.

Walter went to the heavy door, stood on tiptoes to look out the window. It was plate glass with wire embedded in it and a wire mesh screen on each side. Outside, he could see a safety officer in his uniform, leaning against the wall to the right. He was talking to someone.

A minute later, a face appeared at the door - they had probably been watching him with the camera in the corner. It was Staff, not Safety - Safety was, like the doctor, distinct from the rest of Staff. "Howya doin', Walter?" they said.

"I'm fine, I guess. Better. Only... where are all my things?"

Staff leaned back, talked to someone out of his view, whoever Safety had been talking to. He overheard something, just a whisper really: best to tell him while he's in there. Contained.

"Tell me what?" he said, running out of voice.

"You're moving out," Staff said. "We boxed up all your things while you were out. Walter, you're a free man. As soon as you're ready, we'll walk you out to the door, give you bus fare and say goodbye. Congratulations."

"Not only is the Universe stranger than we think, it is stranger than we can think."

Heisenberg

Twenty-One

Walter stood outside the hospital building, by the back parking lot, watching rabbits hide in the tall grass. He hadn't arrive with any suitcases and so was not leaving with any, either. His possessions were all around in him plastic trash bags, the final sign of contempt from Staff. His notebooks alone filled three bags. His clothes filled one more, and various junk items from Christmas and Halloween and New Year's parties over the years yet another.

He would gladly do without any of these things but the notebooks, except those were too heavy for him to carry. And carry where?

"Yvonne," he's said. "Didn't you call my sister?"

Staff had just all looked at each other the way they did when patients said something bizarre.

"Call my sister," he repeated. "I'll do it."

"Walter, your sister has been dead for years. We tried to call Valery, we told you that. But we couldn't reach him in time for this. So you're on your own right now. You've got a month of meds-"

"Meds? I don't want meds. I can't go out there by myself. The red-haired girl-"

"Has never hurt you. She's not real and you don't need to be here. You're free. Go on, life is waiting for you out there. Walk with me. It's going to be all right."

Except it wasn't all right. It was cold out in the parking lot and he had no plan, no support. Forty bucks in his pocket for a bus ticket. To where? To meet whom?

So he pulled a golf pencil out of his pocket, sat down on a pile of clothes, and opened a fresh notebook. It wasn't private, but The Problem still needed to be solved.

As dark was falling, Safety came out of the door to the unit. Walter had been so engrossed in his work he hadn't noticed the guys from his ward come out into the yard and were sitting around on weather-beaten lawn furniture, smoking cigarettes. The red-haired girl was with them, smoking a Pall-Mall slim even though she was too young for smoking. Her teeth sliced up the filter.

"Walter, you have to get going," Safety said. "We've called the local police to escort you off the property."

"Why can't I stay here?" Walter asked, looking back at his notebook. It didn't pay to make too much eye contact with Safety.

"No more money for care for guys like you, Walter. Just for violent perps, sex offenders and guys with good health insurance. Yours ran out years ago. Welcome to Reagan's America. The cops'll be here in a few minutes, give you a ride someplace maybe, if you don't give them any trouble. All right?"

"A ride where?"

"Beats me, buddy. You're free now. For whatever that's worth. I tell you this much: everyone here liked you. We wish you could stay. Directives from above, though. You know how it is."

Walter didn't know how it was, but he didn't say so. It didn't seem like it would help. Safety went away, which was good: Safety made him nervous, made all the patients nervous. Trouble was as apt to start because they were around as to stop because they came to intervene.

Not very long into the night, when smoke break was over and everyone went back inside except Walter, because he was on the wrong side of the fence, and the red-haired girl, because she stayed to watch him, he saw lights break up the darkness of the parking lot. A police cruiser rolled and crunched over the gravel, bumped over the rough curb and through the grass, and came to rest next to Walter and his piles of possessions.

Two officers got out of the car, leaving the headlights pointing at Walter. One was tall and fat, the other was short and fat, and they both kept one thumb hooked in their belt, the other hand near their gun. "You Walter Bradbury?" said the tall one.

"I think so," he said. Nobody had used his last name in his presence in a long time. Even his underwear just had Walter B. written on the tags in black marker.

"Walter, you're trespassing on State property," said the short one.

"I can't help it," Walter replied. "They just threw me out. I was good. I don't know why they did that. I was good. Look, they put all my stuff in trash bags."

The tall one looked at the short one, but the short one didn't look back to get the message. "You need to get up outta here now, Mister Bradbury," he said, and advanced a step forward.

"I can't. I can't carry all this stuff. I can't leave my notebooks - my work..."

"I won't say it again," the short one said, but the tall one came around, put a hand on Walter's arm.

"Walter, can I call you Walter? Good. Walter, how about if we put all this stuff in the back of the cruiser, and we drop you at the bus station? Did they give you bus fare? Yeah? They usually do. Come one. We'll get you downtown, and I'll buy you a cup of coffee, and you can decide where you want to go."

They didn't give him much choice. They were already moving. Before he could really evaluate whether it would be good or bad, he was in the back of the cruiser with half his stuff - the clothes mostly. The seat was really wide across, like being on the back bench of a bus, and there was a steel mesh between him and the front seat. The red-haired girl rode with him, sitting on the other side of the bags of clothes. She didn't smoke in the police car, though.

Walter continued to scribble in his notebook. It was a smooth ride so his work was not too messy. Then they came to the bus station. The officers carried all his stuff inside, set it by one of the benches where people waited for their buses - a Chinese guy got up and walked away as they did so - and left Walter to sit there and watch over everything. The tall officer put a cup of coffee in his hand a minute later.

"There's the desk. They'll open again at six in the morning. We'll swing through here at ten and you need to be gone, OK? My partner, he's not the nicest guy in the world. If it's after ten and you're still here, he might decide he wants to have a little fun, and I won't be able to stop him again. OK? You understand?"

Walter didn't say anything, just looked nervously around the place. He'd lost track of the red-haired girl when they got out of the car. She could be anywhere now, trying to get The Problem from his mind, work out his computations.

"Let's go," the short one said. "Waste of damn time here. Why we always gotta be the ones to drive these bums across town?"

They were walking away, but Walter could hear them as though they were talking right in his ear. "They ain't bums," the tall one was saying, nearing the doors. "They're just unlucky. Sick like, but..." The rest was lost as the glass door swung shut behind him.

Reflected in the door, Walter could see the red-haired girl, sitting right next to him on the bench. When he looked around, though, she was gone again.

With nothing else to do until morning, he worked on his notebook. It was hard, though, because other guys kept coming up to him, waiting for him to look away so they could see what was in his trash bags. Finally he dragged away the bag with his clock radio in it, and his Walkman, and said they could have that one, but they couldn't have the notebooks.

That seemed to work. While a handful of dirty men went through the bag he'd given them, he worked happily on his math, and eventually went to sleep lying on bags of notebooks.

***

"He's where?" Valery said into the telephone. He was in a kiosk outside a hotel downtown, had just been passing by when he had the urge to check up on Walter. It was his lunch hour and Walter never wanted to talk for more than a minute or two, so there was plenty of time. Except he wasn't at the hospital any more.

"We're sorry, sir, but as you're not a direct relative, we can't disclose that information to you."

"Let me put this another way, then," Valery said, doing his best to sound like Telly Savalas. "I'm a lawyer. I might not be the greatest lawyer in the world, I mostly shuffle research documents in the back office, but I work for a firm. That firm has ninety lawyers in it, and all of them like me, because I win their cases for them on precedent. And every one of those ninety lawyers knows forty more. Do you understand what I'm telling you?"

"We've done nothing wrong," the voice over the line said, and they sounded defensive. Valery knew then that he had won.

"You put a mentally ill man out on the street without contacting his next of kin - that would be me, by the way - or making any arrangements for his future care. Any action of his, you are liable for. And any harm that comes to him, you are liable for. Now you tell me where he is, right now, or else-"

"Hold, please."

He held. Dropped another dime in the slot when he felt his time might be running out. Finally, a new voice came on the line.

"This is Doctor Wallenda. Who's speaking, please?"

"This is Valery Leskov. I'm Walter's next of kin. I need to know where he is."

"Our records indicate Yvonne Leskov... Wait a minute, now that's very strange." Valery heard the doctor cover the line with one hand and talk loudly to the people around her. "Did someone change this file? Yes, I mean just now." And then, back with him, "There seems to be some sort of confusion. Walter was discharged on his own recognizance last night, having no surviving kin on record. If you are Valery somehow back from the dead, or if reports of your demise were somehow exaggerated, patients discharged from here with no other resources usually wind up at the bus station, downtown. If you hold one moment more, I'll give you their phone number."

Valery had a notepad in his breast pocket, along with a fountain pen. A minute later, wrath not forgotten but smoldering, he was on the line with the bus station.

"Yes, Walter. Bradbury. Just page him to the phone, please."

Echoing, as if through a building: "Mister Bradbury, Mister Walter Bradbury, please pick up the white courtesy phone..."

"He does not answer," said the bored voice soon thereafter.

"Look, he's sick. Mentally ill. No, I don't think he's dangerous, but he sure can't look after himself. Someone will have to go out and talk to him. He'll have... Notebooks, probably, a pile of them. He's about thirty... Yes, I'll hold..."

Now there were people behind him waiting to use the telephone. A woman with a bag of groceries in one arm, tapping her foot and looking everywhere but at Valery. Where she had gotten a bag of groceries he couldn't say - there wasn't a grocer for twenty blocks, not so much as a bodega.

Finally: "Valery?"

"Yeah, Walter. Yeah, it's me."

"I'm in the bus station, Val."

"OK, Walter. I'm coming for you. Just stay there. OK? Just stay where you are. I'll be there by tonight, come Hell or high water. OK?"

"They said they'd hurt me if I stayed here. I have to take a bus." He sounded very edgy, raw.

"OK, fine, take a bus. Look at the schedule. What's leaving soon?" Valery asked. "Never mind. Give me the agent. Yeah, put her on."

"Look," said the bored voice, "it's not my job to-"

"I don't care what your job is," Valery interrupted. "I care what you're going to do. Now this is important. You put him on the bus to Philadelphia. I'll meet him there. He gets there safe, nobody sues anybody. You got that? In fact, he gets off the bus safe and sound and you're the hero of the story when it breaks in the New York Times this week."

The rest was just negotiating. When Valery hung up then started a new call, the lady outside sighed ostentatiously and there was grumbling in the line of three or four people but there wasn't much they could do. Valery called the office. "Hey, look, I have an emergency," he said.

"Who's this?" asked Marna, the secretary.

"It's Valery."

"Valery? I'm sorry, miss..."

"Valery Leskov. I work there," he said. "Here, write this down. It will make sense later..."

***

Vitali knocked on the door. It was cold under his knuckles despite the bluish sunshine one could only find on the morning of a Rhode Island winter. Nobody came but he didn't mind much. The ocean was beautiful and, even though the house was in the way, he could smell it and hear it, and it was still beautiful.

After a time he rang the bell, and now he heard movement inside, far away. Soon the door opened, and there was Janet, older than when he had seen her last but also more peaceful, more radiant. She wore ecru linens and had some yarn in one hand - a macramé project. "Oh," she said, looking up at Vitali. "Oh, may I help you?"

"Janet? It has been twenty years, I know, or is it thirty? But I thought you would still know me."

"I'm sorry," she said. "Have we met?" But she frowned as if tickled by a memory. "You remind of a man I knew a long time ago..."

"Yes. May I come in, please? Is Brian here? I wanted to see both of you."

"Well..."

"It's Gergiev. You remember? Vitali? I have come a long way to see you."

"But he died," Janet said, mostly to herself. *But who else could be so big, and so bearded, and so Russian?* "He died, an embolism or a heart attack."

"Both true and false. I am here now. Please, may I come inside?"

"Of course," she said, as though ashamed of herself. "Vitali? Is it really you? Can it be true?"

She led him through a hall way where she took his jacket and hung it on a peg alongside many other coats and jackets. There was a red rug on the floor in a Slavic style. Through a door waited a sitting room with a settle, a couch, a wing-back chair. "Drink?" she said.

"Scotch, thank you, Janet. Just a little - I have to look after my heart these days." He settled into the chair. It creaked beneath him and fitted his back like an office chair fit most men.

Janet poured a finger of Glenlivet into a glass. "Excuse me," she said. "I'll run and fetch Brian."

Gergiev looked around the room, saw the trappings of wealth. He had heard about the lottery, was pleased for his friends, but hadn't expected oil paintings and oriental rugs. Brian was always more of a modernist. A tape player and a big television would have been more his style.

By the time Janet returned with Brian, she had forgotten completely about Vitali being dead. "I was so surprised to see him on the doorstep," she said, "that I forgot all my manners and left him standing there. Vitali back from the past and I didn't even recognize the great bear."

"Vitali!" Brian exclaimed as he entered the room behind his wife. Gergiev rose from the chair, imagining he could hear it sigh with relief, and wrapped his old friend in a great hug. Brian was as lost in his arms as Vitali's smile was lost in his beard.

"Life has become strange, my friend," he said, "but I am glad to find you so ordinary after all this time. At the airport, they lose my reservations and have to look me up twice. At the car rental, they are sure my driving record indicates I am deceased. I arrive here and the story is the same: but you cannot be Gergiev, whose heart gave way some years past. But everyone forgets, and then it is like old times again, and I can fly and rent cars and love my friends."

"I know what you mean," Brian replied. "But I didn't know you were involved. Valery, right? Is that why you came all this way to surprise us?"

"Yes, Valery is in some trouble. Bad trouble. I do not know how to begin to understand the trouble he is in. The same trouble that makes you forget I called last week to say I was coming."

"Oh - he's right," said Janet, pouring herself a glass of wine. "You're right. How could we all be so stupid?"

"It is not you," Gergiev said. "It is the universe itself that is stupid, or has gone mad, or is forgetful. The facts of the matter keep changing. We play two games of chess at once and the object is not to win either game but for one to assert itself over the other."

"I don't understand," said Brian. "That's crazy talk."

"Quite," said Gergiev. "But as time seems short, I need your help with some of these math problems. Are you not drinking? I think this is the sort of problem best solved without sobriety."

"Maybe I could use a little vodka," Brian said.

"No, not your American vodka," Gergiev laughed. "I never drink it. Don't you find it so regrettable?"

Brian settled down a minute later with some Irish cream in a coffee mug, sans coffee. "So what is the big problem, old friend? What can be so urgent we don't have time to reminisce for a while first?

"Soon I will be dead again, and you shall have forgotten that I was ever here. Before then, I need to know how to work the equations for a computer chip that can work across realities."

"I don't even understand the question," Brian said, and Janet just covered her mouth with one hand and raised her eyebrows.

Gergiev went into the hall and retrieved a file folder from his jacket pocket. "Here are the beginning calculations. The assumptions are that somewhere in an invisible dimension of space in which I do not exist, and Valery does not, but Yvonne does - his charming wife - there are duplicates of these chips with subtle variations. The goal is to unify the logic between them so that as reality switches back and forth between conditions, the logic between the chips remains smooth and is even enhanced."

"Wow," said Brian, examining the reams of calculations. "You need an expert in higher-dimensional math."

"No, I need the only man ever to solve the Jiminez paradox."

"I'm not the only one," Brian said as he started to make corrections to the equations. "A student did it a few years back. When I grilled him on his proof, he said he didn't really understand it himself. He had help."

"Who?"

"Valery's brother in law. Walter."

"How wonderful that we have met with a paradox. Now we have some hope of making progress."

Bohr

Twenty-Two

Timothy went into the office almost gingerly, his palms sweating. Trant never called him down here to give him good news.

It's been four good years, he thought to himself. *He hasn't really bothered me much since Brian stepped in to provide a respectable funding source.* The military funding that had followed hadn't hurt matters either. He knocked on the door. It was partway open and creaked open further as he knocked, the brass nameplate catching the sunlight through Trant's window.

"Nice view," Timothy said.

"Thanks to you, in part. In large part, if we're being honest. Your success with the magnetometer is unprecedented, and the way you started to secure funding by securing funding - genius. Like the first dollar in the tip jar. Confidence."

"Uh, thanks, I think," Timothy said. All that had been an accident. All he'd done was work the math and take a phone call from a friend. "What can I do for you today, Doctor Trant?"

Trant indicated the seat in front of his desk, a nice leather chair that could lean back a little bit. Timothy perched on the edge uncomfortably.

"You don't play poker, do you, Timothy?"

"No. Why?"

"No good at all at concealing your feelings. Don't worry, I haven't brought you here to dress you down or anything. I just wondered if you knew exactly how successful the program has been."

"What do you mean?" Timothy asked.

"Have you heard of the Texas Superconducting Super Collider project? No? They're calling it the Gippercollider. Billions in funding - that's billions, with a B, and we'll get our cut. Congratulations. I'm making you head of department."

"You'll have to start at the beginning. I'm afraid I got stuck on Gippercollider and didn't really understand that or anything after it."

"Well, let's put it this way. Your position in the department definitely has nothing officially to do with how much funding you manage to secure. At the same time, one measure of the quality of your work is its fecundity. And some of your work has enabled, contributed to, the possibility of this huge project in Texas. We're recognizing you with a promotion. You're welcome. Schmidt will be pissed but hey, Schmidt turned down the high-energy measurement gig in favor of purely theoretical work, a real chalkboard physicist." Trant paused as if for breath, went on, "This isn't my new office, Timothy. Have another look at the name on the door."

He craned his head around until he could see the brass nameplate. It had his own name on it. "This is my office? You mean, I have to supervise a department? I've never..."

"Don't worry about it," said Trant. "I'll scaffold you. Besides, we're more interested in your research than in your supervisory ability. What you get is a raise and a title, and hopefully that title - plus the ability to pick and choose your staff - helps keep the money flowing. Don't worry about any of that now, though. Here, switch seats with me. That's it. Good. Congratulations. You deserve this."

Timothy sat in the big chair, another leather number softer and plusher than the visitors' seat. From that side of the desk he could see the screen of his computer, an IBM PS/2. It had the 3 1/2 inch floppy drive and its own built-in hard drive. The desk was cherry. *This could go to my head,* he thought.

"They started working on it in eighty-three," Trant said. "They just broke ground on it this year. It's fully funded. Lots of factors, lots, but your work was at least a small factor, though you didn't know the DOE would get your stuff through the DOD. Eleven billion dollars is the initial estimate. You know how government projects are, though."

"Yeah," Timothy said, though he didn't really. The Department of Defense had not treated him very badly, except for trying to kill him with paperwork. "Eighty three - not long after the funding came through for the WIMP thing."

"Not a coincidence," Trant said. "Four years to get the math right, feasibility and so on, and finally the Senate approved the whole shebang. Kind of like a satellite, though: most of the technology they've bought for it is already out of date. You know how it is." That phrase again: Timothy didn't actually know. "It takes a year to fund, minimum, then another year to schedule for two years out. By the time the thing is on the launchpad, it's already three to five years old, sometimes older, so we're putting obsolete technology into space all the time. That computer on your desk will be a relic in five years and a joke in ten."

"I bet it works just fine right now," Timothy said, not understanding where Trant was going with any of this.

"Well, I'll leave you to it.," his boss said. "Call me with any questions. We'll meet in the morning and do some paperwork. I'll bet you want to call a few people - if you can figure out the phone." It looked daunting: an array of buttons each with a tiny, inscrutable label. "Ah, last thing: don't park in the faculty lot any more. Your own space. It's right at the entrance to this wing."

Trant leaned across the desk, shook Timothy's hand. Timothy had nothing to say; he was still trying to process what had just happened. By the time he thought to say "thanks," or something like it, he was alone with the formaldehyde smell of new furniture and the crinkle of leather under his weight.

A phone call seemed like a good idea. He lifted the receiver, dialed nine, then Yvonne's number. Walter answered.

"Hi?"

"Walter? Hi, Walter, it's Timothy. Is Yvonne there?"

A pause. In the background: "Sorry, he needs her. Yeah." Then: "Here she is."

"Hello?" Yvonne said. And then Timothy told her about his good fortune.

***

Walter sat in his room eating popcorn. The TV was on: Linda Hamilton and Ron Perlman costumed as a lion. Tomorrow night was Star Trek: the Next Generation. When that came on, Walter would watch it closely. Beauty and the Beast, though, was merely a backdrop for his work.

His room had a whole wall devoted to his notebooks. A fresh one was in his hands, spiral bound, not like the glue-bound books they'd given him in the hospital. And he worked with a real pen, a Bic, so he could work longer without his hand cramping around a tiny golf pencil.

The red-haired girl reclined on the bed next to him. Beauty and the Beast was kind of a romantic show. About the modern, sensitive man. She enjoyed it. While she watched TV, she wasn't watching Walter work, and he liked that. Actually, she was kind of cute, except when her smile revealed her teeth. Sometime after the seventies she'd had some dental work done, replacing her file-sharpened teeth with blue steel ones that were really disturbing.

The phone rang in the front room. There were windows in there, which he didn't like, so he waited in the hopes that Sandra would answer it. Sandra looked after him when Yvonne was at work. It stopped ringing a second later, and he assumed she had gotten it.

Later, she knocked on his door, looked in on him. Walter knew she had to, at least twice per hour. Whenever she did, he was doing the same thing: writing in his notebooks.

"Need anything, Walter?" she asked. She had a nice smile - not like Staff, although she really was Staff, just not at the hospital. She wore a yellow dress with red spots and kept her hair short, close to her head, like LeVar Burton's on Star Trek.

"No," he said. "I'm fine."

"OK. Sorry to keep bugging you. You know how it is though, right?"

"Yeah, I know."

She left. He liked that she wasn't very interested in him. The last one had always tried to start conversations. About what he was watching, what he did all day, what kind of music he liked (he didn't like music: it was full of math, and that interfered with his work on The Problem). Worst, she had wanted to look inside his notebooks.

But she wasn't around anymore, and Sandra mostly let him be.

It had been a weird trip from the bus station four years ago. By the end of the night, all he'd had left was his notebooks. Somehow the rest of his stuff had disappeared when he wasn't looking. A man in a pea coat had sat by him and whispered threats until Walter gave up his sneakers. He'd needed to pee late in the night, and when he came back, even his notebooks had not escaped predation: the bags were split open, and the notebooks scattered around the area.

In the morning, after Valery had called, the bus station people had turned suddenly helpful. One had pulled some suitcases out of lost-and-found and packed Walters notebooks into a mismatched set of suitcases and carpet-bags. He'd been bundled on a bus to who-knew-where. They hadn't even taken the money out of his shirt pocket where it rested, forgotten.

Hours later, Valery had met him at a bus station, someplace where Walter didn't recognize. He hadn't been so glad to see someone for a long, long time. The red-haired girl had sat next to him the whole time (nobody else would). She went away when Valery was there, though. He took Walter to Yvonne's apartment. Later, she had moved out into the suburbs so he wouldn't have to sleep on the couch any more, but Walter hadn't minded the sofa.

Anything was better than the bus stations, even the hospital.

This little house was weird, but he could handle that. Life had been everything but normal since that convention. Fourteen years ago now? When the red-haired girl had started to watch him. She'd gotten younger rather than older. Walter was dimly aware that he himself had aged in some ways and regressed in others, but that thought didn't trouble him.

It vaguely troubled him that Valery was dead sometimes, and Yvonne was dead at others. They had both hired Sandra, though, so that wasn't too weird. Yvonne had written a message on a mirror in the back bedroom they had built for the purpose. Valery had written back. And that was that. Sandra never seemed to notice that she worked for dead people, that sometimes it was one and sometimes the other. It was always completely normal to her, whichever of them walked through the door.

Beauty and the Beast was coming to an end now. The red-haired girl picked up the remote, held it out for Walter to change the station. If he could find something romantic, she would let him be. Otherwise, he was in for a few hours of her staring at him, smiling at him with Richard Kiel's teeth.

***

"I think I understand," Raul said, sitting back in the rolling chair.

"I think you're crazy," Jill said. "You're saying we can't publish this experiment, ever? Whole careers are made on less than this."

"I know, I know. I'm sorry. I am ruining your life. Why have you stayed in my insane secret lab all these years knowing you could not publish any of this?"

"It's so weird, and interesting. I feel," she said, "like we are looking at the heartbeat of the universe or the mind of God. I'd give that up for funding and my name in print? Not on your life."

"That is how I feel, also," Raul said. "Soon you will be a doctor, if that's what you want. And then you can independently 'discover' what we have here."

"Which is what? You said you understand. I still don't. I mean, I think I have an idea, but if this means what I think this means..."

"It does," Raul said. "At the sub-atomic level, these experiments suggest Wheeler was at least partially right: cause need not always precede effect."

"Retrocausality."

"It turns the universe on its head. Microscopically, no big deal, as the kids say these days."

"So why keep it so secret?"

"Because," said Raul, "I do not think these findings are limited to quarks and electrons. I think an effect has preceded a cause. I think we have done something in the future so outrageous, impossible even, that the universe is trying to correct it. Make the current conditions match that future outcome."

"Just like the very first experiment, when the cesium degraded before the entangled quark was forced into a state," Jill said. The current experiment was substantially more complex, and had whole molecules spontaneously degrading fractions of a second before an entangled particle was changed on the other side of the lab. And if molecules could be changed in this manner, in theory whole objects or even organisms could be altered.

"What we are talking about is impossible on its face under the standard model of physics. Large-scale retrocausality would change our whole understanding of the universe. And it would bring quantum physics to a new level of significance - maybe an intolerable level. Maybe it would become a religion, a means to understand the past and future as unified time, all of life as purposeful, with purpose redefined as slavery to future causes."

"Is that why the secrecy?"

"No," he said. "No. Because this is personal. A friend of a friend. Large-scale media attention would not be helpful, and a million hands stirring the pot might obfuscate matters. No, it needs to stay small. But I do not think it will, not forever."

"We may have just explained the big bang. At least, the proximal cause. The singularity exploded because it had to. Because there is a universe. The universe caused the big bang in the past. There is history because there is a future."

"Yeah," Raul said.

"And we can't publish that."

"No."

"I know you don't like cursing in your lab, but..."

"Nonsense is that which does not fit into the prearranged patterns which we have superimposed on reality...Nonsense is nonsense only when we have not yet found that point of view from which it makes sense."
Zukav

Twenty-Three

Gergiev realized his turn signal was on, had probably been on for ten miles or more. It was a long drive home from the airport but at least the turnpike flowed along smoothly. Maybe in the future someone would invent a buzzer that sounded when the turn signal was on for more than a minute or two to help more elderly drivers like him.

Was it age, or mere preoccupation? *I'm not so old*, he thought, running one hand through a beard mostly white but with a few traces of iron gray left in it. *Not so old.*

Did I just wake up? he thought suddenly, the consciousness of the thought jarring. *Have I been sleeping my way down the road? No, I remember being awake, having thoughts. But as I told the Rabbi - that wasn't me. I wasn't there although I am here.*

His car was a Cadillac. Big, powder blue, a few years old. It had sort of sloppy steering and mushy breaks, rolled up and down for half a minute if he hit a bump. He liked it. Plus it had the headroom he needed. Tchaikovsky blared from the speakers filling the cabin with resonances, vibrations, reverbs. It was so loud it almost hurt, rumbled his chest. It felt good, like a massage after an hour in the steam room. Nothing like a good sauna.

Was I dead a minute ago? he thought then. *Did I just spring back to life, as Valery describes?*

Valery's description of events made little sense to Gergiev. Why would he, Gergiev, be dead in one reality and alive in another? If Valery was the lynch-pin of the problem, what had Vitali really to do with it? Some consequence of Valery being alive that kept Gergiev alive?

He thought back to a meeting with Valery a few years back, back when all this madness had started. Valery had shown up with Timothy in tow, had explained how weird the world was getting. How he had dreamed of his old friends, all working together on some grand project. He thought Yvonne wanted him to do something, to start something, and could not quite remember what - only that it had to include her mad brother somehow.

Was that how it had happened? Gergiev felt as fuzzy and indistinct as the big car's steering when he thought of that meeting, as though there were two of him and one remembered it differently.

Was he alive because Valery had noticed how fat he had gotten? "Vitali, is it possible you're even bigger than I remember? It looks like you swallowed yourself, man. There's nothing else you could have eaten to make you bigger than you already were - you were already the size of a cow."

"Good living," Gergiev had replied, patting his ample belly. "My wife likes to cook and I like to eat." And he had - he had loved to eat. But after that meeting had he started to eat just a little less? Was that when lunchtime found him walking around the campus? Stretching his legs, he had told the curious. Stretching his life expectancy though, in reality.

His exit was coming up on the right, so he put the turn signal back on, let the big machine drift over into the correct lane. He knew his destination, cruised unerringly towards it. The Cadillac was like fate: its course could be changed but, at high speeds, only with time and effort. Or like an oil tanker. An oil tanker might take ten miles to reverse course, five miles just to stop. Or like a theoretical interstellar mission: accelerating for half the journey, decelerating for half, as much fuel used in slowing as speeding.

His place wasn't far off the turnpike. Soon he pulled into his own driveway, the smell of his wife's lilacs creeping through the ventilation system. He wished she were still alive to tend them, to force order into the riotous garden, but she was gone these four years. He let the lilacs take over, let them run rampant, and they flowed over the front yard in a mad purple tide. When the gardener came, he told him, just take the weeds. Only that.

Inside the house, he sat on his big, black leather sofa and opened a book without looking at it.

The question appeared in his mind, like the matter of wakefulness on the turnpike:

How do I know what sort of chip to work on? How do I know what problem I am solving?

***

Time keeps on slipping, slipping, slipping... into the future.

"Turn that old crap off," Hugo shouted, grinning and frowning at the same time as the Glenn Miller Band drifted out of Walter's room.

"All I have is old crap," Walter said from his bedroom, but he turned it off.

"He's probably right," Peter said, stretching, cracking his knuckles, interlaced. "We haven't taken him anywhere since he came back. Not the comic book store, not the music store, nothing. The guy could use some new tapes."

"You're right. I'll bring him something good next time we stop in. Metallica, something."

"Nah, let's grab him, take him someplace. It will be good for him," Peter said.

"Who would have thought I would be the stick in the mud?" Hugo said. "I say we stick with what the psychiatrist said. He needs to take his meds and avoid conflict and excitement."

"The same psychiatrist who said he could live on his own and had all his crap put out on the curb to wait for when he was calm enough to exit the seclusion room?"

"Petie, you're getting excited. Let's save that, shall we? The doctor said-"

"Maybe you're right."

Walter came out of his room then, Sandra on the job and on his tail. She didn't say anything, just followed him from a few paces behind, hands in a non-threatening position at her sides, a vague smile on her face the way she had been trained.

"I'll go," Walter said. "If you want to take me. I don't think I should do it alone. We can go in your car and if things get weird, just bring me right back here. Sandra can came with me. I don't think it will be fun, but it might be good. I... I missed so much in there..."

"All right. Are you good with this, Sandra?" Hugo asked.

"He ain't a prisoner," she said. "If he wants to go to the record store, let's go. You want a shot first, Walter? Help with the anxiety?"

"I think I'm all right," Walter said. "Just, let's do it fast, before I change my mind."

They went right away. Hugo took one of the photographs to work from, still on the same Polaroid film after all this time even though better options were available. It worked so they kept doing it. In a minute they were all arranged in Peter's Ford, Sandra behind Peter, who was driving, so Walter was behind Hugo, who worked obsessively on the logic described in little symbols.

There was a record shop about fifteen blocks away, a low structure surrounded by taller ones in a part of town where the trend was more and more towards the tall. That trend might overtake Yvonne's street in a few more years, casting her little house into shadow.

They pulled into the shade of a tall building, parked on the street. The shop was a few paces back from the sidewalk, built in a time when there was more space everywhere. The city was not like the universe: everything was flying closer and closer together here, rather than farther apart.

Inside, the place smelled like dust and old vinyl, like plastic sitting in the sun. Records sat in bins on tables, organized by musical genre. Rock, classical, golden oldies. Rap and hip-hop, categories with which Walter was entirely unfamiliar.

"Where are the tapes?" he said, looking around. A bored clerk in a white shirt and an apron pointed to one side of the store, where the wall was filled with cassette tapes.

"Here," Hugo said, putting headphones on his head. "Look. You can listen before you buy." He put a Nirvana bootleg in the player.

"Oh, not that," Walter said.

He shuffled around, poked this tape and that one, didn't recognize many of the bands or titles. Run DMC. Soft Cell. Prince.

"Oh no, not that, either," Peter said as Walter drifted into Disco. He examined a tape with Bony M on the label, another by the BeeGees. "How could we ever live with an apartment full of that noise? No, please, not the Gloria Gainer..."

"I like Gloria Gainer," Hugo said. Everyone laughed but Walter.

The red-haired girl was starting to catch him up, he was sure of it. He knew it. He could feel it. "Hey," he said, "I don't have any money. This was a bad idea."

"Getting nervous, Walter? Anxious?" Sandra asked, coming closer and standing so she was not quite facing him.

"Yeah, a bit."

"Want to go? Need a pill?"

"Kinda," he said.

"Tell you what, Walter," Hugo said, "You've done great so far. What say I grab five or ten things I think you'd like and we hit the road?"

Walter nodded. Hugo went quickly through the racks, knowing Walter liked REO Speedwagon, Kiss, old Aerosmith. He grabbed newer bands like those older ones. Def Leopard, Quiet Riot. Queen, just because everyone liked Queen these days.

Back at the house, not very much time later, Walter went straight to his room, closed the door, and didn't answer any more questions. Sandra looked in on him as she had to, and noted that he was sleeping.

"Did we push him too hard?" Hugo asked.

"He wanted to go," Sandra said. "He has to take some risks to get better at all. What's good for us is rarely what's easy."

"Seems like not so long ago, he couldn't handle music at all," Hugo said.

"This place is good for him. You boys are good for him."

When Hugo settled back into work, glancing from time to time at Peter with his feet on the coffee table and a textbook in each hand, he worked with a smile on his face. In the back of his mind, he had a picture. Old times, dorm rooms or hotels conferences, before the work got serious, before life did. Comic books instead of texts and equations. The laws of robotics, so much easier to attend to than women, love, rent.

The math fell slowly into place.

***

Walter listened to an old Steppenwolf tape on his headphones, wondering if Hugo would give him a hard time about it if he were around. They only came about once a month because they had jobs to do. But Walter liked when Hugo gave him a hard time.

It was like the old days, when they were all young. Now only Walter was young, because the hospital had stolen a decade of his life.

The notebook in front of him was nearly full, The Problem nearly solved. There was just one more thing to do, and he knew he had to do it soon. So he flipped to the very last page, placed his pen on the last line.

A pain was growing in his chest. Since he had moved here with his sister (or, sometimes, his brother-in-law) there was not a long hallway to use for exercise, and the outside world was too exposed. Yvonne was going to buy him a treadmill as soon as she made a place for it but it was too late for that. Even with constant exercise, though,

Walter knew the drugs he took to stay close to sane were killing him.

He took almost nothing here, just a low dose of antipsychotic and some anxiolytics when he got anxious. And he felt better than he ever had in the hospital. His mind was clearer. Clear enough to know what the pain in his chest meant. It had been building since breakfast, and now it was a clear signal: finish the work, tie up the loose ends.

So he wrote, on the very last line of the journal:

The Gods Themselves.

He meant to write one more line but found he was too tired. One more line, and then fill in the rest of the journal, each line with the math that would ultimately solve The Problem. But his hand hurt, and his arm hurt, and his chest hurt, and he just could not lift the pen again. Sweat trickled down into his eye, and he didn't have the strength left to wipe it out.

The red-haired girl came in just then, turned off the TV. "Hi, Walter," she said.

"You don't talk," he said, although his chest wasn't moving any more, and no air came through his throat to make a voice.

"You just don't hear," she said. "I'm sorry you were frightened, Walter. But it's all right now. You did it. You did what you had to do. You don't have to stay here anymore."

"I don't?"

"No. Come on, I'll show you."

By now there was no oxygen left in his brain. His heart was still, his lungs were still, and his mind was empty now of all thought.

Sandra knocked on the door a few minutes later, looked in, and knew right away that he wasn't sleeping. His eyes and mouth were open, his face slack, a pen near one hand where it had fallen from his grip. She didn't panic, just felt for a pulse, listened for a heartbeat, and sighed. Then she started making phone calls.

"We have a closed circle of consistency here: the laws of physics produce complex systems, and these complex systems lead to consciousness, which then produces mathematics, which can then encode in a succinct and inspiring way the very underlying laws of physics that gave rise to it."

— Penrose

Twenty-Four

Walter's clothes were all in cardboard boxes. The boys, as Yvonne mentally referred to his friends Hugo and Peter, were coming again next week, and she would talk them into taking the boxes to Goodwill. All his tapes, both VCR and audio; his television, Walkman, the few artifacts that proved he had lived, his friends could have those if they wanted or else they could share the fate of Walter's clothes.

I've done this too many times, Yvonne thought, sitting on the edge of Walter's bed while she wrapped an electric cord into a tidy bundle. *Goodwill should write me a nice letter of thanks for all the clothes. Valery's and Walter's.*

It was hard to cry very much for her brother and that made her feel worse. Yvonne had really grieved for him a decade ago, when it became more and more clear he would never recover from his psychosis. If only she had known, if only the doctors had known he could live with her safely... Guilt complicated her grief as much as her close acquaintance with it.

All that was left to do in Walter's room was decide what to do with all his notebooks. There was an offer on the house and she couldn't take all those volumes into the small apartment she had leased. But the task was daunting. There were maybe a thousand of the little books, stacked and piled and dressed along every wall, two or three deep in places and up past her head in others.

Walter has spent close to a month putting them all in order when he'd moved in here, so that the earliest was at the bottom left, starting from the door frame, and the latest

was at the top right as one followed around all four walls.
They had nearly reached back around to the door frame,
reminding her of the time she had taken Walter out to see
Ghostbusters. The line had extended most of the way
around the theater so that the people at the front of the line
could see the tail end of the line.

The very last notebook was on the nightstand. Yvonne
had never looked inside them. She was on one level not
very interested: math just held no attraction for her. And
even if she wanted to, she could not understand anything
more complicated than calculus. Her intelligence ran to
other sorts of occupation: anatomy, systems, oncology.

At another level, she was afraid if she opened one of
Walter's books it would be filled with nonsense, gibberish.
Walter's gifts must have been eroded by his illness. Or by
the drugs he had taken for a third of his life. Everything
from tried-and true medications to sedatives to
experimental compounds. He was so childlike by the end,
so... lost.

She held the book in her hands, imagining she could
feel the warmth of Walter's touch still residing there. Her
fingers brushed the edges of the paper, trying to decide:
find out for sure and forever, or leave him his privacy. And
that was when the telephone rang.

Yvonne carried the book with her into the living room,
set it on the arm of the sofa and picked up the telephone.
"Yes?"

"Ms. Leskov?"

"Doctor Leskov."

"Uh, yes, sorry. This is Jack Sperling at the county
coroner's office. You had asked to be informed of the
results of your brother's autopsy. Um, are you a medical
doctor, Ms. - sorry, Doctor Leskov?"

"Yes," she said. "Oncology."

"Well, this will be a touch easier then. First, let me
repeat how sorry I am for your loss. For your compounded
loss. I'm sure given Walter's condition you've been through
a lot of grief with him." Sperling had a nice voice, an easy

manner. He sounded like someone Yvonne might have liked to have a drink with, maybe talk about theater.

"Thank you, Doctor," was all she said.

"Well, let's see. First, the patient's brain mass was about six or seven percent below expected value." Yvonne noticed he had switched away from Walter's name and wondered whose feelings he was sparing. "I've seen a lot of psychiatric patients. The standard explanation for this is that uncorrected psychosis tends to increase the size of the lateral ventricles. As no means of this expansion is provided by current medical or pseudomedical explanations of psychosis it seems not as likely as we might like to believe. An alternate explanation is that the medications given to psychotic patients have this effect, and the patient's records indicate he was heavily medicated for much of his life.

"No other specific or localized abnormalities were noted in the brain. The size and development of the patient's parietal lobe was slightly higher than expected but within two standard deviations - exceptional but not abnormal."

"He was a mathematician," Yvonne said, not really knowing why.

"That would be consistent," Sperling went on. "His gross anatomy was a little underdeveloped, low muscle tone again possibly induced by heavy medication. His lungs were in good order as was his heart, overall, although there was some beginning atherosclerosis that might have bothered him, the patient, in another ten years or so. Cause of death I've noted as cardiac arrest. I'm not comfortable listing very much more than that on his certificate."

"It was his Q-T interval, wasn't it?" Yvonne asked.

"That would be a very difficult assertion for a medical examiner, Doctor Leskov. Very difficult. Given it is a known side effect of the chief medications on this list and there is no other apparent proximal cause for his heart failure, I'd say that is possible or even likely."

"Did the drugs cause his death?"

"If they didn't," Sperling said, "they would have eventually. But I can't put any of that on the death certificate."

"I think the doctors killed my brother."

"And by extension that you killed him by letting them manage his care? I understand, I think, Doctor Leskov. You have been in a very dicey situation with him, I suspect. The very credentials that might have enabled you to help him have prevented you, through the medical code of ethics, from treating him due to your close relationship. And now you wish to apportion blame in order to achieve some sense of closure.

"There is no negligence here, most likely, and almost certainly no malfeasance or intent to harm. There are just doctors doing the best they can to help people with a condition nobody very much understands right now."

Yvonne thought a little, cried a little - hard tears that felt like diamonds cutting their way out of her tear ducts. And then she thanked the coroner for his help and hung up the telephone.

The house was empty. More than empty: desolate. Silent where quiet would have done. This was not her house: it was Walter's house. Yvonne felt the need to get out, to see sunshine, to encounter humans.

Life had been about Walter for a few years now and she had never been terribly sociable, and so Yvonne's mind came up with nearly no options for human companionship short of ditching work and heading to DC to see Timothy. So she packed a bag, jumped in the car, and drove to the hospital - there was always more work she could do there.

Walter's last journal sat, unopened, on the arm of the sofa.

***

Esmarelda was cleaning behind the sofa. It was on glide pads, so it moved easily across the carpet. There were no young children in the house but there were still toys back there: cat toys. She knelt down. It was hard to get down there and she told herself it was because her uniform was tighter than it used to be rather than because her sixtieth birthday had come and gone. Cat toys went into the pocket of her apron. A green catnip pouch shaped vaguely like a mouse. Some oddments of yarn. Two plastic balls with little bells inside.

She vacuumed the carpet, that job taking less time than getting back to her feet, and shoved the couch back in place with her shins and hips. With the floors done, the next job was the area rug. It would need to be taken outside and beaten. So Esmarelda put the vacuum cleaner back in the hall closet, dropped to her knees again, and started to roll up the rug.

As she knelt the toys in her pocket jingled. She heard tiny footsteps on the stairs, looked up to see the cat coming to investigate. He clearly felt safer with the vacuum cleaner put up. He was a big black cat with enough white patches not to seem unlucky. Big eyes and a nonchalant stance. He sat and watched Esmarelda roll up the rug, haul it and her into a standing position, half-drag, half-carry the thing out through the living room, the kitchen, onto the back deck.

Once outside she kicked the door shut with the back of one foot. It bounced in the latch, swung partially open again. And Schrödinger slipped out of the gap. He watched Esmarelda beat the rug for a while, then got interested in a potted plant, and that led him down the deck stairs and into the large yard. The grass was bluish, tall but even. Schrödinger had rarely touched grass. He let it play across his face, comb through his fur.

Esmarelda was done with the rug, turned and noticed the door was ajar. "Oh no," she said. She turned in a circle, saw the cat in the yard. "Oh, you naughty animal." She went slowly down the stairs. "Here, kitty, come back inside."

But Schrödinger wasn't feeling much like being touched right now. He was enjoying the grass. When she was almost close enough to pick him up, he ran towards her, past her, and up the stairs - but not into the house. He leaped onto the deck railing and from there onto the low roof of the house, and was gone.

***

The lab was quiet. All the experiments were switched off. A low hum wafted from the power grid and, somewhere, a clock ticked.

"I don't understand," Jill said.

"It's as you've always said," Raul replied. "We cannot experiment without publishing, not forever. What we have done here was important. I still cannot explain quite why. But now it is over. You will move on to a new adviser. Please, take these notes, start to reproduce these findings independently. They are my gift to you. No, no - they could not exist without you. They are the product of your work. Go, publish, thrive. I will be retiring and this lab will close, to be replaced with something that makes the university money."

"Nobody else knows how to manipulate the particles we played with. Not at the energy levels we can produce here. This will all be lost."

"None of it is lost," Raul said. "The Superconducting Super Collider in Texas uses much of this technology and is not constrained by our power limitations. I've taken the liberty of recommending you to that project, as well as the European counterpart - although the CERN project is still in the proposal and funding phase. Ten thousand scientists will unite for that work. Ten thousand."

"And it's based on what we did here?"

"No, but partially enabled by it." Raul stood up, extended a hand. "It has been good to work with you. I wish you all the best - and I regret you have delayed your career working here with me. But I could not have done this without you."

Jill took his hand, shook it, wiped tears from her eyes with the other hand. "It's really over?"

"No. It's just beginning."

Later, he drove home with a smile on his face. It was solved. The problem was solved. The math was there, Vitali's chips were close to production at a boutique Silicon Valley manufacturer thanks to funding from the Moldavie Foundation, ground was well-broken at the Collider in Texas, and Timothy's measurements were starting to show the sort of echoes that indicated more than super-symmetry, but the potential that higher-energy measurements could detect the dimensions hidden in space and time predicted by quantum.

That was a lot to feel good about, even though the average person would not understand half of it.

There was traffic. And Raul stopped at Kentucky Fried Chicken - Rosie's favorite - and then at Blockbuster Video. By the time he arrived home it was after dark. As he pulled into the driveway, he did not see the cat sitting there on the pavement. Schrödinger had no experience with the out-of-doors and, as he had when Esmarelda had tried to catch him, ran towards rather than away from the threat.

"Oh. Oh Jesus."

Raul threw the big car in park, engaged the parking brake, edged around the front to see what he had hit. The scream had been horrible.

That night at about nine-thirty, the vet pronounced that the poor cat could not be saved, that heroic measures were futile. By ten that night, Raul and Rosie had forgotten that he had ever been anything but a beloved household pet. By eleven, Yvonne had forgotten that her husband sometimes wrote messages on her bedroom mirror. Hugo and Peter imagined they came by to visit once a month to see Walter rather than to look at Polaroids of complex calculations for chip logic. By midnight, Brian Moldavie imagined he funded various science projects objectively and with no interest in any peculiarities with any special timelines.

Schrödinger was dead.

"Some string theorists prefer to believe that string theory is too arcane to be understood by human beings, rather than consider the possibility that it might just be wrong."

Smolin

Twenty-Five

Timothy looked at the newspaper. October Twenty-Second, Nineteen Ninety-Three. Time was getting away from him. He was closer to forty than thirty now. No gray hairs yet but he felt worn.

The day looked bleak. A long meeting about student retention. Another about alternative funding. Getting people to will their fortunes to the foundation, a strategy that was making millions for big schools like Harvard. Two performance reviews that would say little about teaching and everything about getting money, making money, keeping money. *Does your work have worth? Only if it is well-funded.*

Trant had left him. Left him alone with all of this. He was in Europe working on some huge international project, and Timothy was stuck here doing the scut-work of running a department. From scut-work to a big energy project back to scut-work. Bean counting at the highest level, the dean of science, a grand-sounding title for someone who really just kept the cash-flow in order.

I shouldn't complain, he thought. *I make good money. Great money, for my age. Everyone in the field knows my name. Nice car, a parking spot with my name on it.*

But something was missing.

Maybe she was right, he thought. *She would be fifty-six now. It could never work. Eighteen years between us, the age of most any college freshman down in the quad right now. A lifetime by that measure.* Only he had money, a nice home, prestige, and nobody at all to share it with. *When did I grow so lonely?*

Only there was no time to sit and brood over it. He tossed the paper on his desk - two desks bigger than when Trant had pulled him from the lab and into administration seven years ago - and headed out for the first meeting of the day.

He was a minute or so late but it felt like he was much later than that. The boardroom had an oval table, faux cherry with little black plastic fittings all over the surface to plug in gizmos. The whole department was there, twelve people, mostly men in charcoal grey suits. There was a bit of an uproar.

"Congress has never been a rational body," Jerry was saying.

"This is beyond irrational," Maria replied, raising her voice. Timothy had never seen her angry, had never seen so much naked anger around the table. "We've already spent billions on the project. The cost overruns they're complaining about are their own fault - delaying funding put work behind schedule..."

"There are always overruns," Bruce said. He was head of the theoretical department but his background was engineering. "Part of doing business."

"Congress knows that. This is beyond irrational," Maria repeated. "It's... it's..."

"Politics?" Christine offered.

Timothy tried to call them to order but the room was too hot. He cornered Jerry with his eyes instead. "What the Hell's going on here?" he asked in a voice not loud enough to carry over the arguments.

"You didn't hear?" Jerry said. "Didn't you read the paper this morning?"

"Only the front page. I was running late."

"I'd call this meeting a bust if I were you, then go back upstairs and read page six."

Timothy turned and wrote on the whiteboard at the front of the room: "Meeting adjourned, reconvene next week." Then he did as Jerry suggested.

The front page was all about some scandal involving President Clinton, about land deals and murders. Science was rarely front page news any more, even though this should have gripped national attention.

The Superconducting Super Collider had been defunded. There it was in black and white. Gippertron was dead and Congress killed it.

Suddenly Timothy felt what the rest of his department felt. Rage. Helplessness. Impotence.

Billions wasted. Not because the project was a waste, but because the billions already spent on it could not be recovered. Since the project would never be finished, neither could those billions amount to anything. All they had to show for it was an impressively large hole in the ground in Texas. And if they wanted to restart the project at some point, it would need to be funded over again from the beginning: without care and maintenance, that cave system would become quickly unsuitable for their needs, deteriorate into just another hole in the ground.

They might as well have just thrown a few billion dollars into a furnace. And twenty years of research.

Timothy looked at the telephone on his desk, wondered who he might have been thinking of calling.

***

Yvonne's hand shook near the telephone, but she couldn't imagine who she had been about to call.

The experience was so shocking, and yet so familiar. Like it had happened before, like she knew it was going to happen, and yet she had no memory of it. And something like that would definitely stick in your memory, wouldn't it?

She had been getting ready for work. She felt old for the sort of shifts she was doing, but Yvonne found people responded best to cost-control strategies when you showed up and modeled them - as well as when to break the rules. She'd reached into the closet for a pair of sweats to wear on the train, swung the door closed, and had the strangest impression that there ought to be a mirror on the door. That if there were a mirror on the closet door, like at the old apartment she'd shared with Valery years ago, she might see something in the glass.

So Yvonne had run to the bathroom, snapped on the light -

and screamed.

It was not her face in the mirror. It was a middle-aged man. Well preserved but clearly over fifty. Steel-grey hair, tight little spectacles, a blue tie around an unbuttoned collar. He saw her, she saw him. Neither disappeared at sight of one another.

"Valery?" she'd said, her voice just a breath, the hint of a whisper. He'd said something back but he had no voice, existed only in the glass. She'd reached out to touch him, to touch the glass, and then he was gone. Only her own confused expression remained.

Later, she was at work. The time between that experience and this seemed unreal. Yvonne increasingly felt that way: as though she only existed for a few moments of a given day, and the rest was just memory, just rote. Now she was counting pills in the dispensary. Some of the Xanax had been going missing, supplies short of projections. Since Xanax had a street value, that meant audits every night until it stopped going missing or they caught who was smuggling it out.

This was one of the most stultifyingly dull moments of her existence, and yet now she felt awake and aware, real. Yvonne looked around herself, took stock of her surroundings. Bluish-white light from overheads. The sound of a starter struggling in one of the fluorescents. White tiles underfoot, cold and hard. The pharmacist on duty in pink scrubs pants and a patterned scrub top - pumpkins and candy corns. Her own hands, a liver spot on the back of the left, no nail color, nails chewed short.

Had she been about to call someone earlier? About some shocking experience? Yvonne could not remember. She also found she had lost count of the pills spread out on the clean gauze in front of her, started over.

Is this what life has come to? Boredom, routine, counting tablets? Dropping in to check on myself from time to time, like a skipping stone checks in on the water?

It hadn't always been this way, she knew. Since Walter had died... that was when things had started to fade, when life had stopped having any meaning. After talking to the coroner she'd gone to work and stayed there, sleeping in the on-call bunk room unless she was eating or working. Two weeks of that and finally administration had noticed she was wearing herself out, sent her home on forced vacation for a few days.

Hugo and Peter hadn't come around anymore. Movers had come and taken all the furniture left in the house to her new apartment on the rail line. Now she worked and went home, worked and went home. Yvonne tried to imagine her refrigerator, but the new place seemed unreal in her mind. She imagined Dana's fridge from Ghostbusters instead, full of junk food, leftover Chinese take-out.

Is this my life?

"Hey," said Gertie, and Yvonne jumped what felt like a foot - she hadn't heard her come into the dispensary. "You want a cup of coffee?" It was already in Gertie's hands, a big cardboard cup with a hot-sleeve and a plastic lid.

"Jesus."

"You OK? You look like you've counted those pills like nine times and come up with a different number every time."

"Yeah," Yvonne admitted. "I guess I can use the coffee. Thanks." She sipped, felt better immediately, knew it was an expectancy effect: the brain knew caffeine was coming and acted like it was already there. "When did we stop drinking coffee out of those little Styrofoam cups and start using this big cardboard things?"

"Styrofoam is bad for the environment," Gertie replied. "But I know what you mean. We're getting old. Me, I'm retiring next year. I've been here forty-two years."

Yvonne drank more coffee, looked at Gertie sidelong. She wore a wig these days, and big eyelashes - she was not surgical certified so she could get away with that. But her skin was graying, and she had some pretty good crows-feet going on. And she was heavier, a little more so every year.

"How do you look so young?" Yvonne asked her. "I don't look as young as you and I am younger. Aren't I?"

"I'll never tell," Gertie said. "You have to think about retiring too, don't you? I hate to say it, but you don't look good. You look... tired. All the time. I don't mean old, honey, I mean dog-tired, worn thin, used up. Like, I don't know, like all the life is gone out of life."

"God, that's how I feel," Yvonne said. "I mean, I don't know why. Why I come in here day after day, night after night. You know, I feel most of the time like I'm not living life, like I'm just remembering it. Like it happened to someone else and they told me about it and now I think it happened to me. Don't you ever feel that? Like your life happened to some stranger, that you only just woke up a minute ago and you're scared you'll go back to sleep in a minute?"

"No. But I know someone who does. Here, pack all this up. It can wait. The morning shift can count it. Nobody's going to mess with it now. Come on up to psych. I want you to meet someone."

***

The elevator made hardly any noise, most of the machinery for it being far removed from the car they rode in. A man Yvonne didn't recognize rode partway up with them, got off at the fourth floor. He wore a lab coat and carried a clipboard. There was something heavy in one of his coat pockets, probably a personal organizer.

Yvonne finished the last of the coffee, felt almost human again. When they got to Six, she dropped the cup in the blue recycle can next to the regular trash while Gertie called the charge nurse on the other side of the glass wall and asked for a favor.

The other nurse let them in herself, holding open the thick glass door. "She's awake," she said. "She don't sleep much. Wish she could; only peace she gets."

"Thanks, Juana," Gertie said, and led Yvonne through the ward to a private room in the back. "This is Jane," she said, pausing outside a closed door. "She's a little scary, but don't let her worry you. There's no harm in her." Then she knocked gently, pushed open the door.

A middle-aged woman sat in a hospital bed with a legal pad in her lap. She was dressed in flannel pajamas, powder blue, and smelled like talcum powder. As Yvonne went in, she glanced at the trash can just inside the door and noticed it was full of apple cores.

"Hello, Jane," Yvonne said. "Having some trouble sleeping?"

"Sleeping? Is it nighttime? I just woke up. Just this minute."

Yvonne took the chart from the end of the bed, glanced at the bed check page. Jane had been awake for about three hours.

"Just woke up? OK. How do you feel?"

"Feel?" Jane asked. There was a sharpness to her features, an intensity. She looked zealous. "I feel like I have just awakened after a long sleep. I was here doing things, obviously, I wrote them all down, but only now am I really awake. Now. Just now, as I was talking to you, I woke up as if for the first time. My God, this is consciousness. This is it, now. Now! Excuse me, I have to write this down."

And she did, scribbling in big, loose letters. Yvonne peeked at the page, saw it was filled with this scrawling. Every moment seemed to be Jane's first moment. Every second of consciousness the first awakening to consciousness.

"Jane lost her memory," Gertie was explaining. "To anorexia. You can see she is still quite frail." Jane showed no interest in the explanation. "She woke from a coma about a year ago. Since then, all she has wanted to do is this: explain what it feels like to come alive, to be reborn into the world every second."

"Anorexia. B-complex vitamins. The hippocampus dries up and blows away and no new information can be learned. Most patients with Korsakoff's Syndrome remember at least a few seconds, half a minute at once. They aren't so frantic."

"Her damage is so severe she will likely live like this for a long time," Gertie said.

"The apples in the waste basket. She eats an apple, then forgets she ate it, then the taste of the apple makes her crave an apple. So she asks for it, eats it, forgets. Rinse, repeat."

Right."

"Why are you showing me this?" Yvonne wondered.

"Because, I don't know exactly. But I feel you and she have something in common. She is rising to consciousness every second..."

"Could you keep it down?" Jane interrupted. "I'm trying to write about this feeling - damnit, wow, this is incredible. It's like I've been sleeping all this time-"

"OK, we can go," Gertie said, took Yvonne's arm and led her back outside the room. "She comes up every few seconds. But you... You're gone for hours at a stretch, like you're not really with us, just filling space. I don't always remember you at all, like sometimes you work here and sometimes you don't. Like you're a placeholder for someone else. Thin. Spread out. But sometimes you wake up, become real. Like just now, counting those pills downstairs. You were aware, for a second, of your own unreality."

"I don't know what you're saying," Yvonne said.

"Neither do it. Just think about it. I've got rounds. You want to come?"

"OK."

"God abhors a naked singularity."
Hawking

Twenty-Six

In her office Janet made final arrangements with the travel agent. Two weeks in the Bahamas, no interruptions. No phones, no letters, no visitors. Just the ocean, a bit of booze, and the two of them.

Brian was on the other phone. There were financial statements spread out all over the desk. His computer was on, two different spreadsheet programs open at once, and he was talking two one person on the phone while typing to another through America Online and putting numbers into the computer.

"Yes, completely divest from that one. Well, think whatever you want, I just think it's gotten too risky. No, you may be right - but does money drive every decision? No, I guess you're right - but I DO have enough money to let this one go. Yeah, thanks, Roger. Next? I think real estate for the time being. All right, have a good one."

"What's Roger trying to get us into?" Janet asked.

"He wants us to stay in oil. But you said get out, and I agree. Maybe it can still keep making money, but it shouldn't. The technology isn't keeping up with the placement of the remaining reserves."

"Are you almost ready to turn all that off? I know you won't ever retire for real, but we're going on vacation, and I'm hoping you can think about something other than money."

"Yeah," said Brian. "Yeah, it's a real obsession, isn't it? The eighties were good to us, good beyond all reason. And why not? I'm a mathematician and finance is just math, when you get down to it. But didn't it seem once that all this money was *for* something?"

"That's what I mean," Janet said. "Let's go spend some of it and not really give a crap about anything. A nice cruise, some nice booze. We'll play like we were sixty again."

"Yeah." But Brian looked far away. He tapped a few keys, got out of the chat he was in, put the last numbers in the spreadsheet. "No," he said then. "No, it's not for enjoying. It might be for changing the world. Microloans, clean water projects, college funds. The science is the best. I love those foundations, and especially the way the money seems to magnify. We put in a hundred thousand, lead the charge, and then other people and foundations start to match us, and soon there're millions for some research or other.

"But I feel like we were solving some problem. Like we had a purpose once."

Janet sighed. "It's so hard to let go," she said. "But this is normal. The house has been empty for years. Our kids moved out, you retired, we get calls on birthdays and visits on thanksgiving. But we haven't had jobs, haven't had to struggle to live in so long, sometimes we wonder, what's the point? But there isn't any point, dear. No point at all. Except to eat, and drink, and make merry."

"Maybe you're right," Brian said, and told the computer to save its data and then go to sleep.

Downstairs, in the sitting room, he poured Janet a finger of Scotch and himself just a hint of vodka. He couldn't read the label. The characters were in the Cyrillic alphabet derived from the Greek. Russian vodka. He tried to remember how it came to be on his shelf. Probably a cocktail party gift. But hadn't he had a friend who insisted it was a crime to drink any vodka not bottled in Russia?

He thought briefly of Gergiev, his old childhood friend. Hadn't seen him since college. He'd be eighty now if he were still around - only he'd had a heart attack in his office.

Well, he thought, *Janet's probably right after all. A vacation is just what's in order. Hell, life's a vacation, or it could be. What good is money if you don't go off and see the world?*

***

The unit had reopened four days ago. An extensive remodel had included new floor tiles, semi-private rooms, more, smaller toilets. A safer stairwell into the courtyard. Intercoms, a smoking room with negative pressure.

Anthony had never seen the old unit. The other guys said there used to be cigarette burns on the carpet in the nurses' station where he met with the psychiatrist. And the ceiling tiles hadn't been replaced - they still had that yellowed look rooms got when people smoked in them.

His room was near the back. His roommate was a fat bald White guy who thought he was Jesus. Collected plastic knives for a breakout attempt he'd been planning for a couple of years but the remodel had messed up his timetable. Nice guy - so long as you didn't laugh when he said he was The Christ.

Anthony had made that mistake the first day. "If Jesus had had your pants size, they never coulda nailed him up," Anthony had said. The lunch table had gone quiet. Two guys had laughed then pretended they hadn't. Then Louie had made a show of throwing his pop in Anthony's face, then his plastic plate, then the newspaper.

That's as far as it had gone. Staff, those ubiquitous cool heads, had broken things up before they could get worse. And of course Anthony had got the blame. Just like downstairs. It was the nineties now and racism was supposed to be over, only it wasn't, not really.

All I got's some anxiety, he told himself, spreading some peanut butter on a bagel. *I don't belong up here with these crazies*. Across from him a Puerto-Rican fellow was trying to draw swastikas on his arm with a golf pencil and failing. He thought they were peace symbols and that Hitler had meant to bring on the Age of Aquarius. His theory also included aborted fetuses that lived in the sewers. Anthony knew all this not because he cared especially but because the night before the guy had been locked up in the seclusion room and had screamed his theory through the door while scrawling it on the walls in his own poop.

Might be I could find someplace sorta private.

He went exploring some. Ping-pong tables at this end, looked like they got used about once a century. They were folded up against the wall. Down here was where the groups usually met. Today was Sunday, though, so not much going on for groups. Yard was closed. Anthony didn't smoke - not cigarettes, anyway - so not much chance to get outside. Down here was the smoking room for when it was cold or wet. Further down... a closed door. Inside there was a couch, some nice bookshelves. Magazines, the spines of a couple hundred books.

He went looking for staff, asked them about it. "Hey, what's that locked room for down there?"

"That's the library," Staff said. "These guys, they don't read much, you know what I'm saying?"

"Yeah, I hear you, I hear you. Listen, could a man get some library time? I mean, I like a good book."

"You read? No, I mean, of course you do. But up here, you know... Sure, come on. I'll sit back there with you a bit."

A minute later, Anthony was on the leather loveseat scanning the titles. Someone had been a science fiction nut. Anthony was more of a Lovecraft man himself, or sometimes a good political thriller. And he loved some Stephen King. But books were books and a man had to pass the time somehow. So he started with the first book on top. Asimov. Prelude to Foundation.

***

Gergiev was dead at last, in spite of all his attempts to live forever. By the end he'd eaten little but kale, insisting that a low-calorie, high-nutrient diet was the key to longevity and citing the studies to prove it. Valery had just joked with him that if he ate enough seaweed he would become seaweed, and seaweed did not live forever.

Nothing lives forever.

Is this what it's all about? Valery thought, driving back to the city. His car was a BMW. He had an office with his name on the door. Civil litigation was big money these days and, after being passed over for a partnership yet again five years ago, he'd started his own practice.

Why didn't you do it ten years ago, or fifteen? He wondered that a lot. And the answer was always her. Yvonne. He saw her less and less now. The other morning, her face in the mirror, reaching out as if to try to touch him. He felt like he'd been living half a life, less, but now he was awake, back in the groove.

Maybe he could marry again. He was not quite sixty, looked good, felt good. His son was nearly a grown man now. His second wife had made her peace with him. He felt more alive than ever. And losing Vitali was a kick in the pants.

He thought about Yvonne less every day, too. His third wife had left him because, she said, he didn't seem to be with her but always pining over Yvonne.

"You dream you're her sometimes," she had said. "I imagine I have this whole other life without you, that you're with her someplace. And that life seems more real than this one. More right. Then you wake up and I'm here with you and you don't seem real, or only seem real for a little while.

"I try to remember what it was like to be with you yesterday and I can't. It's like our life yesterday only started today."

"You know how that sounds," he had said, but he felt it, too. When she'd gone he couldn't be angry with her. He'd just grown more and more lonely, by himself in that apartment.

Walter had been the best thing to happen to him. Walter gave him someone to care about, someone he could care about without worrying whether Yvonne might see him, might be jealous. Yvonne would want him to look after Walter. Now Walter was gone, too, and Valery had moved back into the city, but Walter had brought him back to life.

He turned on the radio. Commercials. Buy this car, use that tax service, two lawyer ads. Then, at last, the soothing strains of Rachmaninoff. Road disappeared under the tires.

Valery yawned and stretched behind the wheel. He had done some good crying today, had helped his friend get sent off into the next world - whatever that was.

They hadn't been close lately, not at all. Had they even talked since college? Maybe once or twice? He strained to remember. Was the last time... at Ruth's funeral, all those years ago?

It was not only hard to remember, it was hard to try to remember. Those events seemed bounded off, off-limits somehow. That made him curious. But then the phone rang, the cellphone in his pocket. Shaped like a lozenge, with stiff rubber buttons, it rang with a computer-sounding copy of Beethoven's Fifth Symphony.

He answered it automatically, not taking his eyes off the road. "Yes?"

"Mister Leskov? It's Diane. There's a problem. The Dudikoff file, sir. He's been arrested."

"Arrested? For what? Never mind. I'll be there in ten minutes. Put it all in the file. Call Borowitz, he usually gets us a good rate on bonds." Within a minute or so, he had forgotten that weird, tantalizing sensation that there might be more to life, and become engrossed in living.

"There never can be a man so lost as one who is lost in the vast and intricate corridors of his own lonely mind, where none may reach and none may save."
Asimov

Twenty-Seven

It was a strange retirement party.

Rosie stood at the head of the table handing out cake, a nice chocolate cake that Gertrude had made with her own hands. People came up and took their slice, one by one. But nobody had much to say.

She'd been at the hospital since the seventies, hired into middle management out of the teaching school. Cost controls, mostly. She was good at her job. Not just a bean-counter but someone capable of bridging the gap between caring and cost containment. In the age of HMOs, when caring often took second place, she was beloved by the higher ups and the lower downs.

She remembered being beloved, anyway. But in the moment, she was having trouble remembering who these people were. They looked like they weren't sure who she was, either, but were too polite or conforming to say so. Whispered conversations started around the room, excluding Rosie.

I should have stayed at Teachers', she thought.

But the party warmed up the longer she stayed. The conversations got louder. People started telling stories about her. The guy who had come in with the headache a few years back, too shy to say he'd been having sex when it hit even though his girlfriend was with him and they were both in bathrobes and underwear. How she had got balloon angioplastly into the hospital, saving money on bypass surgery, but Michaels had been angry because there was so much profit in bypasses. She'd come back hot from that meeting.

Rosie ate cake, socialized, shook a bunch of hands. Jenssen was there, the man she'd beaten out of that job so many years ago - he was her boss now. Times had changed. These days she could sue for that. Still, it was a party, so she shook his hand.

"You know," he said, "sometimes I feel like I remember doing your job, although I never did. I'm sorry they didn't pick you in eighty-eight. I think you got to be too good at your job and they didn't want to have to replace you."

"I feel like they didn't want a woman in charge of things, much less a Hispanic woman. But I can't fault you for that. Come on, help me eat this cake. I'm too old to take it home: it will go all to my hips."

"You know, it occurs to me that doctors are a weird bunch? Serving cake and soda at parties is fine for other people, but we know this stuff will kill us eventually." He put his plate in the trash, not a crumb or a scrap of frosting left on it. "Half the guys upstairs still smoke cigarettes."

"I quit in the seventies," Rosie said. "But I know what you mean. Like we're all immune to the things that we treat every day. You know Michaels eventually died of cancer. Pancreatic, I think. Working at some mental institution in Washington."

"Michaels," he repeated. "Nobody used his first name. Yvonne was the only one who ever dared."

"Who's Yvonne?" Rosie wondered.

"Hm?"

"Yvonne. Sounds familiar. Who is that?"

"I, uh, now that I think of it, I don't really know," Jenssen said. "That was weird, wasn't it?"

Rosie sat down. "You know, I've had this feeling, like..."

"Like what? Are you all right? You look pale."

"Like, I can't remember. Like there is something *to* remember, and I can't even remember that most of the time. The strangest feeling. As though everything is a thin painting over another reality, and if I could just get a minute to sit and think..."

Jenssen's pager vibrated. "Oh, Hell. Gotta run," he said. "That's the ER. All hands on deck. Looks like a big train crash." He turned and all but fled the conference room. Another pager beeped, one more whirred. Soon the room was empty of everyone but Rosie, who didn't officially work here anymore, and Lita, the administrative assistant in oncology, and the fading noise of footfalls.

"Oh, what the Hell?" Rosie said, and ran off to join all her colleagues in the ER. It was the best way to go out that she could think of.

***

Raul worked his way through his newsletter. The end of the year was approaching, and he was noting the year's death toll among prominent scientists, a morbid activity but also a chance to review some of the history of his beloved field.

Louis Essen was on the list. Essen had been the progenitor of the atomic clock. A laser counted the oscillations of a single atom, an incredibly stable count. The atomic clock made the Global Positioning System possible. GPS was more or less just a system of orbiting clocks that measured how long it took signals to bounce from place to place then calculated where the receivers must be based on that information.

Something about Louis' death tickled Raul's memory. The clock. The atomic clock was important to something Raul had been working on.

But his memory was not what it had once been. He'd read earlier that same day that high education was an insulating factor against senility, but he thought that relationship might be confounded with money: rich people aged better. He was by no means rich - but he had been a full professor at a high end university and his wife had been a doctor. They did all right.

What else was going on in science? Maldacena's work offered a step forward in grand unifications, showing how two differing models of subatomic physics might be related. Some interesting dinosaur footprints, Deep Blue had beaten Gary Kasparov earlier in the year.

The newsletter done, he saved and shut off the word processor, and decided to flip through a journal or two. Rosie had tried to get him into novels but he found them unsatisfying. His brain was trained to search for academic worth: citations, references, methodology, conclusions, operationalizations.

One of the journals in front of him had an article from Jill Hanks. That name tickled his memory as had the idea of an atomic clock. The article was jaw-dropping: Hanks had entangled photons, and observed them changing their states prior to measurement. That would mean nothing to most people, but for Raul it was an earthquake.

It meant that events in the future might sometimes affect events in the past.

There were plenty of other possible interpretations, and Hanks and her team were careful to note them. Additionally, the effect would be strictly limited to the subatomic scale. Still, a provocative finding.

Raul opened the word processor application back up and started work on a letter to the editor. This finding would almost certainly turn out to be a problem with the technology or something peculiar to the methodology not listed in the design paragraph.

After all, we did this for years, he thought, *and we found... What? What did we find?*
The information would not come. A minute later, he was not even sure what he was trying to remember. His letter had drifted off track, becoming a rambling exploration of the role of women in physics. He wondered if Hanks had had a strong male mentor or if she had needed to struggle against the patriarchal system of science education.

Eventually, Rosie came home, looking not just tired but utterly spent. She was gray in the face and her shoulders slumped. "Rough day at the office?" he said.

"A train derailed as I was going off shift. I stayed to help. We lost over a hundred patients today."

"Do you want to talk about it?"

She did. Raul thought no more about women in the sciences that night.

***

Anthony was back in the hospital.

He sat in the library, contemplating the bruises on his arms. Some of them were from the needles that brought him momentary peace. The rest were from cops manhandling him into the squad car, and the straps that had held him into his hospital bed while he went through withdrawal.

The drugs stopped the anxiety. That's what he told himself. *I'm not an addict. I'm anxious.* That didn't help in the meetings, though. The psychiatrist gave him drugs to help him not need drugs. But with the anxiety at bay, he still wanted the white powder that he mixed with water and injected into his arms.

I'm not an addict, I'm anxious.

The library was a good place. The rest of this unit scared him bloodless. There were rapists and murderers up here. All Anthony had done was yell at a staff guy who said he looked like Steve Erkel. Anthony wasn't even all that tall. Usually you had to be big and black to get sent up here. He was just black.

There was nothing else to do, and a big pile of books on the shelf. During his last visit, he'd read all the Foundation novels. This time he decided to start on anthologies of short stories, in the hope that he would not be staying long. His social worker would find him some out-patient rehabilitation program and that would be that.

Asimov Presents: The Great SF Stories 25 looked promising. Anthony got to work.

A few hours later, he was through with that anthology. He took another with him when it was time for dinner. He read two more over the next three days. Soon he was never seen on the unit without a book under one arm.

"The halfway house won't take you this time," his social worker told him that Thursday. Her name was Sally. She was small-statured, overweight, and had an acne problem despite being forty-ish. "They think you're too risky."

"Risky? I never hurt anyone."

"No," she said, "but you quit the program three times before. Now it's normal to flunk out of a couple of programs. Dual-diagnosis patients are hard to keep clean. We'll just have to find another program. But it looks like you're going to be here at least a little while longer."

"I don't want to stay here," he told her. They were at the lunch table and nobody else was really around. They were in various treatment groups. He should have been in one himself except Sally had pulled him out to give him this news. "These guys frighten me, Sally."

"They aren't so bad."

"You ever go into the bathroom with them? I always worry..."

"Well, the program does have an edge to it. Homeless guys try to use it as winter housing so we can't make it too easy. Just work the program, keep your scores up. It will make it easier to place you."

"You're saying being molested in the bathroom is to keep the homeless people out?" he said, starting to get a little loud.

Sally stood up, started to gather her things. "No sense getting excited," she said, and "excited" seemed to be a code word. Suddenly there were three staff people in the hallway like they had been waiting there the whole time.

"No," he said, "I don't suppose there is. I guess I'll just go to the substance-abuse meeting. Keep my scores up."

"Good idea," Sally said, smiling.

"Energy is liberated matter, matter is energy waiting to happen."
Bryson

Twenty-Eight

Valery put his coat on the hook, kicked off his shoes and left them by the front door. After a long, satisfying pee, he went into the kitchen and put on a kettle. He wasn't much of a cook but soup from a can and a grilled cheese sandwich would go nicely with a cup of tea.

His phone remained cooperatively silent as he toasted the bread and heated the soup. It left him alone while he channel-surfed and chewed. It stayed quiet while he watched Friends and drank his soup.

When dinner was done and the phone still had not interrupted his private life (if that was what his life alone at home could be called), Valery decided it was going to be a good night. Maybe he could make some headway on the unpacking.

He had been in this place for years now, and there were still a few boxes he had never opened. Work kept him really hopping ever since he opened his own firm. Whenever he got halfway through one of the remaining boxes, the phone always rang and dragged him off into something. Which he could not really regret. The last few objects had been packed up for years and therefore were clearly extraneous to his existence, and it was not as though sitting here alone watching Friends was anything like the highlight of his day.

Still, getting the last couple of things unloaded would seem like an accomplishment, would close the door on life with Walter. On some other things, too, maybe, but he couldn't quite think what. And maybe when those doors were all shut, he could get on with the next thing which, he increasingly thought, might be to sell the practice and move to Florida.

Then again, that would mean packing all this crap back up again, unloading it someplace else.

Now he was crouched in front of the bedroom closet with a brown cardboard box in front of him. It said U-Haul on the side, meaning he had paid good money for it. Not enough friends to have access to surplus, reused boxes. He cut the tape, lifted the flaps.

On top was a photograph of him with Yvonne. What year was that? Sixty-eight or sixty-nine, maybe. They were both so young. The film was color but barely. Too much flash, too. But he could see she was beautiful, had always been beautiful to him. He never forgot what she looked like. Even now he could close his eyes and see her face in front of him, imagine what she would look like now, today.

Do I want to set this up someplace, or put it away and let it go?

That was always the question. Sometimes he looked at personal ads in the back of the paper or, more recently, on the internet. And it was the same question then as now. Set her aside, set the past aside. Or, live now. Live for himself, for someone else. Yvonne was gone.

He set it aside, on the floor, choosing to decide later.

Also in the box were an old newspaper, a pair of carpet slippers (*I've been looking for those*), a couple of law journals. A hard case for a pair of glasses, but no glasses. The blanket that went over the back of the couch. And, in the bottom, a yellow notebook.

This box was the last one packed, then. Just oddments from around the living room, the miscellaneous junk that accumulated in lived-in spaces and had no real place. Walter's journal told the story. He'd tossed it on the arm of the couch on his way out to work having not decided whether to read it, whether to give Walt his privacy or find out how much of his mind had remained to him in the end. Whether he'd had any last thoughts back there in the bedroom where he hid out.

That choice came back to him now. The journal was back in his hands, the years between then and now dropping away, the decision fresh and needing to be made.

Just the last page, he told himself. *If the last page is crazy, if there's nothing important there, I'll throw it away.*

The notebook did not want to open. The pages were stuck together along one edge where they had rubbed in transit, merged slightly. The back cover pulled away from the last page, though, and he saw that page was blank except for one line at the bottom, the second to last ruled line on the page.

"The Gods Themselves," Walter had written. Nothing else.

What could that mean? Some sort of religious fervor? Walter never talked about religion. It wasn't a component of his madness, so far as anyone knew, just the little red-haired girl with sharp teeth. She followed him around and made him paranoid, too scared to eat.

He flipped back a page, and another. Three more blanks. Then he started to see ink. It wasn't writing, not words: the journal was filled with dense mathematical notations.

Does this mean anything?

Valery didn't know. He put the journal back where he had last seen it: on the arm of the couch. A different couch by now, to be sure. Then he put away the last of the oddments in the box, carried the box itself outside, down the stairs, into the big dumpster outside the apartment building.

Back inside, he was once again confronted with the picture of him and Yvonne in its silver frame on the floor. He had stood it up but now it was lying flat, perhaps the victim of a draught as he opened the apartment door. Valery picked it up, stared at her for a minute or two. Took her into the kitchen and opened a drawer.

"I love you," he said, putting the photo away out of sight.

***

"Back again, Pierce?" Carl said. Carl had been an inmate of the hospital for twenty-two years, longer than anyone else.

"Nobody calls me that," Anthony said, "except for you. They only use last names like that in the military or in British schools. You been watching Harry Potter?"

"They don't let us watch kid stuff up here," Carl said, his mouth forming a pout that made Anthony's stomach turn over. "Some of the guys, they, you know."

Anthony didn't bother telling Carl he was among the worst such people. He didn't feel like getting smacked in the mouth today. So he just sat on one of the long couches, not too near any of the other guys and as far as possible from the elderly dude with the mullet. That one smelled like pee all the time, couldn't remember where he was or how he'd gotten here, and always seemed to be spoiling for a fight.

The TV was on and, as promised, it was not a children's show. The mandate as Anthony remembered it was that television programming on the unit had to be uplifting, educational, or informative. There was a science show playing. Anthony didn't feel up to watching a science show but Sally wanted to meet with him and it was best to stay available. Truthfully, after a week in jail what he could use was a long, long sleep.

The show was going on about some massive project in Sweden or someplace. They were digging a gigantic tunnel underground. The earthmovers on the screen looked like they might be the ones in Anthony's head, based on his headache.

"Then the particle is guided along an electromagnetic 'rail,' accelerating to nine-tenths the speed of light, and is made to collide in this chamber with an identical particle going the other way around the track." The film cut to an artist's rendering of a big room full of giant, inscrutable machines. "The collision smashes the particles into little pieces and those results are measured here. It will take months of computing to analyze just the first few such impacts. The project is expected to produce so much data that..."

Anthony missed the rest of the talk about data. When Sally woke him later, he was dreaming about petabytes and tera-electron-volts. None of that meant much to him so he forgot about it pretty quickly. But Sally asked him to go over to the lunch table, and the television had switched over to a nature show that was supposed to have great cinematography.

He sat at the table, across a corner from Sally. "Looks like I screwed up again," he opened. "You must be tired of seeing me."

"If it wasn't you it'd be someone else," Sally said. "I'm more concerned with how you feel about being back here."

"Honestly it's starting to feel a bit like home. I mean, some of these guys aren't who I'd pick for roommates, but then again my family wasn't always that great either, if you see my meaning."

"You're a smart guy. You'll figure it all out in the end. Look, we want to try something new with you. We want to keep this visit short. There's a recovery house uptown, and we're sending you there the day after tomorrow. All you have to do is-"

"Go to the groups, work the program, and stay outta trouble?"

"Exactly," Sally said. Then there was the obligatory signing of forms: promise to pay if he ever came into money, agreement to a lien on any property he might own, releases so Sally could legally talk to whomever she wished about Anthony's case, informed consent for voluntary treatment with the implicit threat that if he didn't sign that one they would do the paperwork to hold him involuntarily.

"Pleasure doing business with you," he said when it was all done. Sally said nothing in return.

The nature show was still on so Anthony watched that for a while. A camera flew over the ocean. It was steel-gray, choppy. The image was so clear, he could about feel how cold the water was. The camera went lower, lower, dipped into the sea. Bubbles rose up all around it, and then he was under water. Dark pressed in but did not overwhelm. The ocean seemed empty except for him and these two great whales. The giant animals hung suspended in the water, so lonely and so beautiful that Anthony started to cry.

That felt uncomfortable, so in a little while he left the common room. Tears were best shed while sleeping, grief always too close to allow encounters with beauty. Anthony faced none of that, though, only the anxiety that welled up, that made his feet move.

The best place for peace was still the library. There was another guy back there. He was a big blond man who could not bend the fingers on his left hand all the way because a failed suicide attempt had severed all the tendons in his forearm. He was flipping through a National Geographic, page after page. Judging by the pile in front of him, he'd been at it for at least an hour.

"Man, you know they cut out all the pages with naked women in them," Anthony told him. "I told you that last time. I even showed you where some of the pages used to be."

"I know," said the other man. "I guess I thought it was worth looking again. Just in case. I mean, what the hell else is there to do in here?"

"I don't know. There's a pretty good show on the TV. I'm just too tired to pay attention. You'd like it though. And Wilson has his headphones on - he won't bother anyone for an hour or so." Wilson was the guy who smelled like pee.

"All right. Good call."

Then Anthony had the room to himself. This time he went straight for a novel. A big novel. A couple of days was more than enough time to get through some Asimov.

One book stood out from the others. It was too fat for its spine, as though it were swollen with water damage. He looked at the cover: The Gods Themselves. The cover looked weird and promising, sort of 50's aliens on the cover. Good pulp stuff inside, maybe. He opened the pages to see if they were readable, and some scraps of paper and photographs fell out onto the floor.

Not paper: index cards.

Some of the cards were full of math. Crazy math, the kind of math on the boards Good Will Hunting was always working on when he was supposed to be cleaning the floors. Some of them had writing on them. "She saw Valery again today. Asked me to write it down. Valery was here two days ago. Brought Gergiev's equations. They need some work but I'm too busy."

None of that meant anything to him but it was fascinating, a glimpse inside a mind that was obviously brilliant, based on the math cards, but way out of sync with reality. He read them all, forgetting about the novel. In the end, he was able to squeeze a story out of the whole mess, although it was a crazy story.

"Maybe these are notes for a novel," Anthony said.

"What are?"

He hadn't noticed Sally standing in the doorway watching him.

"I opened this book and all these cards and stuff fell out. I wonder if someone was writing a novel back here." He picked up the novel again, opened to the front cover looking for a name. Sure enough, there was one: Walter Bradbury. "You know this Walter guy?"

"Before my time," Sally said. "I was just checking in to tell you that the doctor wrote a medication schedule for you. Make sure you're at the window by eight p.m. for the first dose, OK?"

"Sure, sure. Thanks. I wonder if we could track this cat down, get him his stuff back?"

But Sally was already gone.

***

"Did you keep all those journals?" Yvonne asked.

Hugo sounded tired. Justifiably so. It was late at night. "Yvonne? Wow. I haven't heard from you in... since... Well, since Walter died. What's going on?"

"I'm sorry I woke you, Hugo."

"No, you didn't. I was just..."

"Yes, I did. And I'm sorry. Just, did you keep all his journals? You were the last one in his room. I never looked back in there. I just found one of them here in a box I hadn't unpacked. You know, kind of living at work, no enthusiasm for the job. And it made me want to know."

"I don't know, Yvonne," Hugo said, sounding a little more with it now. "You know, I think Petie kept them. He has a place, you know, a real house and such. I more or less bunk in this closet. No room for all of that."

"You think he's still up? It's two hours earlier in California."

"No, no, don't call him. You'll upset his wife if you wake him up. Here, let me send him a message. Don't you have Instant Messenger yet? I thought every man, woman and child and their dogs had AOL by now."

"Can you tell him to call me?"

"Is it important?"

"I don't know," Yvonne said. "I just need to know."

She hung up with Hugo, went back to the closet. There were a few things left in the box. A pair of socks that seemed to be Walter's but definitely not hers. The couch blanket. Valery had always hated having a couch blanket. An old picture of her with him, faded, the glass a little dirty. She remembered that night, the dance, the music. He'd worn a real cologne that night. His parents were there looking nothing like the Russian peasants he'd always said they were.

She couldn't decide whether the picture was helpful. Was it good to remember the good times or did it still hurt too much? Maybe if life today had more to it than work and Ramen Noodles. Valery would have made her a grilled-cheese sandwich. She could almost smell it.

As she was deciding, the phone rang. She set the picture flat so she wouldn't knock it over, and went to pick up.

"Hey, Yvonne," Peter said. He sounded like he was in the room with her, not like in the old days when distance made peoples' voice remote, far away, tinny. "I guess you were asking after Walt's books? Yeah, I had them shipped out here. You seemed pretty broke up, kind of out of it actually, and I didn't want to ask you to decide about them. I mean, on top of everything else. So I put them away. You want them back now?"

"No, I, I don't know. It's just that I opened one, and I had the strangest feeling. I meant to just look at the end. But I didn't understand what it said, so I looked backwards through it, and it frightened me."

"What's in it?"

"He just wrote in it, the same thing over and over again. The numbers one to ten, and then back down to one, and back up to ten again. Over and over. That's all he was ever doing."

"Is that so frightening?" Peter asked. "I mean, I guess that's how he stayed calm."

"I think it means he lost himself. He was always in his math, and he couldn't do it anymore, not at the end."

"How long," Peter said. "You want to know how long he was lost, or childlike. When he started to not be able to think anymore."

"I guess."

"Can I call you tomorrow? All those books are in storage."

"Yeah," she said. "I'm sorry to bother you..."

"No, no bother, ever. He was my friend, you know? As much as he was your brother, he was sort of ours, too, since forever. He looked after us in school. Always the brave one, even though Hugo was always the big one, the competent one. I miss him all the time. And whatever you need to know about him, I'll try to tell you. So no, no bother."

"Okay."

"Hey, you said the last line was different."

"Did I?" she asked.

"I thought so. What was it that you didn't understand?"

"I didn't think Walter was religious," Yvonne said.

"Oh. So what did it say?"

"It said, 'The Gods Themselves.'"

"That was his favorite book," Walter said. "He had one autographed by Asimov himself - you believe that? Worth a fortune today, if you could find it. First edition. But he lost it along the way. We got him another for the library up in the hospital. I wonder what he meant by writing it in the back of his book?"

"I don't know," Yvonne said, conscious that she had said it a lot so far that night. What she did know was that gooseflesh was creeping up and down her arms, and the hair on the back of her head was trying to stand on end, and a chill marched from her tailbone to the nape of her neck like a slow-motion electric shock.

"I don't know," she repeated again.

"I think that modern physics has definitely decided in favor of Plato. In fact the smallest units of matter are not physical objects in the ordinary sense; they are forms, ideas which can be expressed unambiguously only in mathematical language."

Heisenberg

Twenty-Nine

The train car shook and rattled, sounding a lot more fragile than it was. It was a long way to D.C. but the ride was nearly over, dark creeping over the East Coast and artificial lights starting to replace the Sun. Soon everything would be halogen-yellow and ghostly.

If he were Yvonne, Valery knew he would have friends to call in town. Hey, I'm in the city for a few hours. Dinner? Drinks? Maybe a show? Valery kept out of the governmental side of law, out of the lobbying and back-slapping, and so he knew nobody down here. New York was where all the action was.

The train slid into the station. Doors opened and people poured out of train cars as others jostled to get in. Washington still wasn't used to the trains and hadn't figured out that you had to let everyone off before there was any sense trying to board. Valery slid and shouldered through the late-night crowd, not enough people for the press to last more than a few feet, then emerged into open space.

From here it was a bus ride to the hospital. Another twenty or thirty minutes to bring this strange quest to an end.

The warm spring night turned wet about the time Valery found the bus stop. There was no shelter, just a bench shaped to be uncomfortable should any homeless people try to sleep there and that was therefore uncomfortable for any weary traveler trying to sit. He read the bus schedule by the light of the headlamps of passing cars, referred to his watch.

"Crap."

The last bus had left a few minutes before he arrived. Traffic had held him up in New York, the train had been delayed by a mechanical problem, and now even had there been another bus, it was much too late to just show up at the hospital and ring the doorbell. And say what? *Hi, I'm the brother in law of a patient you kicked out of here years ago, and I want his books back.* Smooth.

As he was reflecting, Valery failed to notice a car pull up at the stop. By now the rain was all but pelting down, a coastal rain that held nothing back, so he also almost missed the voice that called at him: "Hey, mister, you missed the last bus. You want a ride somewhere?"

He turned, expecting - hoping - to see a taxi, but in fact he saw a Mercedes. Black with silver detailing. "Ah, I wouldn't want to get your interior wet."

"Don't be silly," said the man in the driver's seat. He was youngish, maybe fifteen or eighteen years younger than Valery. *Though that would make him more middle-aged than young now*, Valery thought. Grey suit, yellow tie, not too political-looking or lawyerish. Glasses. Short, dark hair. "A little water won't hurt anything. Come on, hop in, I'll drop you off someplace."

Not knowing why, Valery nodded, trotted around to the passenger side, and slid into the car. The door closed quietly as he pulled it to. Inside, the car quickly began to steam as the water from his clothing merged with the inner atmosphere. "Thanks."

"No problem. I used to ride this line all the time. Kind of a tricky neighborhood. You don't want to be stuck down here with no ride, not this time of night. Where you headed?"

"Well, I was going down to the hospital. But I guess it's a bit late now. Hadn't really formulated a back-up plan."

"Don't tell me you mean Virginia Psychiatric," the driver said, easing the car into the proper lane. There was no traffic to speak of and the headlights showed only falling water.

"Yeah. Why?"

"I was heading there myself. They're expecting me. My name's Timothy."

"Hi, I'm Valery. What are you doing going there this time of night, if you don't mind my asking?"

"You know, that's a good question," Timothy said. "I was going through some budgets when I all of a sudden got this weird feeling. Like something was missing. I don't know, I can't explain it to a stranger, most likely. But then I imagined that whatever it was, it was at this hospital. And I knew the number. It just flashed into my head. So I called down there, and they knew who I was - told me Walter had died years ago, but they still had some of his things. I don't know who Walter is right now but I feel like I did when I set out this morning. And the more I think about it, the more I imagine the psychiatric hospital is just the place for anyone telling that story with a straight face."

"Not a coincidence, I should think," Valery said. "That's why I'm going there, too. Except I know who Walter was. My brother in law. And he left me a note to look for a book, which is most likely there at the hospital."

"The Gods Themselves?"

"Yeah, how did you know?"

"I don't know," said Timothy. "I mean, it's hard to even think about."

"I know what you mean. But this can't be an accident. Something very weird is going on right now, and the answer is in that book. I can't say how I know that, only that it's true."

Both men fell silent. The engine was quiet as church whispers. Warm air kept the steam off the windows and the wipers cursed and muttered and there was no other sound except the rain on the roof, on the glass. Valery reflected that this was how his life had been up to now: insulated, warded off from normalcy, crouched, waiting. An unspoken strangeness in the air.

Timothy made a few turns, having trouble even remembering where he was going and why. But soon the hospital loomed up out of the darkness in front of them.

The sign was illuminated, and the front entrance, but the front buildings were administration: the windows were all darkened for the night. He pulled the car into one of many vacant spots.

"Why are we here?" Timothy asked, as if noticing Valery for the first time.

"Don't you remember?"

"To be honest, no. I feel... strange. Do I know you?"

"We're going to go inside and get a book," Valery said. "I can't say how I know, but I know once we have it, our lives are going to change. Yours and mine."

"The way you're talking makes me afraid."

"Me too. Ready?"

"No, but let's do it anyway." They jogged across the parking lot to the covered entryway, went through glass double doors that creaked and strained, clearly in need of replacement. "Reagan," Timothy said.

"What?" asked Valery, standing over the rug in the hall and dripping. The place was dim inside. There was no help desk like at a regular hospital, but he knew the way.

"Ronald Reagan. He killed this place. Deregulation and defunding. Tossed everyone out."

"Well, not personally," said Valery, "but yeah, a lot of guys who needed care wound up homeless in the eighties. Walter included. It was a miracle I found him in time."

"Who's Walter?"

"Never mind. Come on."

The place looked strange in the near-dark, one fluorescent in six illuminated for safety. Down one long hall and then another, around a sharp bend, and there were the doors to two of the units. Down here the lights were all on and they jabbed harshly at Valery's eyes, now used to semi-dark. There was a stairwell and, while Timothy protested to not remember where they were or why, he was the first up.

At the top of the stairs they saw a heavy door with a card-swipe lock and an intercom. To the right was a mundane door, locked. Valery pressed the intercom button.

"Unit six," a voice intoned, made distant by electronics. "Can we help you?"

Timothy looked blank, so Valery said, "I'm here with Timothy. You talked to him on the phone. We wanted to glance at your library. I know it's unusual..."

The door clicked and a little light on the card-swipe turned from red to green. Valery took that as an invitation. When he and Timothy stepped inside, a man down the hall to the left appeared in the light down there, darkness between him and them. He beckoned to them in a gesture that said both *be quiet* and *come on down*. The place had the feel of sleep to it but not of peace.

"It always smells a little of urine here," Timothy whispered.

They went down the hall and around the corner. There the nurses' station waited, door open, and they went inside. A large wooden conference table took up half the space, and bookshelves most of the rest. There were monitors showing empty rooms, a coffee pot, some telephones. Two men sat at the table and a third waited to shake hands with Timothy and Valery.

"We've had this stuff for years and years," the man said. "When Walter was discharged, somehow none of these books got discharged with him. Someone must've thought they belonged to the library. And later we couldn't find out who was the next of kin to call and send this stuff all to. At night it was his brother in law, but in the morning they insisted it was his sister, and we never could agree. But it's yours now."

On the table were three cardboard boxes filled with books and magazines. They were all science-fiction related, lots of Isaac Asimov.

"He's kind of a legend around here," the man went on. "Pretty nice guy. We never got him figured out, though. Sort of hung out in back and filled book after book after book with numbers. Such a shame. He was some kind of math genius in college, but by the time he came here, all he could write was one to ten, one to ten, all day long. Sometimes all night."

"I used to visit," Timothy said. "He went to my school."

Valery did not argue about what Walter had written in his notebooks. "One book is special," he said. "I came a long way to get it. It's some kind of message. Never mind that now. It's The Gods Themselves. Is it in this pile?" He started to move books aside, to see what was buried in each box.

"Yeah," the guy said. "It's here, in this plastic bag. A patient was back there, in the library, and he opened the book and all this stuff fell out. It's some weird story, like maybe Walter was writing a novel or something."

Valery took the bag, almost snatched it. Grabbed an index card. As he read it, Timothy went over all gray, stepped back, hit the back of his head gently on the wall. He grabbed his head like it hurt, moaned a little.

"Hey, you all right?" said the orderly, and the two guys at the table jumped forward, lowered Timothy into a chair.

"I'm fine, I'm fine. No, really. Yeah, some water would be great. Wow, what a rush. Valery. You're Valery."

Valery didn't feel too steady himself. When he looked at the card, it was like he had plugged into his computer at work, like all the databases he could think of were dumping into his memory. Like he was waking up, for the first time. All his memories were garbage, junk, like normal scenes of mundane life recorded over a horror movie - or a science fiction story.

"Everything I thought is wrong," he said.

"We can fix it," Timothy said. "We need to go to Switzerland."

***

On the TV, David Duchovny was deadpanning through another monologue. Peter smiled, trying to figure out if he was being sincere or having his audience on in some way through the character. Truthfully he hadn't been following the episode; it had something to do with robot cockroaches, but his daughter had a bunch of friends by

for a sleepover so the place was full of little girls. And
they were very noisy.

Ursula was making hot cocoa. Peter didn't say anything
but he knew chocolate was full of sugar and caffeine, so
the odds of anyone sleeping tonight were not so good.
There really should be a bigger warning on the label-

And then it was like a switch flipped over in his brain.
My god, this is all a lie.

With a suddenness like thunder, he recalled his real life,
what had really happened. *Yvonne. Walter. Gergiev's chip
logic - oh Jesus, that crazy chip logic! We knew what it
meant, we had it all figured out, and then Walter died, and
we forgot everything!*

His heart was running away with him, making him a
little light-headed. Peter focused on breathing slow and
steady for a minute, then reached for the phone. He hadn't
talked to Hugo in a couple of years, but now he saw why:
Hugo had been edited out of his history, their close
friendship written out of existence. By who, or what? Time
itself?

As Peter's hand found his phone, it began to ring. "It's
for me," he shouted, so that Ursula wouldn't worry about
it. He knew who it was. "Hugo. It happened to you, too,
right?"

"Right," said Hugo. "I was just sitting here, leading this
whole empty, illusory life, and then like a light-saber
switching on, life just illuminated. From one end to the
other, whoosh, here's everything you've forgotten - and
why."

"Me too," Peter said. "I'm watching some sci-fi on the
TV, and then it's like, no, Fox Mulder could never have
come up with this. We have to go, man. We have to fix
this while we still remember how."

"Yeah," said Hugo. Then, together, they said,
"Switzerland."

They chatted for a few minutes but they had been so
close they didn't really need words.

***

Hugo killed the call, tossed his phone carelessly aside. Rolled out of bed and hunted around the bottom of his closet for his duffel bag.

"Is everything OK?" asked the woman in his bed.

"Yeah, go back to sleep," he said, not trying too hard to remember her name.

"OK," she said. A minute later she was snoring again. There were empty airplane bottles around the bed and he swept them underneath as a courtesy. Wouldn't do for her to slip on them in the morning. Also as a courtesy he pulled his brick of weed from the shoebox in the top of the closet and left it on the bathroom counter where she was sure to find it. He sure wasn't taking that to Switzerland, and there was no sense letting it go to waste.

Then he started throwing stuff in his bag. Shoes first: shoes always went on the bottom. Couple pair of jeans, couple of t-shirts, couple of button downs that weren't too dirty, socks, underwear new in the package. Coat. He packed his toothbrush, toothpaste, soap and shampoo in a brown grocery bag, tossed those in. Anything else?

Then he realized the shoes in the bag were the only shoes he had, unless he wanted to wear the cramped black Oxfords they made him wear at the restaurant. So he dumped everything out, started over.

Ten minutes later he was on his way, cell phone in his shirt pocket, a smile on his face. The last few years he had been waiting for this, for this precise moment, without knowing it. Suddenly he felt like he had a purpose, a reason. He was in motion, the quarrel loosed from the crossbow, while for years he had been lying in the shaft feeling the tension of the string without seeing the target.

It was a train ride and then a cab ride to the airport. The restaurant didn't pay much and tips had been off lately, but mostly he worked there to front his marijuana enterprise, and that paid pretty good. He gave the cabbie an extra twenty for a quick ride when he saw math textbooks piled in the front seat, ran up the steps into the airport.

"I need a ticket to Geneva," he said breathlessly once he reached the British Airways counter.

The airbrushed and carefully coifed woman there took his particulars, tapped a few keys. "But sir, you are already confirmed on flight EU-six-two-four, leaving in two hours."

Hugo laughed. "Nice. Can you see who paid for it? Is it Peter's name on the credit card?"

"No," she said, bemused. "A Brian Moldavie."

***

"I don't know what you're saying," Janet said. She crossed her arms over her breasts, stood up out of bed that way. "Nothing you're saying makes any sense."

"I know, honey, I know that," Brian said, throwing on clothes like he was twenty-two and late for a job interview. "And I can't really explain it. I mean, I guess I could, but you'd call the lawyer about having me committed. It really is just as crazy as you think it is. Just, can you trust me?"

"Have I ever not trusted you?" she asked, a little quieter.

"No. No, I guess not. Hey, look at it this way. You always want me to be more spontaneous. What could be more spontaneous than an unplanned vacation in Switzerland?"

"I can't go to Switzerland. What about bridge night?" she said, putting on a robe.

"You're rich as Hell, sweetie. You can do whatever you want. Almost literally whatever you want. Come on. Don't even pack a bag. Let's just go. It'll be an adventure."

She looked at him like she'd opened a bag of M&M's and found a pistol inside: like he was somewhere between completely mad and very dangerous. Then she put her hands on her hips, smiled, and said, "If this is one of your jokes..."

"Yeah, that's it. A joke. A lark. Come on, a midnight flight to Switzerland. I want some hot cocoa. Let's go."

Then she laughed. "I must be as crazy as you are. They are going to turn us away at the border. Or not let us of the plane, or whatever they do with passengers who don't have passports."

"We have passports," he said. "We need visas though. Maybe? Are they an open country? Well, I'll handle it on the way."

"How?"

"Remember when we went to Senator Franklyn's fundraiser and wrote him that check? Well, he's friends with the ambassador. I told you, Janet. I told you all this money was for something. This is it. This is what it's for. Can you drive? I need to make a bunch of calls on the way."

"You're crazy," Janet said.

"We're rich. When you're rich, you aren't crazy anymore. You're eccentric."

"Fine, then," she said, laughing. "You're certifiably eccentric."

"Physicists like to think that all you have to do is say, these are the conditions, now what happens next?"
Feynman

Thirty

The room wasn't big enough for everyone, Mathilda knew, and imagined it was not what the Americans expected. They would have imagined stainless-steel and glass, maybe a bank of monitors, various electronic devices of uncertain function, accustomed to the technology of the trade and to the rooms at the school with other functions being cheap, strictly utilitarian.

This place was a conference room and had none of the technology of physics in it or near it. The whole building was for administering the Large Hadron Collider project and this room had its function in that grand design, but was built to a different sensibility. A European sensibility.

The chairs were ergonomic and comfortable, black fabric coverings and padded arm-rests at just the right height. Timothy and Hugo stood while the rest of the group sat: Peter, Brian and Janet, Rosie and Raul. Valery on one end. The remaining chairs were taken up by the Head of Projects, Mathilda herself posing as a minion from the accounting department, and Jim Schlauer, a theoretical physicist. The room was richly carpeted, had a tin drop-ceiling, walls papered in gold and yellow. The table was an antique, as was the tea service.

"I'm not at all certain what you are saying has scientific merit," Jim said. "There is really nothing in any previous energy readings to strongly suggest the level of symmetry you propose, and certainly none to suggest some of that symmetry resides in a parallel universe. To be honest, I feel like you are wasting our time. You know, we get two or three thousand requests for experiments per day here. Per day. And the collider won't even be ready for six to eight more years."

Brian looked at Janet, who shrugged. "What else is it for?" she whispered. "Go on, then."

"We're not petitioners come with our hats in our hands to beg favors," Brian said, more confidently than he really felt. If not for his years as a lecturer he was sure his fear would be evident in his voice. "We have quite a wealthy backer who can contribute substantially to the international funds for the project."

"A few thousand dollars won't turn balderdash into science," Jim said. He ran fingers through his white beard, stood, did up the buttons on his lab coat.

The accountant - a woman with a small nose and big eyes magnified by low-profile spectacles, raised one hand a little, and Jim stopped where he was. "How wealthy?" she said.

Mathilda, the woman in charge of the meeting and most of CERN, took off her own glasses and looked up at the people in the room. Brian looked dignified if harried; Janet was dressed simply but in high-end retail fashions. Her jewelry was almost utilitarian but, again, high-end. There was Hugo in the back, slovenly the way only the brightest of scientists can afford to be. Timothy, with the look of an administrator, but she knew his reputation: solid work, and more suggestive than Jim had granted. But Jim was developing a defensive mind: how to screen out and weed out and minimize interference rather than to take risks.

Peter had some published work, solid and creative if not mold-breaking. Valery looked like a lawyer and was an unknown quantity. Could he be the backer?

"How much?" the accountant repeated.

"One point two billion dollars," Janet said.

"Doesn't matter if it's a trillion dollars," Jim said. "You can't buy science."

Mathilda addressed him without looking at him, her eyes back down on the papers in front of her. "You can go, Jim. Thank you for your advice. There are two more super-symmetry people in conference room B who want to form a cooperative for data storage and processing."

Jim turned and left with no obvious show of emotions. "I'll bet they want a first-look exemption," he muttered as he went, clearly already on the next task.

"That would be a generous contribution," Mathilda said. Her white hair spilled down over her face so she lifted it out of the way with one hand as she once again made eye contact around the room. "So much money speaks strongly of confidence. You have more evidence than is in these proposals."

Raul spoke next. "Retrocausality," he said, and waited. When Mathilda's eyes came to rest on his face, he went on. "The Hanks proposal. Feyman and Wheeler have strong and well-supported critiques. But Hanks did not publish everything. I have much stronger empirical support of retrocausality as a physical phenomenon and, as well, experimental evidence that this effect can be observed at larger than sub-atomic scales. Those experiments are unpublished but I can recreate them - with some institutional support. And, and I hesitate to say this, we only confirmed the existence of the top quark in '95. Long before that, I was isolating and manipulating them."

"Impossible."

"Yes. In this set of conditions. But this set has not always dominated. No more questions about this; I will demonstrate the veracity of these claims shortly."

"If you had such evidence, why not publish it? You would be the Einstein of the modern era." Mathilda returned her gaze to the tabletop. "You would be a bigger science celebrity than Leaky or Hawass. The world would be your oyster."

"All the textbooks would need to be rewritten. Yes, I've considered all of that. But basically there are two reasons. The first is, that is not what the experiments are for. They are for what we wish to accomplish here, using the microscopic singularities predicted by some of the math. The second is theological: the principles of evolution were used to justify social Darwinism, eugenics, and eventually not only Hitler's war but other mass sterilizations and genocides. I cannot begin to predict the effects of wide-spread interpretations of these facts, that the future causes the past to the same extent that the past causes the future. I will not be the author of such consequences."

Mathilda thought for a minute, made a decision. "There will be no such singularities," she said, and started to sweep her papers together.

"There will," said Timothy, "and I can prove it."

"With institutional support?" Mathilda asked.

"No. I have the results here. In this folder."

"Go on."

"In eighty-four, I took over the high-energy measurement department at George Washington. At the same time, I worked on the math for extra-dimensional measurements. Looking at cosmic ray collisions, WIMPs, and other exotic interactions, I consistently found - and published - discrepancies in the order of energy needed for these measurements." He stepped to the table, started to lay data sheets in front of Mathilda. They were old, slightly yellowed, with the ragged edges that said they came from big, industrial printers.

"Here, for example. This data shows a measurement of a high-energy particle where no magnetic field was present to disrupt. The overlapping fields were my way to try to create a more-for-less phenomenon, a way to carpet an area so that a disruption too small to change one field would magnify as the fields interacted. I thought that accounted for these data, but it didn't. Your computers can model this easily and they'll verify it."

"So what is this effect?"

"There were two experiments going on simultaneously. In two closely-related conditions. The retrocausality Raul was measuring coincided by accident with this experiment. As conditions changed - the cesium atom he used degraded in advance of a quark changing state in another room - during that time, two universes existed at once. Just at the time this measurement happened. There was another magnetic field, just here, just for a fraction of a second.

Even so, it distorted and altered all these other fields enough to capture this particle's movement."

"That is... what would Americans say? Thin? There could be a thousand other explanations for this data."

"True," Timothy went on. "But, once I worked this out, I went back and looked at all the energy usage for all the equipment. There is more energy in this system than is accounted for by the known input. The fraction is complicated..." he pointed to a scrawled calculation on the back of one of the rip sheets.

"This is not possible."

The accountant pulled a scientific calculator out of one pocket, revealing she was more than a bean-counter, and started tapping keys. "If all these values are correct, this number follows," she said.

"In other words, those microscopic black holes the media is using to frighten people, even though harmless and impossible by the standard math, will be not only possible but inevitable when we precisely align the hadron collisions with retro-causality events. The energy output will temporarily, very briefly, exceed the input by this fraction, resulting in the singularity we need."

"Why aren't you at the Tevatron, Fermilab?"

"Not enough power," Timothy said. "We need the LHC. Even adding power from these effects, not enough power."

"Nobody can know about this," Mathilda whispered into her chest. "Nobody. And I will need first-hand demonstrations within the week."

"I will alert level ten projects," the accountant said.

***

Her first thought was, *Why am I in Switzerland?* Her second: *How do I know I'm in Switzerland?* Then she remembered: sitting up in bed, bolt upright, a rush of information coming at her, and emotion, and trauma - although the memory of all the dread, shock, horror were flat, as if described by a flat, boring author. The knowledge that she needed to go to Switzerland but with no clue as to why.

Yvonne had packed a brief bag, called for a taxi, essentially fled the country. Her passport was good from a conference the year before and it never even occurred to her to call work. Now she knew they would not miss her: she existed only temporarily, an addendum to the universe.

All of that was in her mind like a stranger had told her of those events and she believed them. And this experience, of waking up in a strange bed and wondering why, was filled with hammering heart, sweating palms, appreciation for the way the Sun shone differently here, arcing through the window not like the lance it was through her fourth-story apartment window but with the diffuse beauty of a cool spring afternoon in the mountains.

I'm in Switzerland, and I'm an appendix to everything happening. I've been sidelined in my own story.

All the men had gone to some meeting where she would not matter. No way were they going to mention that reality was fighting itself over ultimate truth, over basic elements of history. So she had slept in, trying not to think too hard about her shadow-life.

Had it always been this way? Yvonne seemed to remember parts of life as less flat, more real, more three-dimensional. Seeing Valery in her apartment, taking photos of the formulae he scrawled on the mirror. Working trauma. Fighting with that schmuck Carl Michaels. When had she faded, thinned out?

Yvonne opened her suitcase, decided she would likely be staying long enough to justify hanging up her clothes in the wardrobe. The hotel room was small but nicely furnished, with a headboard in rich red wood, a little chandelier that scattered rainbows around the room, the wardrobe and a matching writing desk with a tiny chair. This was Europe and everything was to European proportions. Small and serviceable, not needing to accommodate increasingly ample Americans.

There was nothing for Yvonne to do now but wait, and possibly wait a long time, and hope. *How can I stand it, she thought, knowing I will live only a short time each day but remember life as though it were ongoing?*

She was hungry, so once she was sufficiently presentable Yvonne went out of the little hotel room, down some stairs and into the lobby. There was a cafe across the street.

She got a little table outside, a black wrought-iron seat that matched the table and a yellow and black umbrella that kept off the sun. A waitress asked what she wanted.

"Coffee. Perhaps a crescent roll?"

"We 'ave a vonderfull chocolat roll," the waitress said, smiling. Her accent was French and Yvonne looked around with new eyes, seeing all the other people busily walking from place to place, firm destinations in mind. Ten thousand scientists in this city, mostly working on the giant accelerator project that would dominate physics for decades. From everywhere. A whole world of people, with attendant histories, desires, wishes.

"Chocolate sounds lovely," she said. And it was. The buttery warm roll had a perfect texture: just the slightest hint of a crunch to the outside, teeth breaking through into the chewy interior, butter and chocolate and bread flavor washing over the tongue. A lovely chew, substantial but light.

The waitress came back as Yvonne was finishing, watching sunlight creep up over the high-rise apartment being built one block up. "Good?" she asked.

"That was the best thing I've ever eaten," Yvonne said, suddenly remembering the memory patient at the hospital. Awakening again and again to experience as if for the first time. "As long as I'm alive for the time being, perhaps I could trouble you for another?"

Then she sipped her coffee, delighting in the way the steam crept over the lower half of her face, how the flavor started at the front of her tongue and washed backwards, the way it warmed her throat and stomach.

A little bird hopped between the other tables, mostly vacant, looking for crumbs and scraps. It picked up a matchstick, turned its head to one side as if quizzically, dropped the stick again. Picked up a bit of brown leaf, did the same. It seemed to be watching Yvonne, maybe asking her for a favor.

"As long as I'm going to exist only as a story I tell myself, let's make it a story of sensation and hedonism," she told the bird, and imagined he understood. She tossed him a crumb for his service. "Well, Switzerland it is, then."

***

"Two-thousand eight? I'll be seventy-two, if I live that long," Valery said. There was beer foam on his lip.

"You'll live so long," Rosie said. She was across the black-dark wooden table from him, Raul and Brian filling the other two stools. "The way I understand it, if you die before the experiment goes off, none of this happens at all. It is that future event dragging us all into its vortex in the first place."

"That's just what I'm afraid of," Raul said. "That knowing elements of the future dictates the present. We all live in the past so long as we know the future. Life loses its immediacy."

"But if it's true," said Brian, "why not allow people to make their own decisions about it, come to terms in their own way?"

Raul just shook his head.

"Brian, I-" Valery started, but Brian interrupted.

"Like Rosie said, we already did it in the future. We had no choice in the present. That money was *for* something, and it is this. I knew it the way Walter calculated the odds that my house was on fire and told me about it, from the day she told me about that damned lottery ticket." Raul slipped away to the bar for another drink. Brian went on, "All those years we forgot everything, all the weirdness and slippages, all that time Janet and I were looking for something to do with it, building it up and up and up and searching for the right project, the investment that would return more than money. This is it. This will change the nature of the universe as well as our understanding of it."

"Let me say thank you."

"For what? Thank destiny, or fate, or whatever lies at the end of the future dragging us along in its tracks."

"Dance with me," Janet said, coming up to Brian from his left. "You promised me a vacation in Switzerland. I feel like we just bought half of it. Let's go dance in it."

"I feel sixty-five again," Brian said, sliding down off the stool and going off to join her in a corner of the bar that could charitably be called a dance floor.

Timothy wandered over, sat up in the space Brian had vacated. Rosie looked at his face and made an excuse, tried to drag Raul over to the dancing part of the bar.

"I get the feeling I should be uncomfortable," Valery said, looking at Timothy. "You're about to lay something heavy on me."

"Well, yeah. This is so strange, so... impossible. The whole thing from start to finish is impossible. This conversation, I could not imagine having it."

"I already know," Valery said.

"You do? How?"

"Looking at you," he said. "There's nothing else it could be. Nothing in the math or the physics adds up to this awkward approach, this guilty look, to Rosie getting out of the way. You slept with her, maybe loved her. Some of the time, when I don't exist, you still love her. That's why you aren't married, don't have a girlfriend, have no children. That's why you're lost in your work. Why you look awful now."

"Are you just guessing?" Timothy asked.

"I was. Educated guesses keep lawyers successful. But you haven't denied anything, so I'm not guessing any more. If it was a court case you'd be convicted."

"I'm sorry. I mean, I don't know, I know I should be, but I'm really concerned for your feelings. It was a long time ago, and we were young, and back then you were the one who was hazy and insubstantial. You were the one who flitted briefly into existence in reflections and uncomfortable silences, in telephone line static. Yvonne was real, human, warm, lonely. She was sad, always so sad, and yeah, I was in love with her. And she loved me enough to say no."

"What are you sorry for?" Valery asked. "Like you said, it's not like we were married. I didn't exist. I'm somehow creeping into being and pushing her out. One day there'll be only me. She'll be gone completely, the way I remember it: she died in that accident and I lived and that was impossible. But it's becoming possible. If she had some happiness while she was alive, I can't blame you for that or hate you. I can be jealous, yeah. And mad, even though it's irrational. But I don't and never did own her. If she's alive for a few seconds today and she's with you because she can't be with me, help her live. Please?"

"How was it?" Timothy wondered, relaxing a little into a less uptight posture. "How was it to exist only a short time, here and there, in bits and pieces?"

"It was like madness. Like all of life was a dream you could barely recall. Like going through the motions, remembering life as going through the motions. You know, most people my age, they remember where they were when Kennedy was shot? They all remember being in school, hearing the principle's voice over the radio.

"But when you dig into it, people were too young to be in school, or their schools were shut that day in advance of Thanksgiving, and only a few were actually there. They put those memories together from talking about it later, years later.

"That's what it's like. As though half your life is imagined through talking about it with others. But it never really happened."

"I can't even imagine," Timothy said.

"Yes you can," Valery went on. "Because while you're alive in both versions of reality and I'm only alive in one, only in one version did you love her. Here, with me, your love for her is a story you tell yourself. You never met her. She doesn't exist. She died in seventy-three."

"You *are* angry," Timothy said.

"I told you I was. Not with you, though, and I'm sorry if that hurts. But if you love her, want to love her, you have to understand her. That's what she's going through right now: knowing her love for you is imaginary, that she wasn't there. She only remembers being there as if she saw it on a movie and thought it was her."

Timothy didn't talk after that, just nursed a dark beer at the dark table in the dark bar.

"Physicists have come to realize that mathematics, when used with sufficient care, is a proven pathway to truth."

Greene

Thirty-One

The Large Hadron Collider powered up for the first time. It was September 10th, 2008. Excited teams watched the telemetry on screens all over the world. In one room directly below the collision chamber, protected from it by feet of rock and supplementary lead shielding, Valery watched a glass tube about a half-inch thick and six inches high into which a singularity would drop if all the calculations were correct.

He listened to commentary over the in-house channels, sounding like a Moon launch in progress. This bit of esoteric gear checked out; that one was within tolerances; data was flowing from this conduit or that cable. Tighten down the clamp at junction C26, it must have come loose. Clear the tunnels. Test in progress.

Nothing dramatic happened for several hours. Brian napped and Raul tapped a pen anxiously against his teeth.

Soon it will all be over. Once the experiment is complete, Yvonne will come back to me, will live again. We will remember our lives together, together. We will both have lived.

For nearly two hours, technicians guided streams of particles section by section through the miles and miles of tunnels above. Electrons one way, protons the other. Finally, the voices on the speakers all agreed: time to inaugurate the collider with a collision.

Nothing noticeable really happened in the cavern where Valery waited. Timothy had told him to expect that. Valery, Raul and Brian sat in the small chamber with its folding chairs and monitors and screens. Timothy waited in another room, off the campus, with Raul's laser/cesium setup.

A few minutes into the test, when the main teams were satisfied with their data, a red light came on next to the receiving tube. This meant Timothy was switching on the second half of the laser experiment, causing a single quark to change states, causing its partner to also change states, causing the proton of which it was a part to degrade, and the measurement to change slightly in advance of the change. For that instant, timed precisely to the proton-proton collision generated by the collider, two universes existed at once.

Klaxons sounded in the chambers upstairs. The power had amped up, causing a spike in all the readings, just for half a second, less.

The particle they wanted dropped into the receiving tube, its magnetic containment humming: it looked like a tiny point of light, too small to see any form.

"Is that it?" Vyonne asked. "It seems such a small thing." She stepped closer. "Is it safe to approach?"

Brian shook Raul. "It's working," he said. "Only, something's gone wrong. The klaxons. And Valery switched - look, Yvonne has replaced him."

"Yvonne?" said Raul. "No, oh no-"

But it was too late. As she approached the waiting, decaying singularity, it grew, expanded, reached out for her as she reached out for it. She imagined she could see Valery reflected in it, waiting for her there. *If I can just touch him, he will join me here in this universe, just for a second. And that will be impossible, so the universe will have to correct for it, insert him into the past.*

Brian was up, and Raul, too, and they rushed forward to stop her. "No, don't touch it - Valery has to -"

But it was too late. As she had been fated to do since nineteen seventy-three, she put the flesh of her fingers against the yielding, swirling vortex of possibility that emanated from the tube. Valery did the same from the dimension in which he lived. Yvonne was sucked through to the other side, replaced by Valery, never touching, never knowing one another.

"I made it," Valery said. "I did it. We did it. Now it will all be right again."

***

Yvonne awakened in a broken car, a gold-colored LTD. She had on a black dress with bits of glass stuck in it.

What am I doing here?

She crawled out of the shattered windscreen, getting glass stuck in her hands and knees. Her hands looked too young but she didn't stop to think about that. Once in the street, she looked back at the scene she had just left. A wrecked Ford LTD, a real antique, with an old snowplow sticking out of one side. *How did I get in there?*

Oh God, it didn't work. "Val, why aren't you all right? Why didn't it work?"

Also by Jason Dias:

The Worst of Us
For Love of Their Children
The Girlfriend Project
What Hope Wrought

Read on for a sneak peek at The Worst of Us

The Worst of Us

"All right," he said, shifting around in his chair until he was comfortable. "Between the age of thirteen and going to Vietnam, I suppose you could say not too much of any real importance happened. Back home, the rest of the world discovered rock and roll, Jimi Hendrix and so forth. And drugs. Drugs, drugs, drugs. If not for the sixties, why, you wouldn't have a job, Doctor Lisa."

She smiled at him, waited for him to go on.

"I didn't do any of that, though. Well, that's for later. I suppose the next main event happens late in nineteen sixty-eight."

Lisa wrote, "Sixty-eight again," on her blank page.

"I was in prison, on the front lines in the jungle. Well, not really a prison, just a bamboo hut, really. But I wasn't allowed to leave. I was under arrest."

"What for?" Lisa said.

"You want me to tell it," he said, "then let me tell it." But he softened it with a grin, impish and impertinent.

"All right," Lisa said, and sat back to listen.

***

He got that feeling again when she came into the room, into his life.

Elbert had his feet up on a steel desk. His boots weren't shined. There was mud in the half-assed treads, which were really not much more than evenly-spaced thumb-prints in the thick soles. His uniform was dirty but it was camouflage so only his nose made that very plain. The walls were bare corrugated tin over bamboo poles.

She pushed through the door, dismissed the sergeant who had custody of him. The sergeant scrambled away like she was fire and he was made of rice paper. Elbert looked her over, the way a man looks at a woman, but she met none of those kinds of expectations. He looked again. And what he was thinking of was that time with the mirror when he was thirteen, that feeling of sliding right of the edge of reality.

She wasn't tall, maybe five eight. But she was big. "You're a black one, aren't you?" she said.

Out here nobody skirted the racism issue so Elbert wasn't too surprised, but the willies started. Gooseflesh held itself a parade on his forearms. "No blacker than half the boys out here," he said. "I think you got off the wrong stop, lady. MASH is back up the road a piece. This here is temporary jail until they figure out something more permanent."

She pointed at her collar. A subdued blue eagle rested among the random green and brown and black shapes of her camo. Name on her tape said WILCOX. "You forgotten your military bearing, soldier?"

Elbert's eyes widened a little more. He'd never seen a woman colonel before. Even the boss of the nurses didn't usually get farther than major. "I guess I just ain't met a colonel like you before." And he hadn't.

She had ripped the sleeves off her shirt, probably because she'd had to. Her biceps were like rugby balls in size, shape, color and texture. She had a linebacker's shoulders, all straining against the remains of her shirt, against the black tee she wore under it. She had pecs like a bodybuilder. And her face...

"You're in some trouble, MacAvoy," she said.

"My legal counsel advised I stay quiet on that particular topic until I get someplace civilized," Elbert said. The feeling of dislocation increased and he tried to talk steady, with confidence, but he was sure she could see the gooseflesh on his arms.

"You haven't seen a lawyer out here. But you're probably right: shooting an officer is a pretty serious offense."

Elbert crossed his arms, leaned back farther, looked at one of those blank walls like there was a window to see through.

"Black enlisted man shoots a white infantry captain with a shiny service record and a bunch of medals... Well, let's just say your aim was off."

Elbert looked back at her, into her eyes. They were set too far apart, brown like mud. Some folks might have said they were like a doe or a cow, but Elbert figured she was too ugly to be a cow. More like a bull. "I hit what I was aiming at," he said.

"Then you made a serious mistake. You know, your whole unit is mostly likely going down? Rest of the men, they covered for you. I guess they figured Daniels had it coming. Not every day an officer get fragged but it does happen. What doesn't figure is he doesn't fit the profile. He isn't a gung-ho young officer looking for glory and toeing the line. He's on his third tour. Doesn't take unnecessary chances, tried to stay out of the shit."

Elbert looked away again.

"Anyway, you'd have gotten through clean except for one thing. One mistake."

"What's that?"

"You didn't kill him," she said.